Falling Short

Falling Short

Lex Coulton

JOHN MURRAY

First published in Great Britain in 2018 by John Murray (Publishers)
An Hachette UK Company

1

© Lex Coulton 2018

Extract from 'Marina' taken from *Collected Poems 1909–1962* by
T. S. Eliot, reproduced by permission of Faber and Faber Ltd.

Extract from Dennis Scott's 'Marrysong' is reproduced
with the permission of Peepal Tree Press.

A CIP catalogue record for this title is available from the British Library

ISBN 978-1-47366-958-1

Ebook ISBN 978-1-47366-9604

Typeset in Sabon MT by Hewer Text UK Ltd, Edinburgh
Printed and bound by Clays Ltd, St Ives plc

John Murray policy is to use papers that are natural, renewable
and recyclable products and made from wood grown in sustainable
forests. The logging and manufacturing processes are expected to
conform to the environmental regulations of the country of origin.

John Murray (Publishers)
Carmelite House
50 Victoria Embankment
London EC4Y 0DZ

www.johnmurray.co.uk

For John,
with whom all things are possible.

Full fathom five thy father lies;
Of his bones are coral made;
Those are pearls that were his eyes;
Nothing of him that doth fade,
But doth suffer a sea-change
Into something rich and strange.

The Tempest, Act 1, Scene 2

I

She has taken a wrong turning again. A wrong turn on a bloody Friday night, too, when she's already well behind the bank holiday traffic with a long journey ahead. Well done, Pilgrim, she thinks. *A*, excellent.* On the passenger seat, Dog lifts his head to look at her, and sighs.

It's amazing, Jackson always says, how completely useless she is at even finding her own way home, a journey she must have surely done at least five thousand times? The funny thing – is it funny? maybe not – is that Frances knows she can always find her way home, in London at least, when she's drunk. Then, wherever she is, she just seems to put her nose down and trot doggedly on. As she pulls over and gets out her phone, frowning for a moment into the rear-view mirror, she wonders if this is simply because she has spent more of her adult life drunk than sober. Has most of her spatial knowledge been acquired under the influence of over-priced glasses of Merlot (oh, large, please) in the Rat and Gate? *Is the Pope Catholic?* mutters Jackson's voice, in her mind, and, *Do bears shit in the woods?*

She finds it more palatable to think that by now she knows her own turf like the back of her hand, even when pissed. Six years, she thinks, putting her hazard lights on, longer than she's lived anywhere since university, longer than she's lived anywhere apart from the Kentish Weald, full stop. Although she had only come here for love – well, lust as it turned out, which had run out faster than her monthly overdraft extension – it was now her place. It was the rickety studio on Swain's Square that was never warm enough in winter so Dog had to do double duty as hot-water bottle. It was the Heath, and Hilltop, and late night sojourns to those iffy internet dates down the Northern line: Archway, Tufnell Park, Kentish Town, King's Cross. *I don't know why you bother*, her mother tells her shrilly. *They all leave you in the end!*

Frances swipes her phone and taps on Google Maps. There she is now, on the screen, a blue dot quietly swelling and sinking, swelling and sinking, like the light on a police car. She can immediately see what she's done, it's a wrong turn she's taken several times before: left, for some reason, at the Alexandra Park Road lights, so she's going back towards Muswell Hill, rather than right and down the hill towards Colney Hatch and the North Circular, the road that Jackson swears Chris Rea must have been talking about when he wrote 'The Road To Hell'. She usually takes this wrong turn on the Fridays that she's driving back to Kent to see her mother because she's too busy telling Dog about the day she's had, or worrying about something she's just remembered she has left undone: a door unlocked, a gas-ring perhaps still on, a credit card left slightly too close to a ground-floor window. Tonight, sitting in the curdling August heat, she's remembered that she has to give a presentation for House Assembly on Tuesday morning and she's left her MacBook behind.

'Fuck,' she says to Dog, who, with dignity, looks away from her out of the window, pretending not to hear.

'You're a loon,' Jackson used to tell her, listening to her chattering away to Dog in the pub, or in the Green Café at weekends. 'You know that? A certifiable nutter. I've even seen you talking to yourself. One day they'll arrive and take you away. *Boom.*' He would swoop his arms together in front of him, imitating the strait-jacket they'd slap her into before they carted her off, probably to St Anne's on the Seven Sisters Road, and then Frances would always retort that there must be a more salubrious nut-house than that in the North London area. Not for your sort, Jackson would say. *Jackson*, she thinks wistfully. Colleague, confidant, bloody-minded hedonist. And until very recently, pretty much her best friend.

Nonetheless, best friend or not, he's got a point. She knows she ought to stop it, this muttering. She is only running through conversations in her head that she feels she needs to map out more carefully, exchanges where she's asking boyfriends Difficult Questions or squashing that ghastly Mercedes Solomon in Year 13; but still, she's always surprised to find she's actually spoken them out loud. And last term she supposed she had been doing it more frequently than usual, going over in her mind what she'd like to have

3

said to her ex-boyfriend Lucas when she'd still had the chance. Things like, *When can I meet your friends?* Or, *Where do you actually live?* She recognises now that she never asked him because, subconsciously, she must have known she didn't want to hear the answers; but also because she wanted to bask a while longer in that affection of his, that beguiling sense he had given her that he simply couldn't live without her.

Ha.

But although she was too wet to ask the questions then, she wants the answers now; but no one's interested in listening any more. Everyone says she should get over it; after all, plenty more fish in the sea. Silv says she's a dick who's in denial about more things than a dating disaster. Even Hilary in the flat upstairs has taken to changing the subject on dog-walks when it comes to Lucas.

Of course, they're all right. Lucas has gone, and thinking about him now makes her feel sick to her stomach. Frances can cope with most aspects of boyfriend-shittiness. In her iffy internet-dating career she's tolerated perverts and drunks and a baker's dozen of other, more garden-variety weirdos. But Lucas's pathetic little vanishing act has thrown her more completely than anything any other boyfriend has done, reaching as it does back into her past and raking up too many ghosts. *It's not you*, he'd said once, when she'd asked him why he was so cagey about where he lived, *it's me.*

Nope, says Jackson, in her mind. *Believe me, Pilgrim. It's you.*

4

Her mother thinks she should come home, find a nice farmer and get herself married, an opinion that in itself has caused Frances many a long and muttering walk on the Heath.

'You could always marry me,' Jackson used to suggest when she told him about her mother's complaints. 'I could do with someone to look after me in my dotage.'

Thinking of Jackson and his jokey proposals, Frances finds herself biting her lip so hard it hurts, and putting the car abruptly back into gear. She must stop taking these wrong turns. She must learn to concentrate, she's thirty-bloody-nine next month. And something a long way down tells her, quietly but insistently, for reasons she can't entirely fathom, that she must get home to see her mother.

Frances had not liked Jackson to begin with.

He'd arrived at Hilltop at the start of the Lent term the previous year, supposedly as a short-term cover teacher. He was older and a bit battered, but nonetheless exuded a strange sort of glamour in his bright green trousers, tawny hair barely contained by a pair of outlandish tortoiseshell spectacles that he always wore pushed up on to his head.

'How on earth did you find *that*?' Frances had demanded after she'd been cursorily introduced, and Rhidian had shrugged.

'Oh,' he'd said, 'his wife's a friend. You know.'

'No, I don't, actually. How does that qualify him to *teach*?'

Rhidian, looking surprised, said that Jackson had a doctorate in English Literature and had taught at a very successful girls' school already. Did that meet with Frances's approval, or should Rhidian sack him immediately?

Frances was suspicious. 'Which girls' school?'

Out of the office window, in Science Quad, she could see that Jackson wasn't even pretending to do break duty, stretched on a bench in the sunshine and idly turning the pages of a book. As Frances watched, two sixth-form girls sidled up to him, flipping back their hair.

'Oh, I can't remember which one, exactly,' said Rhidian irritably, turning back to a pile of mail marked *Head of English*. 'Why don't you ask him yourself?'

But it was Friday night before Frances had any opportunity to interrogate him. It was a department tradition to take a new member to the pub on their first Friday, Rhidian being of the firm opinion that you only saw someone's true colours when they were drunk. But Jackson, it turned out, was more than happy to be plied with alcohol and insisted that night that he only drank very expensive Sancerre. Over his fourth glass, watching Frances hang up the phone on her mother in a huff, he turned away from Rhidian and said, 'Are you an only child?'

Frances had been too startled to demur. 'How on earth did you guess?'

'Easy.' He regarded her over the rim of his glass. 'You've just been rude to your mother, who by the way sounds like a complete pain in the arse, and now you're obviously crippled with guilt. I suspect if you had siblings you wouldn't feel so responsible. Am I right or am I right?'

Frances conceded that he might be a little bit right, and went off to the bar to get another drink, quickly, before he could finish his last six pounds' worth of Sancerre. When she came back, he said, 'Do you get on any better with your father?'

'No.'

Jackson grinned at her. He was, she conceded to herself, attractive. If you were into that ageing bohemian sort of thing.

'Is he a pain in the arse, too?' he asked.

'No,' said Frances. 'He's dead.'

She's nearing home when she remembers that conversation, having managed for once to take the right slip road at the right junction off the motorway, and to come off at the right place on the A2. Now they are on the higgledy-piggledy, tilty-turny road towards Dryland and her mother's house. She puts a hand on one of Dog's warm ears, just across the handbrake, and feels him stir groggily in his sleep.

Jackson had had the good grace to look mildly abashed when she told him about her father, and they had not pursued the conversation until a long time later, over a year in fact, on the night they walked home beneath the apple blossom. It was only then that she had taken a deep breath and told him the full story: that her father had disappeared from his naval ship, a destroyer named HMS *Wanderer*, in 1981. That he was believed to have slipped and fallen while out on the upper deck. He'd always been a keen

7

astronomer, she said, he'd probably been star-gazing, although no one seemed to know the precise circumstances of what had happened.

It had seemed to five-year-old Frances that one day they'd been seeing him off at Portsmouth, her father pressing a going-away present into her hand and hugging her so tightly to his uniformed front that she had felt the cold imprint of his brass buttons on her forehead, and that almost the next she'd been shepherded gently away by Jean-up-the-lane into a warm house that smelled of cats. Mummy's had a terrible shock, Jean had said to her, but when Frances had asked what the terrible shock was, Jean had only swallowed and avoided her eye. It was about Daddy, she'd said eventually, and Frances had looked away then, out of the window to where Jean's black dog Mack was chasing an indignant-looking squirrel up a tree. What about Daddy? she'd asked. He is all right, isn't he, Jean?

Jean had said in a voice that was not much more than a whisper that Mummy would tell her when she was ready, and in the meantime Frances needed to be a big brave girl. Perhaps, she'd said hopefully, Frances would like to have a cuddle with Mack, or one of the cats?

But thirty-four years later, as they turned into the garden of Jackson's building, where the apple blossom was falling like torn paper on to the warm grass, Frances had admitted to Jackson that she had not been a particularly big brave girl at all. Over the next few days with Jean – her mother was not very well, and it would be better if she was not disturbed, 'yet' – Frances had asked and asked about her father, and when no one would give her an answer she had taken to climbing up to the spare room on Jean's first floor, where she had been installed for her stay with some of her toys from home, and closing the door.

The spare room smelled like vacuum cleaning and air-freshener, but if she climbed up on to the windowsill, Frances had found she could see the first stars coming out between the spiky branches of the damson trees in the garden. At the time of her father's disappearance she'd been going through a period of fascination with stars and planets, she told Jackson that evening, had even been clamouring for a telescope. But on her last night in Jean's spare room, she had pressed her face against the window so that her breath began to fog the glass, and looked out in particular for Sirius, the dog star. There it had been, burning away blue-white in the darkening sky. It was not the brightest star, her father had told her, though it often seemed so because it was the closest to earth.

'Can you see it when you're at the sea?' Frances wanted to know, and her father had smiled. He could see it when he was *at* sea, he told her, yes. In fact, one of the first watches a sailor kept at sea was named the *dogwatch* after Sirius, the dog star. And if Frances ever felt sad, he said, she could always look up at the dog star and be sure that, wherever he was, when her father looked up at it, he'd be thinking about her, too.

But that night, even as Frances watched, something unexpected and devastating had happened.

The dog star had guttered and gone out.

She had blinked, and then, pulling her sleeve down over her hand, had scrubbed at the fogged-up glass, and looked out again.

Nothing.

Sirius had vanished.

And although later Jean would tell her it was probably only the gathering clouds outside that were blocking out the star, that it'd be back by tomorrow evening, love, by then Frances would be quite inconsolable with grief. By then, in fact, she would already have cried and cried until her nose was blocked and she had to breathe through her mouth, and then she would have cried some more until she had humiliatingly retched phlegm and tears all over Jean's plump and comfortable pink-cardied shoulder.

Jean hadn't been cross about the sick, and after she'd settled Frances on the sofa, under a blanket and with Mack – 'to have a cuddle with, he's good at cuddles, aren't you, Mack?' – she had left the room to get them both a nice hot drink and perhaps a piece of cake. But as Mack leaned his old Labrador shoulder against her and licked her cheerfully, Frances had heard Jean talking in a low and indistinct voice in the hall where the telephone lived. And when she came back in, she had told Frances to dry her tears now, because her mother was coming over to collect her, and she needed to show Mummy what a brave girl she was, didn't she?

Afterwards, Frances reflected that she couldn't have done that good a job because when her mother arrived, she had taken one look at her and burst into tears of her own. This

10

in itself was something unprecedented and so shocking that Frances had stopped crying immediately and sat, mouth half open in amazement, as her mother sat down next to Mack on the sofa, and sank her head into her hands. Unlike Frances's, whose wails had caused the cats to leave the room and even the budgerigar to go quiet, her mother's tears had been silent, but her shoulders had shaken; as she watched, Frances had seen the tears sliding through the cracks in her fingers and dripping copiously on to her knees.

Fortunately, Jean had come in then, and they'd all sat together on the sofa. Jean had put her arms around both of them and said that life was a real bugger sometimes, wasn't it, and for years afterwards the camellia smell of Jean's pink cardigan would bring an aching lump to Frances's throat, as if she were fleetingly going down with the flu.

It was only later that night, when she was in bed, that her mother had finally told her the truth. That Daddy had gone to the sea, but that he wouldn't be coming back this time.

Frances, close to an exhausted sleep, had murmured, 'Has he gone with the star?'

Her mother had carried on tucking her in. That was a nice thing to think, she said. That Daddy was a star in the sky.

'But no more tears, now,' she had added. 'They won't bring him back.'

And even close to sleep as she had been, Frances's lip had still quivered to think that her father, in his gold and navy uniform with the big brass buttons, had gone into the sky, which was after all so very far away, and been swallowed up

11

by the darkness where once the star had been. But she had done her best, and next morning her mother, looking pale and composed, had brought her some hot chocolate with her breakfast and a pile of books about ballet and ponies that she'd once liked as a girl. Frances hadn't been remotely interested in ponies or ballet, but she had taken a deep breath herself then, and given her mother a watery smile. Her mother had smiled back: not a particularly happy smile, of course; but there had been a flicker of something in her face then that had awed Frances, for a moment some transcendent sense of her mother's strength of which she had never, when her father was alive, been aware. And later that day, when Jean came round and asked her how she was feeling, Frances had squared her shoulders and raised her chin, and said in a voice that wobbled only a little that she was all right, thank you very much, Jean. She was sad that Daddy wasn't with them any more, but tears weren't going to bring him back, were they?

There'd been a long silence then. Jean had looked confused.

Trying to be helpful, Frances had said, 'He's in the sky with the dog star, Jean.'

Jean had gone *pale* then. She'd looked across at Frances's mother, and said shakily, 'You're sure about that, are you, Mary?' and Frances's mother had looked back at her, unblinking, making Frances think, for a moment, of Merlin, or Morgan le Fay.

Her mother had squared her shoulders and said oh yes, she was quite sure, Jean.

And Frances knew in that moment that Jean had seen it, too, this odd new power of her mother's, because after that she had seemed struck all of a heap, as Frances's father might have said. She hadn't been able to finish her cup of tea, and had left shortly afterwards, her face strangely blotchy and her mouth pressed into a pursed white line.

So after that, when Frances felt like she might cry, she had brought her father's leaving present out of its hiding place in her socks and pants drawer. It was a tiny figurine, no more than two inches high, of a girl standing on the deck of a boat, her hands shading her eyes as she looked out to sea. On the day they returned from Portsmouth, Frances had put the ornament proudly on the sitting room mantelpiece to show anyone who happened to drop in – Come and see my ornament on the mantelpiece! Although more often than not, in her hurry to get her words out, it would come out as *Come and see my ormanteen on the mankenpeen!*

But shortly afterwards, Frances's mother had started to move through the house, taking down all the photographs and insignia associated with her husband, the first stage in a process by which she would, steadily but irrevocably, wave her wand and excise him from their lives. The ornament was a casualty of the purge, luckily found again in the ticky-tack drawer in the kitchen, where small things destined for the bin were sometimes held, and by the time her next birthday came around Frances had learned that most things to do with her father – his vinyl LP of *Sgt. Pepper*, his books on stained glass – were better off concealed. So she hid the ornament under the lining of her socks and pants drawer, and took it out only when her mother was not around to see.

She had told Jackson all this on his doorstep, and he had been so horrified he hadn't even got around to opening the door. 'You poor little scrap,' he had said, when she had finished, putting his arm round her, and Frances, shrugging, had muttered yes, well, crying didn't do anyone any good, did it? You just had to get on with it.

Now, she swings the car left at last, off the main road and up the narrow lane towards her mother's house, and when they reach the hairpin bend a hundred yards before the house, as usual Dog stirs and stands up on the seat, pressing his nose to the crack in the window. Then they round the bend and Frances gasps, stamping on the brakes just in time. Dog slithers into the dashboard and bumps his nose.

A woman in a nightdress is standing barefoot in the lane.

She doesn't move as the car grinds to a stop, but stands looking at them, twisting the hem of her nightdress between her hands. A badly tied headscarf is slipping on to her shoulders.

As Frances unclips her seat belt and opens the door, her mother reaches out a hand, pale as paper. Her face is slack-jawed and blank of recognition, but the word she comes out with shatters the space between them into a thousand pieces.

'Martin,' she says, 'Martin.'

And her eyes fill with tears.

'Really,' says her mother brightly, half an hour later. She's got herself dressed now – 'I've been poorly, a tummy bug going round' – and in jeans and wellies looks almost normal again. 'You mustn't be such a drama queen, Far. I've told you and told you, it's *terribly* tiresome.' And she jolts boiling water into two mugs, as if it is the teabags that are to blame.

She'd woken up, she says, and realised that the dogs were gone. When she went downstairs, the back door was open and so was the back gate, and she was worried they'd stray down to the main road. She'd merely been in the road calling them when Frances's car came bowling around the bend. '*Much* too fast, as usual,' she adds, squashing her teabag against the side of the mug. 'Twenty's plenty, you know, on these roads. You're not in London now.'

That's been her war cry for six years, Frances thinks. It has driven her mother demented that Frances has remained in London, despite her being nearly forty and *still* having to share a draughty building with that coven of peculiar women, what were their names again? But that in itself reminds Frances of another thing. Her mother's grasp on names, cloudy at best since Frances can remember, has become much worse of late. Sometimes she has to run through two or three dog names before she can grasp the right one, so her fox terrier sometimes sits with her head patiently on one side, being called Daisy or Drummer for several minutes before Frances's mother can remember that she is, in fact, called *Dilys*. They have laughed about it in the past, joking about that disease,

15

you know, the one where you can't remember anything, what's it called again?

But recently, Frances knows that there have been other things going on with her mother, things she's tried very hard not to notice. Over the summer, too many cups of undrunk tea in the fridge. Her wallet in the alcove where the fire-lighters live. And other things, sometimes: tiny slippages in her grasp on time, so that, 'Where on earth have you *been*?' she demanded once, when Frances had been out of the room for five minutes. 'I was so *worried*, you've been simply *hours*.' Once, and more peculiarly, when Frances had come in to ask her mother if she knew where her birth certificate was, her mother had said, distractedly, 'Scarborough, I expect.' Glitches, fissures, each in themselves not amounting to much. Her mother is well over seventy, after all, and has lived on her own for years, she's bound to be a bit eccentric. So what if she keeps cups of tea in the fridge? Maybe she likes cold tea.

Now her mother is passing her a mug and saying peevishly, 'I don't know why you never return my phone calls, Far,' and Frances is finding herself unable to tell her mother that she does return the calls, she almost always does. Her mother just doesn't seem able to remember.

And for the rest of the evening every time there's a pause in supper-time conversation, or in the half-second of silence before an advert break on television, she sees again the face staring in at her through her windscreen, that slack jaw and open mouth. But much worse, she recalls the complete absence of recognition in her mother's eyes, as if she had

16

momentarily wandered off the track, and, turning around to retrace her steps, found that the old familiar path had vanished. And although for over thirty years Frances and her mother have never mentioned him by name, they both know that the person she's looking for has gone.

It's only when she's climbing into bed later, pushing Dog off the pillow, that Frances thinks, with a miserable clutch of nausea in her stomach, that *demented* may be a word she will have to stop using so carelessly in the future. As she turns the light off and lies down, she wishes, not for the first time, that she had a father or even a sibling to discuss this with, someone to reassure her; someone perhaps, in the long run, to go through it with her, whatever 'it' turns out to be. She thinks again of Jackson, who's been through all manner of difficult family situations in his life. But they haven't spoken since the end of term, since the night they walked home beneath the apple blossom; and now they're about to be inspected at school everyone's bound to be preoccupied. A reconciliation is unlikely to happen any time soon.

Her phone screen lights up for a moment in the darkness, and she turns to it immediately. But it's just a reminder about a system update, and, a moment later, it is dark once more. Outside, the wind shivering through the sycamore trees reminds her again of the sea.

II

At five o'clock on Friday, Jackson realises that he can't get home.

It's sod's law, he thinks, that even at the start of a bank-bloody-holiday the Jag is buried several cars deep in the tiny school car park. This is what happens when they calendar a school year to begin right on the dot of the first of September, he thinks. He can spot Science Harry's Audi, and that irritating music teacher's Polo stacked behind his car. Damn it! He's clearly going to have to hang about for ages if he wants to move the car. To be fair, it's usually him who's the culprit because he comes in on the nose of eight thirty every morning and not a moment before; it's usually him who someone's ringing up, demanding he come down and let them out, because it's his car squeezed into that tiny little gap just inside the gate. *Come on, mate, I'm a part-timer, I've got to be out of here at two, can't you just come down and move it?* Or, *I have to get out at three to pick up Jemima. Everyone knows that!*

At first, when he was just the cover teacher, Jackson responded to this by simply refusing to leave his telephone number displayed on his dashboard, as per the rules on the common room noticeboard. But then a global email came round from the school office. *Would the driver of the green Jaguar registration Y778 JDA please contact the office immediately?* Jackson never did contact the office, of course, but word got round. There were deep sighs, there were knocks on his door in the middle of lessons. His detractors were mostly peripatetic music teachers, silly little men in bow ties or hipster girls with names like Naomi and Niamh. One day, shortly after he'd been taken on full-time, there was a particularly epic shouting match, and then Jackson's cause was taken up by the Common Room Committee and used as a flagship example of the need for Priority Parking for Full-Time Employees. There was a lot of talk. Emails were sent. Then, of course, nothing further happened, although Jackson's old Jag did get viciously keyed one afternoon. He privately suspected Naomi or Niamh, but gritted his teeth and left his phone number thereafter.

Now, he decides to leave the car and walk, no point in having a row with anyone on the first day of term when Jackson's decided to jack in the job in a few months anyway. The letter to the headmaster is in his bag, although for some reason he didn't get around to putting it in his pigeon-hole today.

'You can't retire at fifty-seven,' Rhidian had pointed out to him crossly. 'You'll go off your head with boredom.' Jackson had snapped that he wasn't *retiring*, just getting out of teaching, and Rhidian had given him an old-fashioned look. Whatever, he'd said, and gone back to his *Hamlet* essays. I'm not retiring, Jackson thinks, shivering: the word conjures up images of health insurance and pension plans, soft food and Saga holidays. To cheer himself up, he tries to remind himself that the walk home to Primrose Hill is a pleasant one: the last light of summer laced now with early bonfires and the waft of garlic and candle-wax from little bistros in Kentish Town reminding him of holidays in France. The leaves are turning in Millbrook Park. It takes under an hour and will be good for him; he really needs to take more exercise. It was one of the few things that even Katy had chided him about. And after all, he always tells himself when confronted with the spectre of exercise, weren't his earliest ancestors in South Africa walkers? *Strandlopers*, beachcombers: itinerants moving restlessly from place to place. Yes, thinks Jackson gloomily. It does, after all, make a certain amount of sense.

And so he turns south on to Thresher's Lane, the precipitous tree-lined road that winds down past the park and the cemetery. One of the few consolations of his newly single state, and of having the job at Hilltop, is that he has been able to choose where he lives. He had hated Kilburn, where they had ended up buying a house two years ago.

'It's a very up-and-coming area,' Katy informed him. 'And anyway, it's all we can afford at the moment.'

Jackson, registering the slight, snapped, 'So why doesn't your father cough up, as promised?' But he knew in his heart of hearts the answer. He's the breadwinner, isn't he? He shouldn't need financial help from his younger wife's

21

parents. Hasn't he got life savings, shouldn't he by now, in fact, have almost more savings left in him than life?

So Jackson submitted grumblingly to what Katy called West Hampstead but which he knew all along was Kilburn really, only occasionally making comments about its demographic which prompted Katy to shush him and say that he couldn't *say* that sort of thing in public any more. It was one of Katy's many very good qualities, Jackson thinks now, as he turns through the black iron gates of Millbrook Park, that she never shouted at him, even when he said really awful things. This wasn't particular evidence of her devotion to Jackson, Katy just wasn't a shouty person. She was calm and equable with her two excitable spaniels, Lachlan and Lorcan, and quietly capable with the neurotic ex-racehorse that she stabled expensively in nearby Mill Hill. It was hardly a leap, Jackson reflects as he crosses the grass, for her to be kind to her discontented, difficult and (he had heard her mother say once to Katy's sister at a lunch party) Much Older partner. It had all been, he could see now, a sort of tuning up for bigger things. Katy had been frank with him about wanting children almost from the moment he met her at a party in Italy, where Jackson had been living for more than ten years, ever since leaving South Africa. He had ostensibly gone there to take up a university post, teaching mostly very basic English language skills to undergraduates, although most people assumed he was having an extended period of what his brother-in-law Clem called *time off for drinking and thinking*. In the apricot light of August, her honey-coloured hair escaping from its chignon, Katy had seemed like a good and sensible idea. She wasn't the sort of dusky lunatic Jackson usually took up with, who might have looked like they belonged in an Almodóvar film but who always turned out to have undiagnosed mental health issues. No, Katy was calm, she was sensible, she was honest. She was also well over twenty-one and not related to anyone he knew.

He wasn't English, he informed her that night, though he might sound to the manor born. No, Jackson had actually been born in South Africa in the sixties, the elder of two children growing up in Cape Town. As a child, he said, he'd been considered almost a prodigy in his government school: at thirteen he'd gone on a scholarship to Stephenhouse, the prestigious private school, and then, at eighteen, on another scholarship, all the way to Cambridge, where, much to the surprise of his supervisor, he had got a First and stayed on to work for a PhD.

Katy had put her head on one side, clearly enchanted with this image of the boy-from-the-backwoods in such a medieval setting. 'Were you terribly sweet?'

'No,' said Jackson, 'I was a wanker.'

Had he been deliberately self-effacing to charm her? Jackson pauses to let a woman with a pram go through the gate into Millbrook Park, and sees, in his mind's eye, his twenty-two-year-old self, a cricket jumper slung around his shoulders but his blond hair determinedly shaggy, 'like some bloody Australian surfer', his supervisor had observed when they first met.

Sometimes, at weekends, he received invitations from other Stephenhouse men, now over in the UK and working

23

in banking, or in the London offices of mining firms like Anglo-American. But Jackson found he had no desire to reminisce about the more sadistic masters at school, the ritual canings some of the boys had received, nor to join in with their discussions about the crassness of the Afrikaner or the Black Consciousness Movement. Jackson's mother had worked in an orphanage in Soweto before she was married, but he had always known that his mother was considered odd by the wealthy parents of his Stephenhouse friends.

There were girls, of course, undergraduates and other graduate students. They were mostly cleverer than he was but had fancied him enough not to show it; to twenty-two-year-old Jackson they simply seemed, beneath their back-combed hair and puffball skirts, jittery and skittish, prone to coltish exclamations like 'Gosh!' and 'That's a bit naughty!' in bed.

It was in Jackson's second year as a postgraduate that his father became ill. He flew home at the end of the Christmas term, but when his sister Edie met him at the airport her eyes were red. Their father had died in hospital, the previous night. Jackson was already in the air, so they hadn't been able to reach him.

'But Mum said—'

Edie's lip curled. 'She didn't want to worry you, Jackson. You know what she's like.'

But Jackson, apparently, should have known anyway that his father's influenza was actually the beginning of a collapsing lung, which would accelerate rapidly as the southern hemisphere's humidity increased through November, until he was hospitalised on the day Jackson got on the aeroplane to fly home. He had died within hours.

Katy put her hand on his arm. 'And you never went back to Cambridge?'

He had shaken his head. He'd transferred his studies to the university at Cape Town, he told her. Within a month it was as if Cambridge had never been.

A year after meeting her, Jackson moved to London with Katy, where she was Head of Geography at a prominent girls' school. He got his first job there, on Katy's recommendation, of course. In the first year, he recalls now, life was languorous and leisurely: Katy looking over her shoulder as she rose from the bed and laughing uproariously at the buttered croissant stuck to her bottom; Katy smiling up at him through a curtain of tawny hair; Katy submitting with surprising alacrity to being scooped up one morning as she stepped out of the shower and thrown, naked and giggling, on to the bed. Even now the memory stirs him a little as he crosses the leaf-littered grass.

But in the second year there were thermometers and charts and special kits from the chemist. When Katy still didn't become pregnant, Jackson began to feel inadequate and guilty, because after all he was, as they knew, Much Older. Katy tried to reassure him by saying that these things took time, after all it was quite a feat for his Little Chaps; it was apparently the equivalent for sperm of swimming from Bodrum to Athens. At school, a Vietnamese Boat Person

25

survivor came in to give a talk about humanitarian aid for the refugees who were crossing from Afghanistan and Turkey into Greece by sea, and after that every time Jackson saw a boat-people photo in the papers he was ashamed to find himself thinking of his own beleaguered sperm, all five hundred million of them risking death as they escaped the war-torn world of Jackson's scrotum and swam towards Katy's womb.

It was during the third year that they began to think that Jackson's Little Chaps, rather like Jackson himself, were not all that keen on exercise. Feeling the pressure, Jackson began to have Problems Downstairs, and they had the first of their major arguments. Katy bulk-bought Viagra on the internet, wanted him to have tests, wanted to know if there was any actual point in their doing IVF. It all threatened to be humiliating, not to mention cripplingly expensive, and anyway they were told that because she was thirty-seven by then and he was of course Much Older it probably wouldn't work; but after a further year Jackson, with a feeling of deep dread, agreed to have the tests. He'd got the appointment, was in fact psyching himself up to jizz in a jar when he came home one day at four to find Katy, unusually, already there.

She had made a pot of Earl Grey tea and shut the dogs in the sitting room.

He stood in the doorway and they looked at one another, and Jackson was never quite sure afterwards whether his dominant emotion was despair or relief.

Now, in Millbrook Park, Jackson finds himself pausing, as usual, to watch a gaggle of girls from Douglas-Allan playing Frisbee in the late afternoon light. They are all rosy and flushed and laughing. He stops for a moment, and watches the one closest to him as she picks up the Frisbee. She wears her tawny hair in a high ponytail, and bends low from the waist like a dancer. Catching him watching her, she meets his gaze before lifting her chin and sending the Frisbee spinning away from her into the summer sunshine.

'Jackson Crecy, you are a *shameless* perv,' Frances had observed one Sunday, a couple of months after Katy had gone, as they sat attempting to moderate A-level course-work in Millbrook Park. She was sitting cross-legged on the rug he'd brought, her unbrushed hair pulled into a bun and a distinct look of last night's make-up about her. Her mouth looked chapped and sore, and it was then that he'd felt a sudden stirring in his groin. Because where Katy had been very much sensible-Surrey-day-school, all scholarships and prizes, he could see in that moment that Frances, with her laddered tights and laissez-faire air of getting-off-with-the-gardener, was pure St Trinian's.

That day, following his gaze to the group of girls playing rounders below them on the slope of the park, she'd stretched her arms behind her head and said, 'Most people your age try and bluff it out when they're slobbering over teenagers.'

She'd cleared her throat then, and struck an attitude. 'Isn't that leggy blonde an Isett-Browne? There, playing *back-stop*? She *does* look like her sister. And isn't that little brunette here in *first deep* Jonty Duff's daughter? Oh, you don't know Jonty? He's been our broker for *donkey's* years.'

Frances, laughing and lascivious, her voluptuous face half hidden behind a pair of scuffed sunglasses, an earlier coffee spill already staining her striped shirt. 'But you, Jackson,' she'd said, 'you just get on and slaver so *honestly*.' She nodded approvingly. 'It's lovely.'

How old was Frisbee girl, seventeen? Yes, seventeen and pert, long-eyed and truculent around the jaw. *Had* he been perving?

(*You fucking well stay away from us, Jackson. You hear me? I swear to God I'll fucking kill you with my own hands otherwise.*)

Fortunately, just then Frances had put out her glass, and Jackson, taking a deep breath, had looked away from the girls and poured her some more prosecco.

It is the first time since July, he realises, that he has thought of Frances almost without rancour. Jackson turns away from the schoolgirls of the present, with their flying ponytails and their voices, all breathless with money and freedom and the unmarked years ahead of them, taking instead the path through the park that curves around alongside the cemetery fence. Over the iron railings he can see gravestones so faded and encrusted with lichen that their inhabitants' names are no longer legible. Occultists climb into the cemetery on Hallowe'en and solstices to perform rituals among the gravestones. While Jackson admires their gumption, he hopes that no pets are slaughtered. Even though he no longer has pets, he likes cats and dogs, and has a weakness even for upstairs's manky cat, Callaghan.

He steers his mind away firmly from Dog, Frances's creaky old Labrador, and instead fingers the crumpled-up letter in his pocket. He threw it in the office bin earlier, and is tempted to chuck it a second time, but knows that if he does he is likely to come back tomorrow to fish for it among the spliff ends and wine bottles and empty tubs of Waitrose hummus in a Millbrook Park bin. He takes it out of his pocket, and turns it over, half closing his eyes so that all he can see is a blur of Katy's elegant green ink, not the actual words themselves. It doesn't matter, though, because he can remember every word she'd written. Her news is a blotch on his mind that will not be erased. He blinks. It's a sadness that is even now settling, like a water-stain into wood, sinking down through the grain until it begins to seep into deeper areas of decay. A hollow feeling, like loss or bereavement; yet when he thinks of how Katy's belly must be beginning to swell, he realises that that's not it, because you cannot be bereft of something that is not dead, can you, of something that is after all the very opposite of dead?

He's reached the gate now. Turning up his collar, he swings left, down towards Kentish Town and the last leg of the journey home.

III

On bank holiday Monday Frances leaves her mother after lunch and drives back to London. She's left an extra-big note next to the phone this time. *Don't Ring Far At Work, Try Her Mobile! X*

School is quiet on days like these. It's often when Frances comes in, not through pedagogic zeal and zest, but out of desperation because she's let so much work back up over the previous week.

When she has to do it at all, Frances prefers to get in mid-morning on a Sunday or a bank holiday, mark exercise books, and have at least a cursory look at what's coming the following week before she takes Dog for a walk on the Heath. In any other job this would count as commitment with a capital C, but in teaching everyone knows you either work in the evenings, which she can never seem to do, or you suck up the loss of a weekend day. It's the Bottom Line. That's where Frances spends most of her time these days, on the Bottom Line. It used to be a ritual between Jackson and her: she'd ring him from the Heath after her Sunday stint and he'd say, 'Oh God, don't make me think about your Bottom Line. Come and have a drink, for Christ's sake.' But that probably won't be happening again any time soon. The long Sunday lunches, falling asleep on his ancient chaise-longue after her fourth glass of wine, the easy way she'd found that she could talk to him about boyfriends, her mother, even her lunatic friend Silv: all finished now.

'Don't you even want to be a head of department?' her mother always asks her when Frances complains about work. The implication is clear. *You're obviously not going to have children, after all*. And, *after all*, most of the people Frances went to Oxford with are now in senior management posts, arranging a mortgage on their second home, and popping out baby number three, all with one hand tied behind their backs. Facebook is full of photos of children who are almost ready to start secondary school, while Frances is still having it off with fuckwits.

She is evidently not the only person last-minuting before the start of term: despite it being a bank holiday, the car park outside Hilltop House is half full, and with a jolt she recognises Jackson's old Jag, hemmed in by several others. Realising with a guilty start that she hasn't had a chance to try and talk to him properly yet, she decides to avoid the department office and heads straight for her classroom on the top floor.

Even after the long summer break, she finds as she pushes open the door that the room still smells faintly of Year 11, her biggest set and the most heavily populated with girls. Strange how July has persisted on to the cusp of autumn, how the empty weeks of sunlight have not quite blotted out the traces of sugary perfume or the groiny smell of boy. Frances instructs Dog to lie down while she works, and he refuses, leaning sulkily instead against her knees as she sits down at her computer, pushing his muzzle up through her arm as he likes to do when he feels that, really, this isn't what he'd had in mind, at *all*. She leans over to press the on-switch on the bulky monitor on her desk, and as she does so catches her breath and draws back a little. Down below, Jackson is standing on the pavement, sunglasses on top of his head, staring gloomily at his boxed-in car. Frances feels her hand twitch involuntarily into a wave; but then, remembering, she draws further back, out of sight.

Dog gives her an old-fashioned look and slumps down, defeated, on the floor. She looks at her monitor and types in her password, then considers the background picture again as it loads. Is it time to change it? Three tall ships with rigging and sails moving on a flat and Merlot-coloured sea. The two ships side-on to the photographer look like they are either about to touch, or pass right by one another: it's hard to tell. But heading at ninety degrees for the tiny space between them is another ship, darker and smaller. The photo gives the impression somehow that it is travelling at speed. Frances likes the photo, although she doesn't know why. She thinks it might be connected to a Larkin poem at the end of last term that ended with a reference to tall ships waving and parting at the mouth of an estuary. Back in July, when she'd just been unceremoniously dumped by Lucas, it had made her go a bit glassy-eyed and sniffy in front of Year 11, who hadn't minded much, being quite used to her fluctuating moods by then.

Moping over Uncle Bulgaria again? Silv would say later, passing her in the hall. 'Shut up,' Frances would say sulkily, and Silv would say, well, he did look like a Womble. And that was what you got, Silv said, for hanging around at a stupid UCAS conference when you could have been doing something more interesting, like coming down to Soho with Silv. You got a *womble*.

'I wasn't *hanging around*,' Frances would protest. 'I had my arm twisted by the head. I had to go.'

'Balls,' said Silv. 'You experienced a complete failure of imagination. As usual.'

The irony was that Frances really hadn't wanted to do the bloody UCAS thing, anyway. Left to herself, she would probably have gone home to cruise her online dating pages and then lie in a bath with her book, while Dog slumped out on the bath mat, waiting for his supper. But then the head, Venning, had caught her over coffee at break-time, and reminded her that all sixth-form tutors should go, it was an opportunity to ask actual admissions tutors important questions and, besides, so much potential for productive dialogue with parents, didn't Frances agree? And Frances, who did not usually give a toss about *productive dialogue* with anyone, was suddenly gloomily aware that her yearly appraisal was looming and that, bouncing about on her Bottom Line, she could probably do with a few brownie points for effort.

'Are you going?' she'd asked Jackson hopefully, as she sat down with her coffee, and he had snorted and said Christ no, he'd rather slam his nob in a drawer than stand around trading value-added statistics with a bunch of chippy state-school teachers. He was, he said, going home to cook himself a delicious meal. It was one of the perks of being on his own again, he could eat and drink whatever he liked. No more foods rich in folate. No more having to sneak glasses of wine when Katy wasn't looking. Tonight it would be a bottle of Meursault and *coquilles St Jacques.* 'You should come over,' he'd said casually, but Frances had sighed and said she couldn't, she'd told *Venning* she was going; it was as good as a prison sentence.

And when Lucas – the Head of Sixth Form at a local comp whom she'd subsequently met at the conference and fallen for despite or perhaps because of what Silv sneeringly described as his *cuddly qualities* – turned out to be married, Jackson had said ha, well, she should have come over to dinner at his that night, shouldn't she? At least she knew *he* was single. And just for a moment, then, she had wondered what it *would* be like to do something with Jackson. And despite the fact that he was thought to be quite sexy even by the merciless Hilltop sixth form, and despite the fact that he had, once, sort of asked her out, she'd swiftly thought, don't be ridiculous. He's your *friend*.

Now, Frances sighs, and looks back at the ships, speeding towards one another on her screen. Looked at one way it was consoling; the two bigger ships were, at least, not parting but moving towards one another, and at that stage, in July, she'd have given her eye-teeth for a splintering collision over a parting, any day. But looked at another way it was morbid, and predictable, and tied in with her latent but lifelong anxiety about her father and the sea. What was it Jackson used to quote at her last term to lighten her up? *The sea, the snot green, scrotum-tightening sea!* And when she'd given him the finger, he had gone off down the corridor with Rhidian, carolling *Oed und leer das Meer* in an accent distinctly reminiscent of Herr Flick in *'Allo, 'Allo*. Pack of bastards, Frances had grumbled to herself, but at least by then she had been smiling.

Now, she opens up PowerPoint to work on her House Assembly presentation. She'd been supposed to do something on poetry and refugees at the end of the summer term, to reflect further on the issues raised by the crisis in Europe; but then of course Lucas had pulled his disappearing stunt and she'd cried off sick on the day it was due. At that stage just getting out of bed felt like one of the twelve labours of Hercules, although as her mother has spent the summer telling her, hasn't Frances brought all this on herself because of her very poor Lifestyle Choices? Frances thinks she probably has, but somehow imminent disaster seems much more appealing than her mother's lifestyle suggestions, which when they are not focused on Frances marrying a local farmer, are about her instead Getting a Hobby. The last time they'd had the conversation it had been her mother's suggestion that Frances might find more happiness in some rare-breed sheep than she would in her fruitless hunt for a human partner. 'Well,' Rhidian had informed her when she told him, 'she may have a point.' His eyes had gleamed. 'Some of those breeds have the most gigantic testicles.'

But Frances, of course, has not given the rare-breed sheep, or their testicles, a try. In fact, she has not done anything over the summer at all, apart from brood, about anything and everything it seems. As usual, the end of an affair has taken away her appetite and left her feeling empty and sick, and increasingly, as the summer's drawn to a close, lacking the energy to do anything at all. Sometimes, at home in the holidays, she had fallen asleep in the middle of the afternoon, waking to find her mother standing over her resentfully. *At your age I had a husband and a toddler to look after!* Bully for you, Frances always wants to retort. Her mother's scepticism about men is not, apparently, matched by an equal scepticism of the value of mother-hood; indeed, sometimes Frances wonders if the reason her mother so often seems so cross with her is that she feels that Frances has, somehow unfairly, evaded the honourable punishment of children, like someone skipping National Service or dodging the draft. *Dulce et decorum est, procreanderum et morietur?* Sometimes she half expects to find a white feather stuffed inside one of her packets of the Pill, or else to find herself somehow immaculately fertilised against her will. But now it's the new term and the House Assembly is coming at her again like an express train, a whole half-hour of holding the attention of seventy pupils, all of whom would rather be doing something else, all of whom would be furtively on their phones beneath the table. *So fuckin bored. Me too. Shall we grab a Nero in period 1?*

Frances' unfinished attempt to construct a presentation on poetry and refugee-dom has been lurking on her desktop since last term. She stares at it, gloomily, knowing it is not awfully good. Last term, Jen McGarrick, dropping in to her classroom, had glanced at it and said, tactfully, 'There's some good stuff in the *Grauniad* about the refugee crisis. I'm going to make some of the stories into a booklet next term.'

'Why?'

'In case people want to use them with Year 11 for GCSE Language practice,' says Jen briskly. 'And also just, well, because.'

Because *we all ought to think about ourselves a bit less*, Frances thinks. But the problem is, she isn't obsessed with herself, she is obsessed with the *lack* of anyone else. Or is one just an extension of the other? Because now Lucas has gone, she feels that she too is vanishing, becoming less solid, emptied of everything except whispers and aches.

It had been lovely with Lucas to begin with, constant texting and infrequent but exuberant dates with far too much wine and a lot of frantic taxi rides at the end of the evening. In fact, her favourite pair of red pants must still be under the passenger seat of an Uber cab somewhere.

But then something had happened.

A week went by and he didn't text. He sent an email from a new account saying he had lost his phone, that he'd be in touch. Frances got drunk and rang the phone to check. A woman's voice at the end. When Frances had gritted her teeth and asked if she could speak to Lucas, the woman had said, 'Hang on. Luke! Sweetheart!' A pause. 'Elsie, love, get your dad, will you?'

Frances had thrown her phone against the wall then, so the screen broke; the next day at work, she'd sent Lucas an email containing a string of compound nouns.

'What's a *fanny-rat*?' Rhidian had asked, looking over her shoulder, and Frances, between gritted teeth, said it was a rural expression.

'Yes,' said Rhidian, wandering away again. 'I suppose it would be.'

After that, Lucas had vanished not only from her Twitter followers but her Spotify and Skype lists too. And now it's been over two months since she's heard from him, three since they've actually met. She isn't quite sure why the whole thing still bothers her so much: Lucas is clearly a twat, after all. But somehow he seems to have dipped a Womble hand (or should that be paw?) into a closed-off part of her mind and stirred up a darkness that, as an adult, she's more or less learned to leave well alone. *When you stare into the abyss, the abyss stares back into you,* Jackson had said that night as they walked home under the apple blossom, talking properly for the first time about their families. Damn it, she's not meant to be thinking about Jackson either, it's as pointless feeling angry and ashamed about him as it is feeling miserable about the state of her love life generally, or convinced that something peculiar is going on with her mother.

Now, after adding some images and tidying up the slide transitions, Frances closes down the paltry PowerPoint and is about to pack up when she hears a distant buzzing, like a trapped bee, coming from inside her bag. She puts her head on one side and then realises, of course, it's her mobile. She'd put it on silent for the drive back from her mother's this afternoon. She picks up her bag and fumbles for her phone among its chaos of coffee receipts and loose tampons. Is it ringing? Is it Jackson, perhaps, calling again to see if they can have a chat about what happened that night? If it is, she's already decided she's ready to talk. She's just about squared with herself that she can muster the words, *yes*, and *of course*, and *no, totally, of course no hard feelings*.

But when she pulls the phone out, she can see two things. It is her mother ringing. But her screen also says *Home: 17 Missed Calls*.

She snatches up the phone and presses the green button. 'Mum?' she says. 'Are you okay?'

By nightfall, it's raining. The heat had broken as she walked home, and for hours now a cool rain has been plashing through the trees in the square, water pooling in sudden puddles on the road and gargling through the plastic pipe beneath her windowsill. When she leans out, she can see pigeons sitting fluffed up and baleful beneath the eaves, and lines of sparrows on the telephone wires beginning to twitch and stir. Lucky sparrows, she thinks, departing for distant climes. Through the mist of rain, the pavement is dappled orange with street lamps and shadows; buses pull in with a whoosh of brakes; taxis hover wolfishly on corners.

Because of the call from her mother, Frances can't settle at home, not to a bath or a book or even a bottle of wine, so in the end she gives in and, clicking her tongue at Dog, sets off across the square. They cross the grass islands in the middle, littered now with Sunday lunch-time sandwich boxes and Coke cans, then drop left down a cobbled alleyway, past the Rat and Gate pub and across the road towards Millbrook Mews. Here, the Georgian houses rise five storeys up to meet the very tops of the horse chestnut trees, and every driveway boasts a Porsche or a Jag. Frances swings a leg up to get over the Residents Only gate into Ellroy Park, hearing herself make an *oof* sound like a sat-on cushion. God, she feels fat, which must be entirely in her mind because she can't remember the last time she ate a proper meal. On the other hand, hadn't someone once told her that her breasts alone would see her through several hard winters? She heaves the other leg over, wondering absently who knew her well enough to say something like that without offending her? Jackson, of course. But now the thought crosses her mind like a leaf, falling unnoticed into the gutter. Because all there is room for inside the broken television of her head is the conversation she'd had earlier with her mother.

For a moment, when she picked up the phone, she'd been sure that her mother was simply going to be in a paddy with her about something she'd borrowed or left undone at home, and had braced herself for a row. Out of the window on the street below, a woman in jeans and smart leather wellingtons had been stopping to watch her dog relieve himself on the pavement, while behind her a toddler in dungarees had begun climbing up on to the low wall that bordered the verge.

'Mum?' she'd said.

And there had been that silence, pregnant with static and held-in breath.

'Mum,' she'd said again. And that had been when the tears began.

'He's left me,' her mother said, and her voice was one Frances had never heard before, dried and splintered as driftwood at low tide.

'Who's left you?' Frances had asked. She'd been sweeping over possibilities as she said it, dogs or gardeners or a bad-tempered old ram they'd once kept called Foggarty for whom her mother still occasionally grieved; but something way down in her belly, even then, had been turning over and over, like a fish.

'He's left me,' her mother said again, but this time sounding very far away. Outside, an ambulance siren had been screaming up the hill, and when Frances glanced out of the window this time she could see that, across the street, the toddler was standing up, wobbling perilously on the low wall while the woman cleaned up after the dog.

'Mum,' she had said, more gently. 'Who has left you? I don't understand what you're saying.'

Her mother had drawn a breath. 'Martin,' she said, the name curdling her voice with pain, 'he's left me. He's *gone*.'

Frances had felt her left hand tighten on the edge of the desk. Her chest had ached. 'Dad died,' she said, and this time her mother's response had been swift and sure as a slap, a flicker just for a moment of her former certainty and power.

42

'*No*, Far,' she said. 'Not dead. Just gone.'

The siren was rising to a shriek somewhere near, on the High Street, and Frances had watched quite absently, phone still in hand, as across the road the toddler fell off the wall, crumpled, and began to howl.

As the gradient of Ellroy Park becomes more and more precipitous, Frances can hear them all – Rhidian, Jackson, even Silv – saying they *told* her so. She should have taken action sooner, should have arranged some proper home care for her mother as soon as she noticed that her behaviour was off-kilter. She's been far too preoccupied, hasn't she, with her hangovers and one-nights, with her missed milestones and status anxiety, with the wreckage that floats around the boat of her blind, stupid heart. Wouldn't anyone else, anyone normal, have known at once that her mother was slowly but steadily going bonkers, and, moreover, wouldn't they have been better at doing something about it?

She's on the Heath itself now, leaving the lights of Ellroy behind her. Dog is up ahead in front of her, just a pair of green eyes gleaming at her through the dark as she pauses to drag her sleeve across her eyes. She must grow up, she must start taking responsibility. She must get on to the local GP; she must go home at the next possible opportunity; she must tell her mother, at last, that it's time they sat down and talked about her father. Martin Pilgrim, only sometimes beloved husband although totally worshipped father, who had died thirty-four years ago in an accident, at sea.

43

They have never spoken about him because her mother hasn't permitted it. Like Gandalf in the mines of Moria, she has kept that door closed by sheer force of will. But the conversation is evidently now long overdue.

Up ahead, the rising moon sluices a slatey light across the path towards Lachlan's Copse and in the darkness she can see Dog turning round to stare at her, eyes gleaming and muzzle outstretched. She read somewhere once that animals can smell your past and your future, your hope and your fear, so does this mean that all along even Dog has known that she's a total fucking idiot? *Answers on a post-card*, says Rhidian's voice in the distance. The ridge in front of her looms, cresting like a tidal wave in the dark and she shivers. Her mother has never wanted to discuss her father's death, has in the past seemed to vanish within herself if pressed on the subject, but Frances knows that the time has now come. The facts need to be laid out in black and white, once and for all, for both their sakes. But the prospect makes her feel watery in the mouth and sick, and as she whistles for Dog, Frances can't help wishing, again, that her father had left her with at least one sibling, a brother perhaps, or a sensible, reliable sister. Someone, at any rate, to help her deal with whatever it is that's coming.

IV

Jackson wakes late on Tuesday, wondering, as is often the case, where he is.

In the half-light, the shape of the room gradually reasserts its familiarity: its sloping ceiling, long windows, the triangle of darkness where the door has been left ajar into the shuttered bathroom. Is this dementia, Jackson wonders, putting a hand out to look at the clock on the bedside table, or is it simply that as one got older, everything contracted and condensed, so that five years became more like five minutes, and all attendant shifts and changes bunched together and became that much more frenetic and unsettling? He'd been dreaming, too, but as was becoming habitual since Edie died, he couldn't remember the shapes and outlines of the dream clearly. This morning, as on so many others throughout August, he wakes with a sense of his dream retreating like a tide, leaving his mind beached and smooth, marked only in places by abstract things. One of his sister's shoes, a fragment of something that might once have been his father's pipe, a scrap of lace that might (Christ!) have been his christening gown.

But stranger than that are the stray words, heard from above and far off, as if cried by plaintive gulls wheeling somewhere out of sight. *Langtande. Breker! Hou die blink kant bô!* Colloquial phrases in the Afrikaans of the schoolyard, words that no one Jackson knows now would use or understand, but mixed in with them this morning are quieter phrases, in English voices that are at once remote and familiar, blurred at the edges as though broadcast on a crackly radio. Is it his father's voice telling how he feels *clapped*, *seen into*? Is it his mother telling him it's warm enough to go for a *goof* or that he really needs a *bonnychop*? Jackson screws his eyes shut for a moment, feels his fists bunch on the bedsheets. He wants to reach out and pluck the words from the air, catch them like birds or falling leaves. They are his and his alone. Sometimes, since Edie died, he feels absurdly that these lost and washed-up words are the closest he comes to his childhood and his family. *Langtande, breker, goof!*

Because he forgets that his car is still in the school car park, Jackson has to take the Tube to work and only gets to school a minute after the start of Headmaster's Briefing. Monday briefings are a three-line whip, but ordinarily he'd think nothing of skiving off to the sixth form common room to have some hot toast and a chat with Jackie, the catering manager. Given last week's confirmation that the school inspectors are coming, however, today's briefing will likely be one of such gigantic and vibrating self-importance that Jackson wouldn't be at all surprised if Venning took a register, or sent a tick sheet round.

46

The staff common room is crammed, as he'd expected, and the howling autumn wind outside only seems to reinforce a grim, collars-up sort of camaraderie among the eighty or so assembled teachers, many of whom are clutching their Teacher's Planners and a pen, so that they look to Jackson like very officious disciples. Even burly Roger Cobb, Head of Games, has taken his hand away from his crotch for long enough to grasp a bitey-looking Biro, attached by a bit of string to a clipboard.

As Jackson slinks in, Venning, nattily power-dressed in charcoal pinstripe and a Trinity College tie, has already begun telling them all about the upcoming inspection. He's telling them that the school is now a different place from what it had been five years ago, how it's forging ahead in a new direction. Nonetheless, it is a good time for them all to reflect on how they present themselves in their, ahem, *day-to-day business*. Is it Jackson's imagination, or are his eyes sliding round the room as he says this, as if looking for someone in particular? Oh, God, is it him?

Accountability, Venning is saying, that was what an inspection was ultimately about, and it was he and the governors who were, of course, ultimately accountable for the ways in which the school had been running for the past five years. But they should all be looking on the positive side: *accountable* was only another way of saying *responsible*, and they were, all of them, acutely responsible practitioners. They were good teachers, good planners and, above all, good record-keepers. There really was nothing to fear from an inspection. Nonetheless, just to make sure they

47

were all singing from the same hymn sheet, Venning was convening a rotating series of lunchtime working parties to make sure they were all properly briefed on key school policy documents. Lunch would be provided; all other commitments were suspended. An almost imperceptible sigh runs round the common room, like wind through wheat. *Safeguarding and welfare*, Jackson thinks. *Special Educational Needs.* Christ, even the thought of it is enough to make him want to retire on the spot.

Venning is now asking them to please take some time this week to consider how they would like to be seen by a complete stranger. Impressions were often subtly formed: the way they dressed, the way they deported themselves around the school, the way they interacted with pupils *and* colleagues.

Right behind him, Jackson can hear Frances whispering to Rhidian that Venning looks like a total penis in pinstripe; but when he turns around to try and meet her eye, she looks away, and starts fiddling, like a teenage girl, with her hair.

By lunchtime, Jackson is feeling even more fed up.

The problem starts, as usual, with the girls in his sixth-form set. Well, with *the* sixth-form girl, if he's honest. The girl who was plain Mercedes Solomon on the dotted line; who was Sadie, she told him, at home; but the girl who, in his class, gazing at him with those big dark eyes, was always just Solly. Mercedes Solomon, not nearly as clever as she thinks she is, but who for reasons too complicated for her ever to guess, preoccupies him at times rather more than she should.

The whole set sit in front of him this morning in their usual lopsided square, three on the left, two on the right, Mercedes of course at the head of the table, sucking her pen lid and spiralling a lock of dark, wavy hair around her finger. They stare down at the *Guardian* article, which Jackson has photocopied from Jen's booklet, without enthusiasm.

'I thought we were starting our coursework today?' says a girl called Amadea. 'Mr Sayer's set started theirs last term.' She glances at Mercedes for affirmation; she wants some support if she's going to be stroppy, and she knows, as they all do, that Jackson has a strange weakness for slim, raven-haired Mercedes.

'Sir,' Mercedes always puts that particular inflection into the word, that tilted pitch, that dying fall. She must be able to read his mind, he thinks. Now she's cocking her head, a little bit Princess Di, a strand of hair spiralling tight round the flesh of her finger. 'I think what Amadea means is, is this article going to be *relevant* to our coursework? Is it, like, context? Or is it just meant to be, you know' – here she smiles confidentially, dipping her head a little more to the side, so that he can see the side of her slim, pale throat – 'to Make Us Think?'

Jackson gazes at her. Mercedes gazes back, lids lazy over her dark eyes.

You fucking well stay away from us, Jackson!

He drops his eyes first, and sighs. 'Everything, Miss Solomon, is meant to Make You Think. We're meant to be

49

pushing you beyond the curriculum here, aren't we?' To the others, he says, 'But the article in question has a wider application to the coursework task, yes. Can anyone perhaps see what it might be?'

They gaze at the photocopies in front of them, at the image of the family in the dinghy, clutching one another; at the endless expanse of bleak grey sea and the complete absence of a shore.

'Oh,' says Amadea suddenly. 'I get it.'

'Does anyone else? Inigo? August?'

Inigo, who has recently shaved his head and who these days prefers to be called 'Go', scowls at the use of his full name, but eventually after a few seconds' silence mutters, 'Sea.'

'Exactly!' says Jackson with a hearty enthusiasm. 'Would anyone else care to expand on Inigo's brilliant thesis?'

Mercedes puts her pen in her mouth again, her glossed-up lips working round the lid.

'Is it, like, something about *loneliness*?' she says, looking right at him.

Don't take any notice, Jackson thinks, her father clearly doesn't pay her enough attention. So he puts his head on one side in a mocking echo of hers. 'Loneliness?' he says, and then, simply because he doesn't want to agree with her too readily, doesn't want the others to exchange glances and shake their heads in exasperation (*Dr C, so fucking obsessed with Solly!*), says, 'Isn't there another way of looking at it?'

Mercedes pouts at the rebuff, and it is surprisingly Inigo who says, suddenly, 'Yeah.'

Amadea shakes back her hair and gives a little laugh. 'Of

50

course it's about loneliness,' she says. 'And, like, *despair*. I mean, look at them, they're miles out to sea in a grotty little boat which is probably going to sink any minute. It's hardly like, quick, let's have a selfie, is it?'

She glances at Mercedes for affirmation and they exchange a smile. Jackson expects Inigo to be quashed, but is surprised when the boy shrugs and says, 'Yeah, but the thing is, it's a family, isn't it? Look.' He stabs at the photograph with his finger. Jackson can see an inky tattoo on his hand. *Make Peas, Not War.* 'Mum, Dad, little kid, baby.'

They all stare again at the photograph, at the father whose arms loop protectively around the woman's body to hold on to the shoulders of a little girl, whose face is a rictus of consternation. 'There isn't a baby,' Amadea is snapping but even as she's saying it, Jackson sees that Inigo is right. Shrugged into the mother's body is a papoose, in which Jackson realises suddenly there must also be a tiny baby. He looks across at the boy and nods.

'Go's got it,' he says, and out of the corner of his eye sees Mercedes mouthing, 'Oh. My. God,' at Amadea, and flipping back her hair.

At lunchtime, as Jackson is emerging from the lesson, he feels a tap on his shoulder.

'Lunch,' says Rhidian meaningfully.

'No, thanks. I've got to—'

'It wasn't a question,' Rhidian informs him, then, standing aside to let two girls pass, 'Hello, Mercedes, hello Amadea. I'll see you in the Rat and Gate,' he adds.

'Thanks,' says Mercedes. 'Mine's a gin and tonic.' The girls giggle.

'You're *such* a slut,' Jackson hears Amadea saying as they go on down the stairs, shaking back their hair, files clasped to their breasts. The girls disappear around the corner, Mercedes glancing back at him as she goes.

'Jackson,' says Rhidian. 'Stop it.'

'I am,' says Jackson. 'I'm retiring.'

'Good,' says Rhidian. 'You'll end up in prison otherwise.'

As he follows Rhidian down the stairs, he finds himself glancing at a flyer announcing auditions for the school play.

'I know, I know,' says Rhidian, following his gaze. 'Too clichéd for words, isn't it? *The Tempest*. But it's just come back on to the GCSE syllabus and' – he sighs – 'of course the head thinks it's topical.'

'Topical how, exactly?'

'Oh, God, you know. Refugees at sea, all that shit. I would have gone for *Hamlet*, myself.'

'That's because you're also a hysteric,' Jackson points out, but it is too late, Rhidian is away, peering theatrically from imaginary battlements and informing some passing Year 7s that in the gross and scope of his opinion, it bodes some great eruption to our state . . .

They pause outside the office. From within, they can hear the telephone ringing, on and on.

'Leave it,' says Jackson. 'It'll just be parents.'

But Rhidian sighs, and goes in.

52

'City morgue,' he says blandly, and then, 'Oh, hello, Mrs Pilgrim. No, not at the moment. Probably still teaching. Yes, I did tell her . . . she didn't, oh dear . . . Yes, yes, I'll put it on her desk this time. Okay. Try not to worry.'

Jackson raises his eyebrows. 'What on earth does she want?'

'Wait till we have a drink,' says Rhidian, scrawling down a message for Frances before picking up his coat.

Now, as they settle down at their usual table in the back of the Rat and Gate, Jackson says, 'So. What's up?'

He suspects Rhidian is going to give him a talking-to about Mercedes's flirting, and is gearing up to reassure him that he hasn't *done* anything, and of course he bloody won't, when Rhidian says abruptly, 'It's about Pilgrim. No, don't,' he adds, seeing Jackson's face. 'Whatever happened between the two of you over the summer is none of my business.'

Jackson doesn't reply that Frances has made it quite clear that it's none of anybody's business. He remembers for a moment the shape of her back as she sat on the edge of his bed that morning, the watery light coming through his window broadcasting her misery, a shadow a thousand times the size of itself, against the far wall. The way she'd tiptoed out without so much as a half-hearted excuse, and the way he'd pretended to be asleep, so she could. He thinks with a flash of anger of the message he'd sent her from Edie's bedside. *Can I call you? It's all a bit grim.* But there'd been no reply, and even when he called she didn't pick up, didn't call back later.

'Jackson,' Rhidian is saying gently, 'there are one or two things I think we need to bear in mind about Frances.'

He pauses.

Jackson takes a slug of his wine, and waits. He doesn't feel inclined to help.

'The woman who keeps ringing the office,' Rhidian goes on, 'is Ma Pilgrim. Frances's mother.'

Jackson raises an eyebrow. 'The not-so-merry widow?'

Rhidian sighs, curling his fingers delicately around the stem of his wine glass. 'What would you say if I told you she'd rung the office eight times in the last two days?'

'That she was fucking annoying.'

'And that she often doesn't seem to remember having rung the previous time?'

'Then I'd say she was clearly a piss-cat, just like her daughter,' says Jackson sulkily. He's not interested in Frances's mother. He's not, he tells himself, interested in anything about Frances any more. But Rhidian is giving him a look, and so he sighs and says, 'Do you think she's starting to—'

'Yes,' says Rhidian, 'I do. It happened to my father. I recognise the signs.'

'Well, what am I supposed to do about it? I'm not a doctor.'

'You're a human being. Officially.'

Jackson groans. 'You mean you want me to play nicely with Pilgrim?'

Rhidian shrugs and says, 'Just bear it in mind.'

*

At four o'clock, Jackson goes home, finding he can't face returning to the Gut for start-of-term drinks and having to pretend to be nice to Frances. He doesn't give a toss about her family problems any more, not after the summer that's just gone. He'd thought she was different then, but, sure enough, she's a common or garden girl like all the others. Vain, manipulative, self-regarding. It occurs to him fleetingly to wonder whether calling a thirty-eight-year-old woman a *girl* is flattery or insult. Perhaps it depends on the girl. Woman. Whatever.

At home, he yanks a bottle of Sancerre out of the fridge, fills a wine glass with ice, and briefly checks his email. Something from the lawyer handling Edie's estate and something from his friend Alison, *re: dinner next Tuesday?* Jackson sighs. Alison will want to fix him up with a Delicious Girl. She says he's got performance anxiety, he just needs to get back on that horse, cowboy, pun very much intended. But nothing, not even porn seems to rouse him these days. In fact, apart from that startling occasion in the summer, with Frances, when the apple blossom was out, his cock's been hiding out in his pants like a rat in a storm drain for the best part of six months. Jackson is beginning to think, gloomily, that the Problem may be in his prostate. After all, he's the right age for all that sort of thing now. He tosses his iPad on to the sofa on his way to the bathroom.

It was Katy who had introduced him to the idea of baths; she could lie in them, he'd discovered, for hours. But now, as he watches the hot water running into the bathtub, thinking about Katy only makes him think about all the missing girls in his own life. The daughter he thought he'd have one day; his sister Edie, scattered now beneath a distant sun. Even Frances, to an extent, although she has never really been 'his', has spent the summer suddenly missing, leaving a surprising hole in his life for someone he has known for so little time. Jackson puts his wine down on the floor next to the bathtub, and despite all his resolutions begins to think about Frances.

Even when Jackson was still living with Katy, he had been dimly and idly aware of Frances, in the way that one is aware of a picture displayed in a shop window that one passes every day. There is no occasion for it, and one doesn't particularly need another painting like that anyway, but still. One always knows it's there.

'You're completely retarded,' Rhidian would explode at her, when she hadn't got her reports in on time, or had turned up late to a meeting. 'Thirty-eight, going on zero.'

But in Millbrook Park that Sunday, still in last night's make-up and with a coffee stain on her shirt, to Jackson she seemed suddenly, startlingly, perfect.

The following week he'd suggested to her that they went for a drink somewhere that wasn't the Gut, and she'd agreed readily enough, making Jackson feel that his cleaning the flat and changing the sheets, his buying flowers and filling the fridge with trinkets and sweetmeats probably hadn't been, as he'd suspected at the time, pathetically previous. He took her to Le Poisson Blanc, a bistro run by his friend

Laurent-Olivier, and didn't know whether to be delighted or outraged when the pretty waitress arrived with the wine and smiled at him, saying, '*Ah, Jackson, ta fille est très charmante.*'

They looked at one another for an awkward moment.

'I suppose I am much too old for you,' Jackson had said, filling up her glass.

'Oh God, yes, far too old.'

And he'd noticed then that the corners of her mouth were turning down, as if she were suppressing an enormous private joke, and had to resist the urge to reach across the table and run his fingers over her lips. Down, boy. Later.

'Old as the hills,' he'd said instead, 'unlike all your lovers, I suppose. Old as Methuselah.'

'*Old as balls*, as Rhidian always says.' Seeing his expression, she had added, 'I think it's an Auden reference. Didn't someone say that if Auden's face looked like that, *imagine the state of his balls?*'

'David Hockney,' Jackson had said, examining the label on the back of the wine bottle. Then, looking up, he'd added lightly, 'So, how many are there?'

'Two, one imagines? Oh, sorry, you mean my lovers. Um, well, only one active one at the moment.' He was a television actor she had met online.

Jackson had been horrified. 'Isn't that terribly dangerous?'

But she'd just shrugged. Everyone did it, she said, like everyone did Facebook and Twitter and Snapchat. Jackson, who did none of them, remained mystified, but before he could pursue the topic of her love life, she had been asking him about himself. How on earth, she'd said curiously, had he made the jump from being a university lecturer in South Africa to a London schoolteacher?

Jackson sighed. 'The teaching bit was Katy's idea. When we first met, she was teaching at Grove House in Notting Hill, and a vacancy came up there. Part-time, train-on-the-job sort of thing. And we were getting a mortgage, and the money was good, so I said I'd give it a try. And it was okay.'

Frances had smiled at him: a genuine smile this time, which made her look much younger than she was. 'That's just the icing. What I want to know is how you met a London schoolteacher in South Africa?'

Jackson hesitated for a second, then said, 'Actually, I was in Italy when I met Katy.'

Frances had looked at him over the rim of her glass. 'What on earth were you doing in Italy? Holiday?'

He had paused for a moment, then – a fraction too long, perhaps, under ordinary circumstances. But fortunately Frances, despite being drunk enough to ask personal questions, was also drunk enough not to notice his pause.

'Something like that,' said Jackson.

Frances had not probed any more. She had merely poured herself some more wine, and said, 'Well, you've been a complete hit, anyway. Half the sixth form wants to shag you.'

Jackson had said lightly, 'What about the other half?'

'Probably in denial.'

He had really wanted to say, 'And what about you?' but was momentarily deterred by the thought of Richard the television actor, some smug bastard in his thirties leaning against her door with an arch expression like the man in the old Nescafé ads. Then the waitress had arrived and he had been gently diverted into advising her on the best things to have so that she had asked him all about his time in Italy, and then about meeting Katy; and then the critical moment had passed and it had been an easy hop, skip and a jump to talking about dull, urbane things: the theatre, music, how her favourite composer was Benjamin Britten, and how she kept meaning to go to Aldeburgh on a sort of Britten pilgrimage with Dog, only she didn't much like the seaside so she never got round to it.

'Don't like the sea?' Jackson had asked. 'Why on earth not?'

But she had only shrugged again, then, and changed the subject. And at the end of the evening her phone rang, and she was in a cab down to Wimbledon to see Richard-from-the-Nescafé-adverts. When Jackson got home he had drunk all the champagne in his fridge himself and woken up the next morning with a hangover.

And indeed, he would discover that there was always a boyfriend in the way. She lined them up, one after an unsuitable other, so that as one exited, another entered, like a bloody French farce.

'You're the human equivalent of Battersea Dogs Home,' Jackson complained every Friday night in the pub. On one occasion when he had had too much to drink, he'd said, casually, 'You should just marry me, you know. I could do with someone to look after me in my dotage.'

But she had just laughed, and elbowed him in the ribs. And so they had gone on as before.

Until the last night of last summer term.

Jackson finally climbs into the bath, and picks up his glass of wine. He'll cut down soon; his doctor said he really needed to get his liver enzymes down. But not tonight.

It was the night after the phone call from Edie's husband Clem.

By that stage Jackson and his sister had not spoken for almost ten years, and he had not seen her for much longer than that. Like most other people, Edie had stopped talking to him shortly before he left South Africa, and she had never backed down, a bloody-mindedness clearly encoded in both their genes.

'You need to come to her,' Clem said, in the sepulchral tones of the messenger. 'Now.' In the background, Jackson could hear someone asking if anyone knew where the medicine box was, and had Clem seen the chart lying about, it needed to be signed off.

He said stupidly, 'Why?'

Clem had snapped, 'Because she's sick, goddamn it. Really sick.' Then he'd said, apologetically, 'I'm sorry, bro. She didn't want you to know. She said you'd only make a fuss. But I thought you should know, before . . .' There was a pause. 'The doctors aren't sure if . . .'

Jackson had shaken his head, discovering he was tearing the petals of the lilies he'd bought the day before between his fingers so that they bled pollen on to his cuffs. 'Is it—'

60

'Cancer,' Clem had said. 'Yes.'

When Frances had tumbled into the office the next day with Jen McGarrick, Rhidian's second-in-command, both of them breathless with end-of-term prosecco and exhorting, 'Jackson, Jackson, come with us to the *spit*-roast!' he'd had to shake his head, already clearing his desk and getting ready to go home and pack.

'Grumpy *cat*,' said Jen, ruffling his hair. 'Whassa matter, Pilgrim still won't sleep with you? You're a bad girl,' she added, turning to Frances, who was standing swaying on a chair, trying to reach some files on a high shelf. 'Why won't you sleep with Jackson?'

'Shut up, Jen-Jen.'

'You can sleep with Jackson now, can't you?' And then Jen was looping her arms round his neck, and put her face down to his to nuzzle him, to whisper, 'She's single again, Jacksy. New bloke turned out to be married, she found out last week.'

The tickle of her hair and the sweet reek of prosecco suddenly sickened him, and he pushed her away. 'Get off.'

'Grumpy *cat*.' She began to pirouette in the middle of the floor. 'Come and dance with me, Pilgrim. Jackson's being a grumpy *cat*.'

But Frances was looking at Jackson. 'You okay?'

'No.'

And while Jen pirouetted until she fell face first into the office door, Frances stretched out her hand.

They'd walked together across Millbrook and down through Kentish Town, and all the way Frances had held his hand, as he at last told her all about Edie, and Nicko, and Carly, and why none of them had spoken to him for sixteen years. Well, if you discounted Carly's occasional flirtatious emails. *Had a dream about you last night, Jacksy. We had fun, didn't we?* Timestamp typically 12.43 a.m., in South Africa.

When he got to the end, he had looked at her for signs of contempt or pity, but Frances's eyes had been soft. 'Poor Jackson,' she'd said, and squeezed his hand.

Later, when they were cooking supper, she came up behind him and wrapped her arms round him, resting her head on his shoulder. He could smell the vanilla scent that she wore.

'Don't,' he said. 'In my deranged state, I might try and kiss you.'

'Pervert like you,' she'd murmured, kissing his forehead and then his eyes with a softness he'd never imagined in her, 'I suppose you might.'

How much had they had to drink by that stage? A lot, he thought. Was that all it was?

But whatever it was, as he kissed her on the mouth, he felt it. That unmistakable tingle, the glorious heaviness in his groin. It had occurred to him – rather disloyally, he supposed later – to wonder for a moment if it was the mention, at last, of Carly, that had broken the drought; if it was Carly as she'd been then who'd been set loose in his sitting room, Carly and her voluptuous, devouring mouth, her bubble-gum breath and cool, *Charlie*-scented skin. But the thought did not last long because Jackson and Frances had started to undress each other in the kitchen.

Thinking about it now, he sighs. He'd been too eager to get at her, hadn't he, too afraid that after a year of impotence the wind would drop and his sails would sag. He'd crashed on her like a wave, drowning her in a jittery surge of enthusiasm, knowing as he was doing so that he was failing her but too anxious to slow down, in case . . .

Neither of them had enjoyed it much. Afterwards, she'd clearly only pretended to sleep for a few hours, but after she'd crept out, after he'd heard the front door click behind her, he'd remembered Jen McGarrick whispering, 'Her new boyfriend's dumped her.' God, he'd thought, there was always a reason, with her even an absence was as strong as a presence. Why would she never give him a proper chance?

The next morning he'd found one of her earrings in the untouched *boeuf bourguignon*. He'd rinsed it carefully, and put it in the soap dish to give to her later. It was still there, like a tear drop on a thread, or a shard of glass.

Now, spread out in the bath, Jackson looks down at his cock, floating like a wrinkled pink sock in the bubbles. Then he groans, and pulls out the plug.

V

It is Wednesday before Frances decides to take her courage in both hands and talk to Jackson.

Turning to wipe clean her whiteboard of the chaotic mind-map she's made from Year 10's ideas about *The Tempest* – Prospero: loving father or ruthless fixer? – she is reminded again, by her own board-marker scrawl, that it is, indeed, the second of September. Not only the second day of the new school year, but a full two months since the Thing happened. Two months in which she has not communicated with Jackson, a fact that she has tried to put down to his having spent a lot of the summer in South Africa with his sister, but which she knows, in her heart of hearts, is because of their joint inarticulacy regarding the Thing.

'Was it just, like, really shit?' Silv enquired cheerfully, the day after it happened.

Had it been really shit? Frances had shaken her head to that, then immediately wished she hadn't, because her head seemed to be full of an evil black liquid that rolled about with each movement of her neck. It had been a firecracker of a hangover, ambushing her out of an uneasy sleep at

4 a.m. and sending her unsteadily to Jackson's bathroom to take down frantic gulps of water. Hours later, her mouth had still ached with the mineral taste of the tap.

Silv had sat back in her chair and surveyed Frances with amusement. 'Can you actually remember any of it?'

Frances had buried her head in her hands, mugged by a recollection of herself standing behind Jackson as he stood at the stove stirring the *boeuf bourguignon* they had tried, drunkenly, to cook but never actually got around to eating. His neck had smelled of warm lemons, a smell that had seemed at once echoingly familiar and intensely new. When he turned around and made a crack about trying to kiss her, she had called him a pervert, as usual, but then leaned in and kissed him herself. God! Not that this wasn't her usual MO when pissed, but with someone she actually knew, with someone she'd have to face again afterwards – what had she been *thinking*? Worse, what had *he* been thinking? That was a hard one to fathom, because rational discourse had not figured much after that. She had been surprised, not by her own ardour – she was, as Rhidian liked to point out to her, like the Wife of bloody Bath, *a lickerous mouth and a lickerous tail!* – but by his, such a contrast to the dry and laconic Jackson she'd grown to know since his divorce, the Jackson who on a Sunday after-noon would sprawl elegantly on his chaise longue, still admirably loose-hipped, one corner of a striped collar always, somehow, turned up, something that had always made her want to reach out and turn it, gently, back down.

The act itself had been over relatively quickly – but then,

first times so often were, weren't they, everyone too nervous to take their time and enjoy themselves. Pleasure, Frances had learned, so often came later, as if taxed, the first time being more like an exchange of contracts, a will made explicit in the skin to do this more often, and better. The trouble was that neither of them had seemed very sure if they did want it to happen again, had they? Afterwards, Jackson had muttered that he was sorry, mumbled something about being rather out of practice, but by then wine-dark shadows had been dancing on the wall and she'd been too close to just passing out to say very much in reply at all.

When she woke in the night, his arm had been thrown out, across her body, and as she slithered out of bed he had murmured, 'Are you all right?' to which she could only, by then, groan a reply. And when she got back from the bathroom, the hangover had her by the throat, that head-thumping, heart-racing bastard of a hangover, which rolled over her like a vast black wave whenever she tried to lie down and find relief in a pillow, so that she'd ended up sitting dizzily on the edge of the bed for about half an hour, wondering dully if she was going to be sick, and whether Jackson's walls were thin enough for him to hear if she was.

And it had been then, head bowed on the edge of his bed, that she'd been assailed by a sudden and violent self-disgust, as unexpected as a hand over her mouth. *Chemical guilt*, she could hear Rhidian saying, in her mind. *The long dark teatime of the soul!* But Frances had experienced plenty of those, and this had been completely different, as if she were, for the first time, seeing herself through

67

someone else's eyes. Jackson's, perhaps, although he was obviously asleep and not actually looking at that precise moment. Jackson, who despite his filthy and irreverent sense of humour had, after all, chosen to get married to Katy, a woman of regular blow-dries and manicures, whom Frances thought probably even had sex in long rubber washing-up gloves, with a finger bowl next to the bed for afterwards.

And it was Katy who had left him, wasn't it? It wasn't that Jackson had got bored of her, was it? He evidently hadn't woken up one day and decided that Katy was just too clean and blonde and all-round-bloody-perfect and that what he really wanted when he was a bit low was to get jumped on by his mad friend Frances, had he? No. Frances had made that decision for him, when they were both maudlin and drunk and when he was obviously flattened by the news of his sister's illness. When Jackson had flirted once before with the idea of Frances, it had been before he knew her properly, and even then he had conducted himself like an adult, taking her out to a nice restaurant and asking her all about herself. Trying to get to know her the old-fashioned way. And she had laughingly drunk all the wine he offered her and then scooted off to South Wimbledon to jump into bed with bloody Richard-the-TV-actor, hadn't she? And now, two years on, Jackson would know what she was really like with men: a simultaneously maudlin and libidinous drunk, the sort of girl who shagged you when she was feeling lonely and pissed and then was (probably) sick in your bathroom afterwards.

No wonder none of her relationships ever lasted; she was stuck in a rut, somehow, trapped, unable to move forward. Or, as her mother liked to tell her, she was a disaster looking for somewhere to happen, although the more Frances thought about it, the more it occurred to her that she was a disaster who didn't even know *what* was happening, or why. Was it just her hormones? Breed and die, Rhidian always said disdainfully when yet another of their Hilltop colleagues went on maternity leave. *They lay their eggs, and sting and sing And weave their petty cells and die!* And Frances had read an article in one of the Sunday colour supplements recently, on Jackson's sofa in fact, about what happened to women's ovaries as they neared the end of their reproductive life. The body, according to the article, went into a sort of kamikaze fertility mode, often releasing two or more eggs at a time in a last-ditch bid for procreation. This late surge of hormones was apparently why women over forty so often had twins or triplets. Three glasses of wine down on a Sunday afternoon, Frances had found the article hilarious, imagining her remaining eggs all lined up on her ovary wall like a line of truculent Humpty Dumpties. She had even started to read a bit out to Jackson, before she'd remembered that perhaps women's ovaries weren't quite top of his list of favourite things to talk about at the moment.

And so at six o'clock she had got up, and crept out into the watery dawn. When she'd turned around at the door, Jackson's eyes had been closed, and yet as she turned away she had that same, discomfiting sense that he was awake, and watching her. Probably overwhelmed with relief, she'd

69

thought, as she opened the front door and almost tripped over something on the mat outside.

'Bugger off, Callaghan,' she'd muttered. But as she went on her way down the stairs, she was convinced that even the cat was watching her with distaste.

Now, as she finishes wiping the whiteboard clean of everything except the date, she glances out of the window, which is when she sees the taxi sitting in the mouth of the tiny car park. Must be a pick-up of a pupil going home early, she thinks, but even as she turns away something about the vehicle is niggling at her, and when she looks back, she can see exactly what it is.

The taxi has a logo on it with which Frances has been familiar since her teenage years, before she had her licence. *Singh's Cars, Dryland.*

And the small figure who is struggling out of the car in a slipping headscarf, with what looks like a phone pressed to her ear, is also immediately familiar. Grabbing her jacket and her bag, Frances hurries out of her classroom and down the concrete stairs to the lobby.

It is another thirty minutes before she gets to the office, thoughts of any lunch other than a large glass of wine completely forgotten. It has taken her half an hour to manoeuvre her mother to the Green Café and sit her down with a cup of tea – 'I don't like that frothy coffee rubbish' – and to ask her, gently, why she is here.

At this, a frightened look crosses her mother's face. Her eyes bulge like a rabbit's, and when she looks down into the depths of her gleaming glass of tea, Frances notices that underneath the muddy Barbour she wears to walk dogs and feed chickens, she is wearing only the T-shirt and the leggings that she usually sleeps in.

'Mum?'

Her mother folds her hands in her lap, and says, with dignity, 'I had something I needed to tell you, and you wouldn't answer your phone.'

'I was teaching, Mum. I have to have the phone on silent.' Frances reaches across and takes one of her mother's hands, cold and dry as paper. The hand shakes, and she squeezes it, desperately. 'What did you need to tell me?'

But her mother cannot answer right away. She looks away from Frances, out of the window on to the busy High Street, where double-decker buses are stopping and starting in both directions, and where chattering pupils in uniform are emerging from the deli over the road with cans of Coke and baguettes. Frances waits, and after a moment her mother manages to look up at her, aghast.

'I can't remember,' she says, and buries her face in her hands.

In the sanctuary of the Ladies, Frances sits down fully clothed on the loo seat.

She is shaking. Seeing again her mother's muddy leggings and rabbit eyes, Frances finds that she wants to take hold of her, wants to put her cold, papery hands inside her own and make them warm, to blow on them or put mittens on her, as you would to a child. More than anything she longs, as she always has done, to put her arms around her mother

71

and hold her. But she knows what reaction that evinces: a stiffening of those chicken-wing shoulders, a tightening of the sinews in her back as her mother immediately pulls herself apart and away, like a fan.

On a more practical level, Frances wants to put her mother in her car and drive her back to Kent herself, but it's already twenty to two, there isn't time to find any cover because everyone's at lunch and, anyway, what would she tell them? Her mother is not dead, has not had any evident cardiac event or stroke, she is not lying bleeding in the road, and Year 11 do need to be taught, Miss Pilgrim!

So Frances pulls out her telephone and rings the only person who she knows she can rely on – their neighbour, Jean. She tells Jean that her mother is unwell, and that Frances is putting her in a taxi home. She will give the taxi driver Jean's number, so could Jean come out and take her mother in when she arrives? No, no, she doesn't need to go to hospital, and Frances herself will be home this evening, she just needs someone to keep an eye on her for a couple of hours. Jean is bright and breezy. Of course, she'll pop in and keep an eye on Mary, such a worry isn't it, being on your own when you're older, perhaps the moment has come for – well, anyway, that's a discussion for another time, isn't it? See you later, then, love!

Putting her phone back into her coat pocket and getting up to go, Frances catches a momentary glimpse of her reflection in the mirror: she looks pale and puffy, too much bloody wine, she's got to slow down soon. For years she's been young-looking, a female Peter Pan or Dorian Gray, but she's starting to look a bit, well . . . *raddled*? suggests Rhidian's voice in her mind. Behind her, by contrast, is a poster advertising afternoons of Structured Play for toddlers in Millbrook Park. A young couple, tanned and laughing, balance a small child between them, each holding on to one of its plump, starfish hands. In the mirror the poster shines brightly against her own reflection, and she turns away quickly, but not before she has seen it, at her side parting. A sudden sliver of white, glinting under the toilet's strip lighting.

It strikes her as she unlocks the loo door that she and her mother are probably running a bit short on *another time*. They seem to be running out of time, full stop.

Jackson is the only person in the office when she gets back. He's sitting at his desk, writing, a coffee at his elbow, with what looks like a crumpled piece of notepaper propped up on his desk. He is wearing his spectacles on his face for a change, and it makes him look older and less rakish. For a moment he looks professorial, almost avuncular. Frances feels something turn over deep in her chest, then she takes a deep breath and says nervously, 'Are you busy?'

He doesn't look up, doesn't stop writing. 'Fairly.'

Outside in the corridor, she can hear a burst of exuberant noise as the next year-group are released from the holding pen of the Science Quad outside to go down to lunch. Jackson pauses from his writing and tilts his head up as if thinking, or reaching for a phrase, and Frances tries again, helplessly, 'Could we maybe go for a coffee?' She desperately needs to talk to someone, anyone, about what is happening, and she knows she and Jackson have been a bit awkward around each other, but it was only a one-night stand, wasn't it, people do have them, it isn't exactly the end of the world.

But Jackson says nothing, merely gestures to the coffee that is sitting on his desk.

Frances tries again. 'I don't mean now, I just meant, you know, later. Maybe after school? When it's convenient. When you're not, you know . . .'

Now he's put down his pen and turned around to look at her, which she hopes is a good sign. Is he going to make some crack about her inability to finish sentences, maybe even give her some sort of a softening, a Jacksonish half-smile? But he doesn't say anything, he only waits until her sentence withers and peters out. Frances is pleating part of her pinafore in her hand and trying hard to think of something shallow and amusing to say to break the silence when Jackson sighs, and pushes his spectacles up on to his forehead.

'Rhidian tells me,' he says, 'that I ought to be kind to you at the moment.'

'He did?'

'Yes,' says Jackson. 'He says it's rather obvious, from the frequency and the nature of the telephone calls your mother's been making to the office, that she's becoming quite unwell.'

Frances feels sick. Even though she had of course been thinking the same thing herself only five minutes previously, actually hearing someone else say it out loud is still

74

shocking. It brings something blurry and indistinct inside her head into fine, pixellated focus. Jackson's impeccable vowels make her own private fear seem suddenly like a concrete medical reality, like a documented fact.

Jackson looks at her meditatively for a moment, and then says coldly, 'You might remember a conversation we had at the end of last term, when I told you my sister had been diagnosed with cancer.'

'I do, I've been meaning to—'

But he cuts her off. She's seen him bollocking kids often enough to know what's coming, and feels her fingers curling around the edge of the chair behind her. He goes on, 'I spent the summer sitting at her bedside. On the other side of the world, with a family who barely spoke to me. Helping to change her nappies. Feeding her with a spoon.'

Someone is knocking at the door, but neither of them answers it. They remain frozen, staring at one another.

'I'm sorry,' she whispers, 'I'm sorry.' And in her mind's eye she can see herself in Kent, lying on her mother's sofa, hearing the phone ringing or pinging that night and, seeing Jackson's name on the screen, feeling that horrific sense of shame washing over her. He'd been ringing to have the Chat, she'd thought, to tell her that they should write it off to too much wine. Knowing Jackson, he'd be ringing in order to make a joke of some sort, and then say, 'So, we're all right then? No hard feelings?' and Frances would have had to lie and say no, of course not, no hard feelings, Jackson. Because it wouldn't be his fault that she feels, again, so soiled and disposable, will it? He didn't make the pass, did he? He was probably just too polite – no, come on, too drunk to refuse what, after all, had been some nice, no-strings sex presented on a plate and tied up with a bloody ribbon. As she watched his name continue to flash on her screen – *Jackson Calling* – she had remembered, again, the way that the back of his neck smelled like warm lemons, and she'd felt ridiculous tears filling her eyes. No, she couldn't pretend it was all okay. *But his sister*, she'd thought then, and *poor Jackson*. But by then the screen had gone dark. I will ring him back, she'd thought. Just to make sure he's okay. I will.

But she hadn't, had she?

'I'm sorry,' she says again. 'I was a shitty friend, I should have been there, I should have—'

'Oh, shut up,' says Jackson.

There's a pause. Frances does shut up, stinging in spite of herself with outrage at his tone but knowing she hasn't a leg to stand on.

At length, Jackson says, 'I don't know if I've made this point before, but, unlike you, I don't live in the country of my birth. I don't have a million and one friends on Facebook. Both my parents are dead. There weren't' – he pauses, and for just a moment, turns away from her – 'there wasn't anyone to talk to.'

'I'm so sorry,' she whispers again, and with a stinging sense of shame feels her eyes beginning to well. *No more tears, now.*

Jackson notices it too. 'Don't try any crocodile tears with me,' he snaps. 'Your mother may be losing her marbles, but at least she's still alive, along with your various toy boys and girlfriends.' More friends and relations than Rabbit, he'd said once, laughing, although she'd had to correct him on the relations bit.

He isn't laughing now.

There's another knock at the door, and Jackson gets to his feet. Frances is tall, but Jackson is taller, and he looms over her for a moment, eyes narrow.

'Don't come snivelling to me to make amends,' he says, putting his hand on the door ready to wrench it open, but his eyes never leaving her face, 'when you couldn't even be bothered to answer a simple text message for two whole months, and all because you were embarrassed about what happened that night. *You* were embarrassed,' he adds contemptuously. 'Christ!'

This last is directed at the knock that comes again at the door, louder now, and then Jackson is wrenching the door open, shouting before he can see who's there, 'No, for Christ's sake, not now. GO AWAY!'

'Oh,' says Jen McGarrick, peering around the door and taking in the scene with interest. 'I've just been sent to tell you you're both expected at the working party upstairs. It was meant to start five minutes ago.'

VI

Clearly Jen doesn't want to miss an opportunity to thrill the deputy head, Lauren, with her policy-document acumen, because she is hurrying up the stairs again before the office door has even closed on Frances, who, when Jackson looks back, is sitting, looking glassy-eyed and stunned, on the edge of her desk.

But as Jackson finds himself following Jen's neat navy calves up the concrete stairs, he wonders why the hell he is bothering to go to the working party. He could have just told Jen that sod it, he wasn't going, and taken himself off for a walk instead. After all, he's about to retire, or rather get out of teaching, so what are they going to do, sack him? But already his outburst at Frances, and her evident anguish, has left him limp as a burst balloon. It isn't just that he doesn't have the energy to resist the working party edict, he also knows he's gone far enough today already. A stupid seminar on school policy is sufficiently penitential, for now, but, gritting his teeth, he knows he will have to apologise to Frances, if only for the sake of everyone else in the office. Jackson groans inwardly, and follows Jen into the seminar room.

'What are we doing?' mutters Jackson to Rhidian, sinking into the chair next to him, and Rhidian murmurs blandly that it's Special Educational Needs. A pause. 'Thick people, basically.'

Despite himself, Jackson has just started to laugh, when Lauren, Venning's principal deputy, clears her throat and says okay, everybody, they can probably get started. 'Now the stragglers have arrived,' observes Rhidian cheerfully, and Lauren gives a tight smile, before proceeding. They are *very* lucky, she says, to have with them today Professor Christopher Appleby, of University College, who is a government adviser on special educational provision in schools. There is a polite smattering of applause before a slight man in corduroy trousers, with a straggly beard, gets up and says heartily that he expects none of them can think of anything more dull than attending a seminar on SEN in their lunchtime!

No one contradicts him, so Christopher Appleby quickly clears his throat and says that they should all have found a handout on their chairs, which they can refer to as they go along. Jackson realises he is sitting on his, and as he shuffles forward on his seat in order to pull it out he becomes aware that Rhidian is busily sketching what looks suspiciously like a large penis on his copy of the handout. But before Jackson can work out, definitively, that it is a phallus, Christopher Appleby is suggesting that they might like to turn their attention to some slides that he's going to show. So Jackson sighs, and pulling his glasses down on to his nose, looks in resignation at the smart board at the front of the room.

The first slide is headed *Somebody Else's Problem*. It includes a picture of an institutional-looking door, on which is hung a blue sign saying Special Educational Needs Coordinator in big white letters. Christopher Appleby strokes his beard and then tells them that this is so often the attitude of subject teachers to children with particular learning needs: they are simply shunted off to the overworked SENCO, who until very recently might not actually have been a qualified teacher at all!

Jackson can see Lauren, who is sitting next to the smart board, shaking her head mournfully. Meanwhile, Rhidian is cheerfully using his red pen to give his penis what looks like a straggly beard.

These days, Christopher Appleby informs them, using a clicking device to point a red laser beam at the wall and switch slides, schools are working towards what is called a more *graduated* approach. This graduated approach begins and ends with the subject teacher. In other words, he says, looking sternly over his spectacles at them, it has become their individual responsibility to scaffold and monitor the progress of those children in their care who are *differently abled*. Jackson watches with interest as Rhidian, with a flick of his wrist, adds some spectacles to his penis, and then a speech bubble saying *Hello, I'm differently abled!*

But then something happens.

Christopher Appleby has switched slides, and Jackson finds that, quite inadvertently, he is leaning forward to look at it more closely. There is a picture on the next slide of a teenage girl standing apart from a group of her peers. She is tawny-haired and slender, and Jackson guesses that she is about sixteen. She clutches her schoolbooks to her checked school blouse, looking down at her feet. In the background is an ugly school building, made of glass and concrete and the sort of pale blue panels of which all schools and hospitals in the sixties seemed to have been constructed. In the photograph, the sky is grey and the trees are bare. Now Christopher Appleby is flying in a heading that announces SMART. This, he is informing them, stands for *specific, measurable, achievable, realistic* and *time-bound*. As Christopher Appleby points his red laser at the photograph and reminds them that girls with learning difficulties are more likely to be treated or assessed differently to boys, Jackson is aware that Rhidian is nudging him in the ribs and murmuring that see, he'd *told* Jackson they had to be nice to Frances, hadn't he? But Jackson cannot take his eyes off the slide.

Tawny hair. Slim.

It isn't Carly. He knows that. And the building in the background doesn't look anything like the genteel hill-houses in Muizenberg or the faded brick façade of Cape Town University – there's no flinty shadow of a mountain, no bougainvillea, no jacaranda trees on the grass, no distant misty sea. The grey and chilly scene is definitely, uniquely British. But something about the scene is nonetheless creepingly, discomfitingly familiar, and it makes something deep in his heart start unfurling, like a worm.

*

'I'm thick, you see,' Carly had informed him, the first time they met.

She had been lying on her parents' mint-green sofa when she said this, underneath a long and brutal canvas of what Jackson realised later was the Sharpeville massacre of 1960. Above the pale pastel of the sofa the scene unfolded in a stew of broken brown flesh, streaked with crimson. In the distance, three spiked white figures, running.

The ice in his gin had already melted in the January heat. He'd spent most of the evening wondering why Edie and Clem had invited him along with them to this tedious dinner party at Tory's place – well, it hadn't been so much dinner as a dusty *braai*, had it – until in an idle moment he'd asked where Tory's husband, Nicko, had got to.

Silence.

Tory had fussed with a strand of invisible hair, and Edie had kicked him under the table.

And that was when Jackson had made an excuse, something about checking on his car or going to the loo, anything to get away from the silence which was stretching into a several-second awkwardness. But as he'd made his way from the garden towards the patio windows, he'd thought: of course. Tory and Edie had been friends since school. Tory had always been the plump and sensible friend, chosen, Jackson had always thought, to enhance rather than detract from Edie's cover-girl good looks. Tory had been good at exams, uninvited to parties unless Edie remembered. Edie said airily that there was no point asking Tory to parties at the beach as she hated stripping off. 'She's got thick ankles, poor thing. And webbed feet.' So Tory had married Nicko, a square man boasting Scottish ancestry, and they had produced three children in quick succession, two boys so generally burly and ruggerish that no one would have especially noted their ankles and then, last of all, a girl, Caroline, who up until now had been away at school in Scotland.

As Jackson stepped over the threshold from the garden into the sitting room, he'd been thinking that if he hadn't given Tory Potter a second look when she was seventeen, he was unlikely to be drawn to her at an unhappy thirty-eight, her skin sagging sadly but determinedly from her bones as though she were trying to shed it, as if something glossier might miraculously lurk beneath. If Edie had invited him out here in an attempt to get him off with Tory, Jackson decided, he really would take umbrage. *You don't live in the real world, Jackson*, Edie told him frequently. *You live in a fantasy land.* Jackson knew the rest of his family had, in their various ways, agreed. *Good-looking*, his Great-Aunt Vi had always said, *but quite useless of course. Poor fellow.* That had been Great-Aunt Vi's gleeful postscript on all her husbands, and indeed most other men she encountered, a muttered slight and then a robustly insincere *Oh! Poor fellow.* Nevertheless, as Jackson stood at the door, still breathing in the suffocating sweetness of the old roses which were, Edie said magnanimously, 'such a feature' of Tory's garden, he was thinking yet again that he saw no reason to live in a real world where one was expected to be both bored and boring as a matter of course.

84

Which was – of course – when it happened.

'Giving up already?' drawled a voice to his right.

Jackson, whose gin glass had been at his lips at that moment, had swung around then, with the glass still against his mouth. It had knocked into his teeth, sending a shock into his gums.

Years later, he would come to think that there had been something fateful about the way the girl chose to address him in that moment, as he stood there on the threshold of her parents' pastel sitting room. He would tell her, feverishly, that it was as if she had known what had been in his mind at that particular moment. She would shrug, and laugh, 'No, silly. You just looked bored to shit.'

At the time, though he had said nothing, aware that his mouth, because of the shock of the glass, was half open like an idiot. He'd only been to Tory and Nicko's place once or twice previously, before the separation, and did not instinctively remember the layout of the sitting room. He had evidently forgotten the layout of the family, too, about the daughter whose name he had occasionally felt they bandied about more because of the school in Scotland than because she was theirs.

'Sorry,' the girl said lazily. 'Did I frighten you?'

She had a round cat face. Somewhere further down the sofa, bisected by a scatter cushion that she was holding lightly, were long smooth legs tapering, he couldn't help noticing, to hard, thoroughbred ankles. Someone on Nicko's side must have contributed those. One of the ankles was girdled with a silver bracelet which glinted in the evening light. The girl had not bothered to kick off her white sandals, through which peeped her toes, each nail dipped in crimson nail polish.

Afterwards, driving home with Edie, it was not the girl's round cat face that came and went in the light that sliced down from the lamps on the highway. It wasn't her sleepy drawling voice or her truculent smile or even her rather surprising ankles.

It was what she had said when, at last, he had said, 'I'm sorry – I didn't even know you were home.'

'No.'

'I mean' – he groped for something better – 'your mother never mentioned it. That you were home.'

Shit.

But the girl only raised an eyebrow, and drew the scatter cushion up to her chin. Jackson took a slug of his warm and watery gin, and was looking around to see where the door to the kitchen was, when the girl said, 'My mother never talks about me if she can help it.'

Jackson looked at her.

'I'm an embarrassment.'

'I doubt that.'

'If she had talked about me,' the girl said, shrugging, 'she'd have had to tell you I was kicked out of my smart school, wouldn't she? In *Scought*land,' she added cruelly. The mimicry was effortless, and in that moment Jackson had a discomfiting image of Tory's melting flesh falling away to reveal this gleaming creature beneath, the new skin like a precious suit of scales, like armour.

He took another swallow of his drink to banish the thought. 'Why were you thrown out?'

That eyebrow raise again. Such a small gesture, yet it acknowledged an intimacy – no, more, a conspiracy – between them, and it was in that moment that even without looking, Jackson knew how aware he was of the glossy sprawl of her, limbs and midriff and shoulders not covered nearly enough. He didn't need to look with his eyes: his whole being registered her, the way animals in the bush knew when a storm was coming.

But it was what she said next that caught him out. He supposed later that if he had been thinking anything in that moment, when most of his mind was preoccupied with trying not to look at her, he had probably been expecting a litany of mundane transgressions: a bottle of vodka rolling out from under the bed, a stray joint falling from a careless back pocket. Curfews and condoms and insubordination.

'I'm thick, you see,' Carly said.

She tilted her chin defiantly when she said it, as if to show she didn't care. But she glanced away from him for a moment then too, towards the mantelpiece. Jackson followed her gaze. Propped on one side of it was a photo of her brother Hanno, in gown and mortarboard. *Stephenhouse*, Jackson could hear Tory telling him. *He was head boy.* And, on the other side of a vase of lilies, a large trophy, against which leaned a photo of the other brother, Robbie wasn't it, in rugby gear, running, his lips snarled back against his gum guard.

There was no photo of the girl anywhere.

Outside on the terrace, he could hear Tory's voice tinkling away, and Edie laughing. He didn't know what to say then, and wished, suddenly, that Nicko were there to break the silence. Big, bullish Nicko, whom he barely knew, who would nonetheless have clapped Jackson on the shoulder, would have ushered him away on to the terrace or into the kitchen or another part of the house entirely. Nicko, who would have stood between Jackson and the girl on the mint-green sofa, who in that moment was looking away from him and clutching the scatter cushion to her chest as if it were a stuffed toy.

In the present, in the classroom, Jackson realises that people are putting their hands up and talking, and, a moment later, Christopher Appleby is looking around the room and asking whether anyone else has any suggestions for ways in which subject teachers can facilitate the progress of the differently abled child?

'Jackson,' whispers Rhidian, 'you've got to *pretend* to at least be interested. Honestly. Lauren is looking.'

But Jackson barely hears him.

The following day, Edie had telephoned him.

'Can I give Tee your number?'

Jackson had sighed, gustily, into the receiver.

'It's all right,' said Edie drily. 'She knows you're going out with what's-her-face at the university.'

'She does? Who told her that?'

'I did,' said Edie, 'during the awkward twenty minutes when you didn't come back to the supper table.'

'It wasn't twenty minutes,' Jackson said sulkily. But it probably had been. He'd got lost trying to find a way of returning to the garden that didn't involve going back through the sitting room. For a moment, the girl floated before his eyes again, with her lascivious mouth and her tilted, turned-away face.

Edie was still talking.

'. . . so can I?'

'Can you what?'

'Oh, for Christ's sake, Jackson. Can I give Tee your number?'

And Jackson had groaned out loud this time, but given in. Tory had phoned him after lunch. She had sounded suitably apologetic, although for what, Jackson hadn't initially been sure. Then it had come out.

'I gather you met Caroline last night?'

Jackson had tensed. 'Only briefly,' he said. 'I mean, I was just walking through the sitting room looking for the kitchen and—'

'Oh, I know.' Tory had given a little laugh. 'She does like to lurk. I suppose it's her age – never actually comes forward and introduces herself, never puts in an appearance. Just, you know, does her own thing.' She took a deep breath. 'Anyway, we've had a tiny little problem with Caroline, Jackson. It seems she had far too much fun at school last year – you know she was at Robertstown, in Scotland – and she failed most of her exams and now they're saying they won't have her back for sixth form . . .'

And as she chattered brightly on about how outrageous it was, such a betrayal, no sense of pastoral responsibility at all, just turfing a child out like that, all Jackson could think was, *she must be nearly seventeen, then.*

Because although he had not got within touching distance of Carly Nicholson, had in fact made his excuses and left soon after she'd told him about her being thick, and even though Jackson knew there was nothing unnatural in itself about the fact that he had – well – *noticed* her, in that moment, holding the phone reluctantly against his ear he couldn't help feeling it all over again.

The shock of his glass against his gums.

The dark flicker of her eyebrow.

The warmth he'd felt rising on his face.

Yes. There had been a moment when Carly Nicholson, aged almost-seventeen-surely had silently but clearly said to him, *Hi, Jackson.*

And before he could check it, Jackson knew that he had said, slowly, *Hello,* back. The unvoiced words had been exchanged, like contracts. So when Tory finally got round to saying wistfully, 'I don't know if you know of anyone who could perhaps tutor her, Jackson?' Jackson had said immediately that he knew of an excellent woman at the university who did freelance tutoring. He would email Tory her number, if she liked?

At the end of the line, he could hear a tiny sigh, as Tory said, thank you, Jackson. That was what she'd been hoping for, yes. It really had.

*

After the session, when everyone is piling into the corridor and making for the stairs in order to make it to period five on time, Lauren stops them.

'Wasn't that *excellent*?' she demands of Rhidian, and Rhidian murmurs that it was, Lauren, it was.

As he heads for the stairs, Jackson can hear Lauren saying, curiously, 'Is Dr Crecy all right, do you think? He looked a little preoccupied, I thought,' and Rhidian replying blandly that he expects Jackson is just getting his period.

VII

Last lesson of the day for Frances is Year 11, and despite an urgent desire to go home and lock herself away with Dog and a bottle of wine, she squares her shoulders and makes her way back up to her classroom to teach it, wearily conscious of her puffy face, her greasy hair and the ladder she's just discovered in her new and stupidly super-sheer tights. The events of the lunch hour, and perhaps her lack of lunch have left her feeling dizzy and a bit sick, and so, where she would normally bound up the four flights of stairs to her classroom, today she steps into the dilapidated lift which they're not really supposed to use on account of its many Health and Safety issues. As the door closes behind her, the smell of cigarette smoke and, Christ, is that actually *urine*, makes her jaw begin to quilt with saliva. She looks down at the ground, flecked with chewing gum and grime, and for a panicked moment feels herself beginning to gag. Deep breath, she tells herself. Still, as the lift creaks to a halt at the fourth floor, she realises that the combination of her mother and Jackson has really knocked her for six, and the thought of the drive back to Kent makes her want to lie down and die on the spot.

Thankfully, Year 11 are usually late to this particular lesson because they have to make their way over from another part of the school's sprawling site, and so she takes herself into the book room at the back to collect herself for a few minutes. She is still sitting there, staring blankly at the wall, and wondering how long it will take her to get home in mid-week traffic, not to mention what she'll do when she gets there, when the pupils begin to arrive. Clank, thump, grumble. (You can't sit there, Smithy, that's my seat.) (Have you done the prep?) (Is she actually *here*?)

Just for a second, the thought of stepping out among them seems overwhelming. They will be raucous and chatty with lunchtime sugar, but too close to the end of the day to be malleable, in need of marshalling and shushing and cajoling to do anything approaching work. In the past, Ceci Vale has been tactless enough to ask curiously, 'Miss, what's wrong with you?' and Frances wonders, if she does, what she will say this time. *Well, Ceci. Where would you like me to begin? My mother has either had a stroke or has advancing Alzheimer's and my best friend won't speak to me. In addition to this, I'm nearly forty, perpetually broke and am probably going to die alone and be eaten by my dog. Does that answer your question?* She can imagine Ceci Vale's china-blue eyes widening, the way she will flick her hair and mutter, 'Sorr-ee, Jesus.'

Through the wall, the noise level is rising. If she is going to teach them, rather than run away to Matron, she needs to get in there and get on with it. *Up and at 'em, Pilgrim*, Jackson always used to say cheerfully when she was languishing at the end of the day, or *Once more into the breach, dear friends!* Jackson, she thinks desperately, feeling her throat beginning to constrict again. Never before has she wanted to throw herself at him and weep so much, but it's no good wanting that any more, is it, and at any rate it's already five to three, the lesson should have started ten minutes ago. So Frances gets to her feet and, taking a deep breath, pushes open the book room door.

'Oh,' says Ceci Vale, looking disappointed. 'You *are* here.'

'Miss, can we watch a film?'

'Miss, we've just had maths, we're exhausted.'

It is Frances's favourite, lanky Callum Smith, who says, 'Shut up, everyone. Miss, are you okay?' and Frances is opening her mouth to tell them to sit down, bags on the floor, please, everyone, when all of a sudden the classroom in front of her eyes begins to flicker and buzz. 'Miss?'

'I'm fine, Callum,' she says, more sharply than she had intended. Then, to soften it, she adds, 'Could you hand out those sheets that are on my desk, please?'

'Oh, God, miss,' says Ceci Vale, putting her head on the desk, 'not a poem, I just *can't* today, I'm so tired.'

For one of their GCSE Literature papers, the pupils have to be confident in commenting on Unseen Texts. Unseen Commentary is approved of by the head as it gives them what he calls 'a pedagogical platform', from which to make the pupils practise what Venning sanctimoniously markets as the skill of Independent Learning. 'Or in other words, time off for teacher,' as Rhidian always points out. Only *lazy* teachers, he says, enjoy just chucking things at their students and leaving them to make a pig's ear of it.

'I have no scruples whatsoever about being a lazy teacher,' Jackson always muttered in her ear. 'Do you?'

Frances does not, and today she is relieved that she has a set of Matthew Arnold's 'Dover Beach' to hand.

'How come you don't mind teaching "Dover-bloody-Beach",' demands Jackson, who can't stand Arnold. 'Surely it only compounds your ridiculous hydrophobia?'

But as Frances always points out, 'Dover Beach' is not really about the sea, it's about the sadness the sea provokes, and she rather likes that. *Oed und leer das Meer*, he mutters by way of retort. *Oed und leer das Meer, Pilgrim!*

Now, as Year 11 reluctantly get out their highlighters and their different-coloured pens for annotation, Frances says, 'Who'd like to read? Amelie?'

Amelie wouldn't like, really, but she will if she has to, miss.

'It's okay, miss,' says Callum Smith kindly, 'I'll read.'

'Thanks, Callum.' Frances takes a breath, 'Okay, people, before we begin, what about the title? What do we associate with Dover? With beaches, generally?'

And they're off, rattling into gear like a car on a cold morning, reluctant at first but then, as ever, competitive, perhaps – yes, just perhaps, but shhh – a little interested. Dover's white cliffs, isn't it, miss, it's bluebirds, it's nostalgia, it's all about coming home in wartime, about *familiarity* and, like, safety.

96

'And a beach is about what, exactly?' Frances asks them.

'Sandcastles,' says a fat boy called Duncan, grinning. 'Ice cream. Donkeys.'

'God, Duncan,' says Ceci Vale. 'You're so *basic*.'

Duncan scowls. Frances can see him thinking *smug bitch*, a sentiment with which she herself has often had a fair bit of sympathy, after all. So she smiles, briefly and encouragingly, at Duncan, and then turns away, saying, 'Go on then, Ceci, what else is a beach about?'

Ceci widens her eyes and lifts her chin. 'Well, miss,' she says. 'It's the space between land and sea, isn't it? It's – what did we call it before? – oh yes. It's a *liminal space*.'

Frances can hear Duncan muttering, quite audibly, that *Ceci* is a fucking liminal space, but for once she pretends not to hear.

'So,' she says, 'what sort of mood does this perhaps impart to the poem, even before we start reading?'

Uncertainty, says Ceci. Ambivalence, *ambiguity*.

Frances sighs. She doesn't dare even look across at Duncan.

'Thank you, Ceci. Very good. Write it down,' she says to the others, then, 'Cal, still happy to read?'

'More than, miss. More than.'

He's such a nice boy, Frances is thinking vaguely, as she hitches herself up on to the edge of her desk, poem in hand. But as Cal begins to read – *The sea is calm tonight. The tide is full, the moon lies fair Upon the straits* – something odd begins to happen.

Frances feels herself lose her balance for a moment, on the edge of the desk, has to reach out a hand, quickly, to grab the edge of her computer monitor. Careful, miss, says Duncan in the front row, giving her a wink, and Frances is trying to raise her eyebrows in a self-deprecatory way, trying to look, too, as if she is still focusing on Cal Smith's voice.

But the words, somehow, seem to be coming at her as if over a far longer distance than the third row back. She can see Cal's mouth moving, yes, but the sound seems to reach her, echoing and staticky, a moment or two afterwards, as if she's on a bad satellite link-up. She shakes her head. *Come on, Pilgrim*, she can hear Rhidian saying in the distance. *Pull yourself together, for heaven's sake.* The poem, she thinks, focus on the poem. *Listen! you hear the grating roar Of pebbles which the waves draw back, and fling—*

But the world itself seems to be drawing back, doesn't it, and it is Cal Smith's ordinarily husky voice that is becoming a low and grating roar, and is in fact petering out now because he's stopped reading and is saying, 'Miss? Are you okay?' and she is trying to gesture him to go on, to get to the bit she likes most, about the waves with tremulous cadence slow, bringing the eternal note of sadness in—

But he doesn't get that far. And when she next looks up, slowly, Callum Smith has become a dark smudged outline in front of her, like a charcoal sketch. Perplexed, she looks up at the strip lighting in the ceiling, but even that sudden movement of her head seems to do something peculiar to her vision, because all of a sudden now, the room is sliding very peculiarly sideways. The edges of the whiteboard are turning on their side and illuminating like a spaceship about to lift off, and, closer to home, Callum Smith's blurred grey school trousers suddenly seem to be turning left and sideways across her vision, like the second hand moving backwards on a clock face.

Frances can just about hear Ceci Vale saying, 'Oh, my, actual *God*,' before her head hits the side of a desk and everything goes black.

When she comes round, for a moment she thinks that she is alone. She is looking straight through the legs of some desks to the scuffed and dirty skirting board that edges the blue carpet. Near the bin, there is a white scatter like old confetti where someone has messily emptied a hole-puncher, and outside the door she can hear pupil voices in the corridor, a swarming sound that suggests they have recently been vigorously shushed down from a state of near hysteria by an irritated teacher. Have they just bolted en masse because she's passed out? Opportunistic buggers, she thinks, and tries to move, only then becoming aware of something soft under her head and a man's voice telling her not to move too quickly. Jackson, she thinks hopefully, but when she looks around, it is Rhidian who is sitting on a chair pulled up next to her.

'Oh good,' he says, bending down to look at her. 'You are alive.' When Frances blinks, he adds, 'At least I shall be spared the bother of advertising for your replacement.'

But she notices that the hand he offers her in order to pull her upright is shaking in a very un-Rhidian-like manner.

'What happened?' he asks, and Frances can only shake her head.

'I was trying to get them to do "Dover Beach",' she says. 'And then something happened, and I . . . I just—'

'Blacked out?'

She nods.

Rhidian eyes her for a moment, looking doubtful. Women's problems, she can see him thinking. Above my pay-grade! 'Have you eaten today?' he says at last.

When she shakes her head, he frowns, then says they'll have to go and complete an accidents-in-the-workplace form – 'That should cheer you up' – but that after that he is taking her out for some food.

Frances opens her mouth to say that she can't, she's got to go home to her mother's, but then closes it again rapidly. If Rhidian finds out she's thinking of going anywhere near her car, he'll probably lock her in the department overnight. So she nods meekly, and waits for him to go out into the corridor and send her Year 11 away.

Half an hour later, as she collects her jacket and bag from the English office, where Rhidian has put them, there is a knock on the door. Dora Valentine, the head's secretary, is standing outside. 'Ah, Frances,' she says, 'your mother's been ringing the main office. She seems a bit confused. I told her I'd make sure you got the message.' She sounds like she's being kind but she's not. Frances knows Dora can detect a drama at a hundred paces, like Dog sniffing out scraps under a park bench. Dora is snooping. After Frances has gone she'll write a note on her file. *Mother unwell*. It'll be soft information, off-book, not talked about. But it all gets noted; at some stage, it will all be taken into account, will all add up to the bigger picture of her yearly appraisal as they consider, again, whether Frances is Fit for Responsibility (she isn't).

'Thank you,' she says now, as briefly as she can. It doesn't do to be rude to Dora.

'Do you think you should perhaps call her back?' Dora is alleged to be the great-great-granddaughter of a famous English explorer, although this has never been corroborated. Frances thinks she is certainly the nosiest person to have existed in several generations.

But now she just sighs, says she expects so. Says, 'Thanks, Dora. Thank you for being messenger.'

'You do have people at home, Frances?' Dora calls after her. 'You really shouldn't be alone this evening, in case you faint again . . .'

I bloody should be alone, Frances thinks. On her already quite considerable list of most embarrassing things ever, fainting in front of Year 11 trumps them all. Once she was on her feet again, Rhidian had led her discreetly out of her classroom and down to the medical centre, but she'd still had to walk past a Year 7 boy sitting miserably outside with a sick-bag, and a weeping sixth-form girl being propped up by a weary and solid-looking friend, feeling like she was one of them, the sick and sorry, the walking wounded. Christ!

Frances realises Dora is still talking at her.

'What?'

'Your phone, dear. It's ringing in your bag.'

'Oh. Right.'

On her desk is a note from Rhidian, saying he has been called to a meeting with a parent, but that she is not, on any account, to leave before he gets back. Frances waits until Dora has reluctantly withdrawn before she slings her bag over her shoulder and walks out of the office, making for the main lobby. She can't cope with her mother just yet; she knows she really needs to find Silv and have a drink before she attempts the drive home, but the minutes between her emerging from the book room and her fainting keep unspooling now, like the CCTV footage of a mugging, almost paralysing her. Had the pupils seen her pants? And, God, would any of them have been crass enough to have taken a photograph? As she slips through the electric doors on to North Road, she finds herself inadvertently tugging at the hem of her pinafore, as if that will, in some way, help restore her dignity.

But inside her bag now, her phone is buzzing again, tangling and choking the spool of images, and when she retrieves it she sees that she has seven missed calls and three unanswered texts. She turns it off and puts the phone back in her bag. Then, feeling ashamed, she gets it out and switches it back on, scrolling quickly through the list of missed calls, still, in spite of it all, trying not to hope one might be from Jackson, asking if she's okay. As if he might somehow have caught a trace of her fear across all the distance between them, and come to find her. But the calls are all from her mother, insistently. Seven calls in a row.

When she opens the front door of the flat, Dog flings himself at her straight away. Picking up his lead from the hallway table, she clicks it on to his collar and takes him out to the square. As he relieves himself and then hunts for left-over sandwiches under a horse chestnut tree, Frances looks at her watch. Only half past four.

Her phone is buzzing again. *Accept incoming call?*

'Mum?'

There's a pause at the other end of the line, then a shaky-sounding gasp.

'Mum,' she says again stupidly, watching Dog hunting in circles in the shadows beneath the trees. 'It's okay, I'm coming home tonight. I'll be there in a couple of hours.' Somewhere in the background she can hear Jean bustling in: *Now, Mary, love, what did we say about using the telephone this afternoon?*

But her mother is still on the line and her voice, when she speaks, is now thin and high, like a child.

'Gone,' she says, and when Frances asks her if she can speak to Jean, she starts to cry.

'He's gone,' she says, her voice tipping up into a wail. 'Please, Far, find him. Bring him home, do.'

VIII

'Have you seen Pilgrim?' Rhidian demands of Jackson as soon as he arrives back in the office at four o'clock.

Jackson looks at him warily. 'Why are you asking me?'

Rhidian stares at him. 'You mean you haven't heard? She passed out in front of her Year 11 class.' He shakes his head. 'Cal Smith came and found me. He looked white as a sheet.'

Jackson frowns. 'What's wrong with her?'

'Oh, God, answers on a postcard. But I told her to wait for me here after she came back from the medical centre.' Rhidian is pulling out his mobile phone now and scrolling to find Frances's number.

'She'll have gone home,' says Jackson, turning back to his desk, and trying to banish the memory of Frances's white face as he had laid into her earlier. It's not my fault, he thinks. A moment later, Rhidian is hanging up. 'No joy?'

'Straight to voicemail. Do you think we should go round there?'

'No,' says Jackson. Then, when Rhidian raises his eyebrows, he adds, 'She'll be fine. Getting pissed with that mad friend of hers, I expect.'

'The love child of Greta Garbo and Margaret Thatcher?' Rhidian looks doubtful. 'Is she really a reliable babysitter?'

Jackson shrugs. 'She'll be fine,' he repeats. 'She's probably just, you know . . .'

'Hung-over?'

'Knowing her.'

'Well. You know best, I'm sure.'

And with that, Rhidian departs towards the Tube.

IX

'Oh,' her mother says, when Frances comes through the back door at seven o'clock on Wednesday evening. 'What are you doing here?'

Jean bustles in then. 'Ah, look, Mary,' she says in a nursery voice. 'Here's Frances. I told you she was coming, didn't I?'

'No,' says Frances's mother, sniffing, 'you didn't.'

Jean opens her mouth, but Frances gives her a bright smile and says, 'Tell you what, Jean, shall I pop over for a cup of tea in the morning?'

Jean returns the bright smile and says that would be super, she'll look forward to that, Frances. Lovely. And then she's gone, scuttling through the door and side-stepping Dog's friendly goosing, turning back only when she is safely outside to make a telephone gesture, her first and fourth fingers near her ear. Frances pretends she is waving at Jean, and tries to give her a thumbs-up without her mother noticing. Her head is ringing from the drive, and although on one level she feels too exhausted for this pantomime with Jean, she finds herself watching the other woman's retreating back with something approaching horror.

'She's so nosy,' says Frances's mother, sniffing again. 'She always has been, typical only child, always on the lookout for gossip. I should think she drove that nice Brian up the wall, back in the day. No wonder he had a heart attack at forty. Hen-pecked to death, I'd say.'

There is a strong smell in the air, although Frances can't identify what it is. It reminds her of the smell of chicken stew in the school canteen, something warm and pungent and meaty. Is her mother cooking something? The oven doesn't appear to be on.

'I told you earlier, Mum,' she says. 'I thought I'd pop home tonight. See how you are.' But her heart is sinking. Her mother seems to have no recollection of the taxi journey to London, the glass cup of tea, or her shamed tears in the Green Café. How has this happened so fast? Has she had a stroke?

'I can't keep up with you,' her mother is saying testily, and to give herself something to do, Frances turns away and starts to fill up the kettle for tea. In the darkened glass of the kitchen window she looks ghastly, half of her face in shadow, the other half unnaturally white, like a skull. For a moment she remembers the streak of white she'd glimpsed in her hair earlier. In the glass, she can also see the blurred reflection of her mother, who has now sat down at the kitchen table, and seems to be trying to remove something from one of the terrier's ears. Nearby, her cat is crouched on the table, lapping milk from a dish which sits alongside four or five mugs of cold undrunk tea. Perhaps some of them are Jean's, she thinks hopefully, but in her heart of hearts she knows that they are now beyond counting mugs. They are in much deeper water now, each of them as out of their depth as the other.

'That Evans girl is getting married,' says her mother suddenly, jerking her head sourly towards the lane by the side of the house. 'At twenty-one, I ask you.'

It isn't clear if the Evans girl's marriage is offensive because she is so young, or because it rubs yet more salt in the wound of Frances's mulish spinsterhood. Frances pours boiling water on to two teabags and puts them down on the table, waiting for her mother to make some dry, contingent comment on the state of Frances's own personal life. Her mother has always viewed men, even when lucid, with the waspish resignation she also reserves for doctors or the police: on some level only portents of trouble, yet perhaps just a modicum better than the anarchy that prevails without them. Frances has always assumed that this reaction stems, somehow, from her father's death – perhaps her mother has never moved out of the anger stage of grief into sorrow and then acceptance? But today, at least, her mother is distracted and so no comment about Frances's own nuptial prospects is forthcoming: instead, her mother is busy examining something she has pulled out of her fox terrier, Dilys's, ear. Dilys, meanwhile, takes the opportunity to wriggle away from her and jump on to the floor, where she sits down balefully, and starts to scratch her ear with her paw.

Frances frowns, and pushes one of the mugs of tea towards her mother. 'Who is she marrying?'

But her mother only looks at her as if she were mad. 'Who's who marrying?'

'The Evans girl,' she says, biting her lip.

But her mother is shrugging. She can't keep up with all Frances's questions, honestly, she's always had a mind like a butterfly, ever since she was tiny. Then she picks up her tea, takes a sip and saying, 'There's no milk in this,' she grabs the old Evesham ramekin that has the remnants of the cat's curdling milk in it, and pours it straight into her tea.

Frances waits until she isn't looking before taking the mug off her and quietly pouring it down the sink.

Later on, when her mother is at last asleep, propped up on her pillows with the light still on and her half-moon glasses drooping on her nose, Frances goes on a hunt for a radio. She's not been big on 'the wireless', as her mother still calls it, since she was at school, and over the summer has got used to watching television in the dark with Dog after her mother has gone to bed. But tonight, although she is so exhausted she just wants to go to bed, she nonetheless feels the need for some outside voice, speaking in joined-up and non-peevish sentences about breezy, day-to-day things.

Perhaps, she thinks hopefully, there will be news on the radio, or a documentary or play? Even the shipping news would be a relief. She's got a feeling that there is a miniature battery radio knocking about somewhere, perhaps in her mother's room, and pushes the door open, stealthily, to look.

The room is quiet, and Frances stands for a moment, feeling as she always does when she chances on her mother unawares that she is, somehow, spying or stealing, taking something from her mother that she would not ordinarily give. In sleep the bitter brackets around the corners of her mouth have relaxed, and her lips have softened and fallen apart, like a child's. She is holding something in her hands which at first Frances takes to be a large book, but which, as she steps closer, she can see is, in fact, an old leather-bound photograph album, the sort every household had had in the days before Facebook and Instagram. It is heavy, and already beginning to slip on to the hump of duvet that lies over one of her mother's still-raised knees, so she steps forward and takes it gently, intending to put it on the windowsill behind her mother's bed. But curiosity, as usual, overcomes her, and before she does so she opens the cover, wondering what it is that has prompted her mother to dig out this unwieldy artefact from some muddled and furtive drawer.

The frontispiece is flecked and yellowed, but still just about discernible is what she realises must be her father's handwriting, spiky and brown with age. *Dryland, 1976–82.* The album, then, begins in the year she is born, and runs until his death. Disappearance, her teenage self insists for a moment, but she overrides it savagely. *Death.* She is too old now to believe anything else, even though she had been told at the time that she was too young to go to the funeral, and even though of course his body, lost at sea, has never been found. Nonetheless, her breath catches for a moment in the back of her throat, because she's never seen any of the family photographs, her mother having purged the house of memorabilia in the weeks after her father's death with all the reforming zeal of a Puritan stripping an altar.

For a moment she feels the urge to text Jackson and tell him that she's found some photographs of her father, at last; but then she remembers him telling her how selfish she is, how she really needs to just grow up, Christ! They might be talking again – well, shouting, anyway – but she is on her own with this small find for now, with her father's actual writing, considered and spiky in fading brown ink, and with these precious images of them all from almost forty years ago. *Full fathom five thy father lies*, she thinks, but it doesn't make her smile; in fact, once again, she feels tears threatening in her throat, just as they had done at lunch in the office. She carries it stealthily back to her bedroom, and climbs into bed.

'Move over,' she says to Dog, but her voice has cracked a little, even before she turns the pages to find the first photographs in the album.

X

Although somewhere in the distance he is sure he can hear a woman's voice calling his name, Jackson is adrift in a dream about Edie.

This time, the landscape is surprisingly clear. They are children again, sailing across the burned grass of their garden in Cape Town towards the made-up land they'd always simply referred to as the Ashores. Jackson is sitting behind her as they swing forward together, rowing against the air with their hands; occasionally his chin, reaching forward, grazes against her warm baby flesh. She smells green and damp, like a young shrub. He can see the tiny mole on her shoulder. Somewhere in the distance, he can hear the dream-laughter of his mother; somewhere beyond that, the laconic, deadpan tone of his father. In the street, someone is selling mealy corn with that old mournful cry of 'Meee-leeeees! Meeeeee-leeeees!' which to young Jackson had always sounded like a plaintive, 'Me, please! Me, please!'

But when his sister turns around to look at him, he draws back as if she has spat in his face, because the face looking back at him above the chubby folds of a baby's neck is not his baby sister. The face is almost adult, and round, like a cat's. The tip of a pink tongue pokes out childishly, and the face giggles.

'Hi, Jackson,' it whispers, but even though Jackson is pulling away, he can hear himself saying, again, from somewhere inside his skull, the word, bewildered and exhilarated and slow.

Hello.

He wakes up tangled in the quilt, and hears a door banging and a woman's voice calling, 'Jackson! Jackson, are you here?'

It's Thursday morning, he thinks. It isn't the cleaner's day. At the back of his mind he is aware that there is something else for him to worry about today, something immediate and visceral, but the baby dream has wiped it out, and now he is distracted by the sound of the sitting room door opening in the hall, then more footsteps, coming closer now.

'In here,' he calls, and then he hears the bedroom door opening, the steps near enough now for him to recognise the familiar tap and clink on his wooden floor. Riding boots with short spurs sitting low on the heel. In the gloaming he can pick up the warm tang of horse, a whiff of sweet hay.

'Jackson,' says Katy disapprovingly, standing over him. 'What on earth is going on? I've been trying to ring you for days, I even wrote you a *letter*—'

114

'Yes,' says Jackson. 'And now you've let yourself into my flat.' Although this is entirely his own fault, he realises. He'd given Katy the spare key when he moved in because she was, quite simply, the most reliable and organised person he knew. Frances would have lost it instantly, leaving it sitting on a pub table, probably, or dropping it down a drain.

Katy lifts her chin, tucks a stray strand of blonde hair behind her ear, and looks like she is about to say something when her gaze falls on something lying beside the bed. Jackson looks, and curses inwardly. It is Frances's earring.

'Oh,' says Katy, raising an eyebrow. 'Have you got company?'

The earring is what Frances calls a dangly, and is shaped like a teardrop, cut from a strange milky-coloured stone. It is the companion of the one Jackson had, all those weeks ago in the summer, fished out of their uneaten *boeuf bourguignon*, to place, so carefully, in his soap dish. It does not look precious, but in its length and style it looks, distinctly, like a young woman's possession. Jackson groans. He wants to tell Katy to go away, mind her own business, but suspects that that will only protract the other conversation she's come for, the one he doesn't want to have. Katy wants to know he's all right about Edie, all right about her baby news, and Jackson is far too proud to tell her that he is anything but about either.

Because what Jackson hasn't told anyone, not even Frances, is that what Katy's news has re-aroused in him of late is his terrible sense of smallness, his bleak and sterile separateness in the world. Now his sister Edie is gone, he alone of all his family persists, not just the only one who remembers his family home high up on the mountain slopes and the holidays near Cape Agulhas; not just the only person who remembers Edward Maroli the gardener and Lisette, their barrel-chested, belly-laughing maid; no, far worse than this sense of there being too many memories for one mind to hold on to satisfactorily is the knowledge that he, Jackson, is now the only living vessel containing any vestiges whatsoever of his sweet, laughing mother and gentle, lugubrious father. He's the only one left who knows what it is to feel *clapped, tethered, seen into*. And imagining Katy's baby, he does, even now, imagine the child they might have had together, a grave, blond baby whom they'd been going to name Eve or Grace or Agnes, Ben or Henry or Sam. It underlines to him, in a way that nothing else can, the very great darkness that will one day enfold him, and the roaring silence that he himself will leave behind. Not for him the great act of necromancy that is a child. No. Nothing at all of him will persist on this side of the grave. When he goes, that'll be that, lights out, and nothing left to show for it; well, apart from some first editions of D.H. Lawrence and the misplaced affections of upstairs' manky cat, anyway.

He sighs. He's not all right about it, at all. On the other hand, if he tells Katy to bugger off now she will leave thinking that he has probably relapsed and been indulging his well-documented urges for Much Younger Flesh. Once upon a time, Jackson would have told her to fuck off and think what she liked, but the injustice of her assumptions, on this occasion, rankles too much.

'I can see you're not, you know, right now,' Katy concedes, sitting down on the chair opposite and taking in the absence on the other side of his double bed. 'And, obviously, it isn't any of my business.' The thank goodness may be unspoken, but it rings across the space between them anyway, like a glass struck with a spoon.

Jackson struggles to sit up, remembers he has no pants on, and clutches at the duvet.

'It's Frances's,' he says, and can't help enjoying the way that Katy's pursed mouth sags suddenly, like a pricked balloon. She has always known that Jackson and Frances were friends, but now he can see doubt clouding her pink face. Rather quick, she is thinking, and then, had they, perhaps, been . . .

Jackson relents, and says, 'She stayed over once, in the summer.' He's bloody well not going to tell her any more than that, and certainly not that Frances crept out at dawn and has not really spoken to him since.

There is a pause. He can see that Katy's expression is altering subtly, her eyes softening from suspicion into – Jackson groans inwardly – pity. He knows what she's thinking: poor old boy, obviously still can't, he really ought to see a doctor if he's to have any hope of . . .

To deflect her pity, he says, 'Can we perhaps talk in the kitchen?' Katy's presence in the bedroom, only inches from Frances's long-abandoned earring, is making him feel sick with a very redundant sort of performance anxiety.

Katy reaches a hand out to touch his shoulder and Jackson tries not to flinch. 'Of course we can.'

A few minutes later, when he comes into the kitchen, she says, with sincerity, 'Sorry. Sorry for just walking in on you, and being, you know, suspicious. I just . . . worry about you, Jackson.'

So you bloody well should, thinks Jackson. Even as she's squeezing his hand, and passing him a cup of coffee, he finds himself staring balefully at her stomach, but she is still wearing her waterproof Musto jacket, so there is not much to see. Even so, the imagined swelling in her belly makes him feel again that blown-apart emptiness in his own. He thinks, fleetingly, of a poster he's seen lately around school, an image of a sculpture that supposedly sums up the plight of the refugee, the man-in-exile. The man is carved from iron, wears a bowler hat, a suit, and carries a briefcase. But there is a gaping hole below his shoulders where most of his torso should be: no belly, no guts, no lungs, no heart.

He sighs. Katy, on the other hand, is chock-full: two hearts, two sets of lungs. She is bellied with luck. It'll be a modest belly, though, if he knows her, right up to the day she gives birth. Then she'll be off to Pilates and back to the stables. Her new partner, Phil, whom Rhidian tells him is 'a bit of a playboy, on the Forbes Rich List last year, apparently', would surely provide a nanny. And then, being a bit of a playboy, probably roger her, he thinks. But he's such a sentimental berk that the fact that Katy's shacked up with an evident prick gives him little pleasure.

118

'When are you due?' he asks. When she tells him, he counts back on his fingers and raises his eyebrows.

'I know,' says Katy, looking down into her mug. 'We only met at Christmas. It was all quite quick. Given my age.'

She glances across at Jackson quickly, and then says, 'I'm not saying that—'

Jackson holds up a hand. 'It's fine.'

'Some people are just – well, just a better . . . fit.' At least now she has the grace to look embarrassed. Jackson is still trying to banish the unfortunate image of Phil-from-the-Forbes-List fitting himself between Katy's legs like a piece of Lego when there is a loud bang and a scrape from the window box outside the kitchen. They both start, spilling their coffee, and look over, only to see Callaghan the cat hurling himself off the window box and through the open kitchen window, landing on the floor with a thump like a prop hurling himself into a scrum. He picks himself up nonchalantly, and strolls across the tiles towards Jackson, his ginger tail vertical, and what looks like a dead sparrow gripped in his orange jaws.

Callaghan is quite disgusting. Nonetheless, Jackson isn't sure who out of the pair of them is more relieved to see him.

XI

On Thursday morning, Frances stays in Kent, and takes Dog for a long walk up on Dryland Common so that she can ring the surgery without her mother overhearing.

It's bright and blustery and Frances watches as Dog tears away from her after sheep, watching them blurt out of his way, not realising of course that he's just a soft old Lab who couldn't bring down a kitten. The receptionist tells her she'll have to wait until tomorrow for an appointment, unless it's an emergency. Is it an emergency?

'Yes,' says Frances, after a pause. 'It is.'

'Eleven o'clock, then.'

Frances suspects that, despite his initial concern, Rhidian will be wound up by her pulling a sickie, just when they're all meant to be psyching themselves up for the arrival of the inspectors on Monday. So, as Dog cavorts in circles, she taps out an apologetic email on her phone, promising to be back in to teach her only two lessons later this afternoon. But she also knows, deep down, that it doesn't really matter what Rhidian, or the inspectors, think. It doesn't matter about losing half a day of school.

Her mother appears to be losing her mind; and now, with the appearance of the half-empty photograph album, Frances wonders if she might be joining her. *Two for one on tickets to Wonderland!* she imagines Jackson saying sardonically. *One mental woman travels free!*

Because now, on the common, watching Dog quartering the ground with his nose glued to the turf, Frances finds herself unable to stop thinking about the photograph album, and the way in which what she found there has started to dissolve her longest-held assumptions about her parents, and their shared past. As she watches Dog follow the trail of an invisible rabbit, it seems to her that another past entirely is beginning to develop in her mind, a past that seems, discomfortingly, to be more the stuff of suppressed memory than revelation: as if the images have always been down there, just below the surface. She's simply never bothered to retrieve them from the fluid, and let them dry.

Because Frances has grown so used to her mother being frayed and caustic, hasn't she? In fact, her total memories of her seemed until last night only to begin on the night the dog star disappeared behind a cloud out of Jean's spare room window. The night her mother stood in Jean's sitting room doorway and took in her daughter, blotchy and sniffling under a blanket on Jean's sofa, with Mack the long-suffering Labrador watching worriedly over her, before giving way to the last tears Frances had ever known her to shed. Until now.

Since then, she has never been conventionally motherly,

she's developed brusque philosophies of *tough love, too bad*, and (her favourite) *well, life's not fair!* prompting a teenage Frances once to tell her she was like the love-child of Nurse Ratched and Attila the Hun. Theirs has always been an uneasy union. *You've put on weight*, her mother used to like saying truculently when she hadn't seen her daughter for a while, or, if she was feeling magnanimous, *You've got to be so slim to carry off your height, you know.* Sometimes it was her daughter's hair that bothered her. *You'd be better off with some highlights, really. They give mousy hair such a lift!*

It is only as Frances has grown older, only after she has observed hundreds of mothers and daughters sitting in front of her at Parents' Evenings that Frances has realised that it doesn't make a blind bit of difference how much weight she loses or what she does with her hair. When her mother looks at her, as Frances has seen so many mothers look at their daughters, in tight-lipped exasperation, she does not really see Frances. She sees, fearfully perhaps, only a younger version of the self she knew she would eventually become, not a sorceress any longer but a woman old and alone, wild-haired and weather-beaten in woolly leggings from the seconds shop, a strange collage, in her slipping headscarf and outdoor galoshes, of defiance and defeat. Her reproaches, which to a younger Frances had seemed so piercing and so unkind, are really only meant as a species of warning. *You're not immune to all this, you know. Life will come for you, too, in the end!*

But the photograph album doesn't bear out Frances's private conviction that her mother was born disgruntled and picky.

In the first photographs in the album, before Frances was born, her mother stares up at the camera, the quality that has since become a wild-eyed defiance then more of a sweet and expectant pertness, such as Frances remembered seeing in Dog when he was a puppy, waiting to be taken for a walk. In a photograph from early in 1977, her hair is set in a shoulder-length bob that flicks coquettishly out at the ends. In another photograph, she wears a tweed cap and flared trousers; in yet another, she glances back over her shoulder from a restaurant doorway in a fur coat and heels, hair in a wave, eyes dark in her luminous face like a young Jackie O. Sitting in bed with Dog and staring down at that photo, Frances had had a sudden memory of opening her mother's wardrobe one rainy afternoon, looking to play a furtive game of dress-up in the full-length mirror. How many dresses there had been, in how many sleek and sinuous fabrics, like the rippled loins of leopards or panthers seen once in the zoo; and there, right at the back of the closet like a secret, had been the fur coat itself. Had it been real? If it had, her mother has long since thrown it away, and now donates money by monthly direct debit to all manner of animal charities. But young Frances had not been bothered by the politics of the garment, she had just pressed her face into its slithery, tickly surface, and breathed in its strange musky smell, a mixture of her mother's perfume – Arpège, wasn't it? – and something expensively smoothed and treated, like leather.

Later photographs had shown her mother holding a very young Frances with the fierce combination of propriety and alarm that Frances had seen over the years in her own friends' nervy, new-mother faces; her mother in a Laura Ashley dress holding Frances, in her first school uniform, by the shoulders. Even at five, the brim of Frances's green school hat is pulled down a little too low, so she looks more like an indignant Kermit than a keen-bean Second Year.

And then there are the occasional pictures of her father, too, more often the photographer, it seems, than the subject: standing in the garden with his arm around her mother's shoulders, Frances lolling more comfortably in front of them in jeans and a sweatshirt, her first ever tricycle grasped between her knees; her father watching over her as she played on a Space Hopper; her father walking beside a grinning Frances in a sunhat sitting on what looked like a very bad-tempered mule.

Nonetheless, all the photographs had the posed quality of a Peter and Jane book to them: you could almost feel the fussy hand of a neighbour or relative behind the lens in the strained smiles and awkward leaning postures that they all kept. *Just a bit closer to Mary, now, Martin! And, Mary, can you just turn your head and smile at him a little? Super! Now, everyone, say cheese!* But in the tricycle photograph in the garden, Frances's mother's jaw had seemed quilted and set as she turned her head towards Martin. Perhaps she had been smiling. But to Frances, the overall effect seemed more like an animal, baring its teeth. *Dryland, September 1981*, her father had written under the picture.

It was the last one in the album. The pages after that are empty, the transparent layers that are meant to hold photographs in place fluttering agitatedly against the blank, unyielding backs of the unfilled pages.

XII

In London, Jackson says, 'Where's Pilgrim?' to Rhidian as they walk to the office from their pigeonholes.

'Not here,' snaps Rhidian. 'She sent me an email this morning, said something about having to take her mother to the doctor.' He shrugs, barely concealing his irritation. 'She says she's coming in this afternoon, but it's Cover City, USA this morning, *and* another dose of inspection-related bullshit at lunch.'

Jackson frowns. 'Her mother?'

'Apparently. Although I imagine that having fainted in class gives her a fairly solid platform for a little lie-in.' In front of them, Lauren pauses to hold the door open for them, and Rhidian has to lower his voice to add, 'Sometimes one wishes the lady-folk among us had a *little* bit more spine.'

Jackson fidgets. Somehow, yesterday's seminar has only intensified his anxiety about the way he'd flown at Frances, taunting her about her mother and laying it on thick about Edie. He needs to see her. Only last night he had woken up in the dark convinced he could hear someone crying. But it had only been Callaghan, of course, his scrawny face pressed up against the window, begging to come in.

Rhidian, pushing past him to get to the door, says, 'Don't forget the working party at lunch, Jackson.' His eyes gleam for a moment. 'I'm sure Lauren is *longing* to hear some of your policy initiatives.'

In the end Jackson gets to the working party a minute after one thirty, having decided he can't possibly sit through it without a coffee. This time, the carousel has lumped him and Rhidian in with what looks like a load of games teachers and NQTs in a maths classroom that smells robustly bleached, as if someone has recently been sick. As he looks around for an empty seat, the one next door to Rhidian having this time already been taken, Jackson notices the rigidly symmetrical wall displays. *Year 8 tackle quadratic equations!* Every sheet in a tessellated pattern, covered in a savage storm of red ticks. On the wall facing him are pictures of famous mathematicians, and a slogan poster that informs him that *Mathematics may not teach us to manufacture love or conquer hatred, but it does teach us that all problems have a solution!* Fuck's *sake*.

'Ah, Jackson,' says Lauren. 'Do have a seat. We're just waiting to start.'

Waiting for you, she means. Lauren is a master of passive-aggressive communication. Despite the fact that Jackson is sixty seconds late, at best, he is now a small speck of grit in Lauren's machine – although, come to think of it, he suspects that nothing has been near Lauren's machinery for some time. She has the Teflon gleam of a newly wiped kitchen surface.

Lauren scans down her list, and then looks around for Rhidian. 'No Frances?'

'She's ill,' says Jackson.

Oh dear, says Lauren blandly. Nothing serious, she hopes? Jackson is just opening his mouth to inform Lauren that actually, Frances is not in bed with a hangover, but away looking after her demented mother. But he is too late: Lauren is already saying thank you to them all for giving up a lunchtime for what she hopes will be an informative and useful session on the ever-developing issue of Safeguarding and Welfare in schools and reminding them that the purpose of the session is to enable them all to be able to respond appropriately if asked by an inspector about the school's policies on Child Protection. Behind him, Jackson can hear Rhidian grinding his teeth.

'We're going to be using a selection of scenarios which you'll find on your sheets,' says Lauren. 'You'll have an opportunity to work through them in pairs, and then we'll discuss each one as a group.'

'Group work,' mutters Rhidian. 'Oh *joy*.'

Could they get into pairs, please? Jackson looks to his right and finds that the stripe-haired games teacher with the orange tan is already talking to the person on her right. He looks to his left, and discovers a tall, angular man in his early twenties from – oh Christ – the physics department.

'Do you want to read it?' Jackson says politely, gesturing to the printed sheet, and the young man shrugs. His jaw is massive and bony, and the eyes behind his thick lenses are cold as pebbles as he reads.

In the course of a duty in the sixth-form centre, you encounter two pupils in a compromising sexual situation in a sixth-form study. One is in Year 12, but the other is in Year 11.

Jackson narrows his eyes. Is this a joke? Is Lauren showing signs at last of the surreal and even rather sinister sense of humour that Jackson has long suspected of members of the Senior Team? But when he looks around the room everyone is bent seriously over their scenarios. A low rumble of earnest chat is beginning to rise through the sicky, bleach-scented air. Jackson looks round hopefully, but Rhidian has his back to him.

'So,' the physics teacher asks him. '*What questions do we need to ask?*' His accent is slow and nasal: what *quaaiystionns do we nidd tuh aahsk?*

Jackson says crossly that, as far as he's concerned, the only question that needs to be asked is why on earth they couldn't hang on until they got home. The physics teacher stares at Jackson, implacable. Is he Scottish? Did anyone actually *have* sex in Scotland? Probably not and certainly not outside; you'd freeze your bollocks off. Jackson thinks with a sudden surge of longing that if it were Frances sitting next to him, she'd have been offering the lewdest possible answers in an audible stage whisper.

'So what action would you take?' the younger man persists, and Jackson notes the subtle grammatical shift, as if the physics teacher is psychologically re-aligning himself, away from Jackson and all his frivolous disregard for Child Welfare.

'I'd throw a bucket of cold water over them,' he says sulkily. What a total fucking waste of time this all is. Anyone in their right mind stumbling on pupils shagging would obviously just turn the other way and walk on. What were you meant to do? Tap them on the shoulder and ask them if they were old enough? Or hang about watching until they'd finished? The options were all obsessive or silly or slightly sinister. Jackson decides again that he can't wait to retire. Get out of teaching. Whatever.

Luckily, at that moment Lauren stops them to go through their answers. It depends, she says, on the actual age of the younger pupil. If they were both of age, then it was a simple disciplinary issue. Both pupils would be suspended and parents informed. If, however, the Year 11 was not yet sixteen then technically there were statutory rape implications, even if the act appeared to be consensual.

Behind Jackson, Rhidian is muttering mutinously that it should be if the Year 11 *were* not yet sixteen, because *if* takes the subjunctive, Lauren, you bloody idiot. If Lauren hears him, she shows no sign, and reminds them all that the correct action in a situation like this is to immediately contact the Designated Child Protection Officer – Lauren suggested they add her mobile number to their phones at the end of the session – and outline the scenario to her. Always pass it up the line, advises Lauren. That way they are not personally accountable. And of course, the welfare of the pupils would be well served, too.

Jackson drinks some of his coffee, and wonders what he will have for supper.

'Now,' says Lauren brightly. 'Shall we move on to Scenario B?'

Jackson sighs and looks at his watch, but in order not to have to listen to the physics teacher's dreary nasal voice any more, he offers to read it out himself.

Later, he will wonder if he would have done this had he known what was coming. Would he have smiled politely at the physics teacher instead, and suggested he do it, in his scratchy Scottish brogue? Would he have excused himself to the loos on the first floor, so that he was nowhere near Lauren when she began casting about for answers? But by then, of course, it will be too late. The questions will have been asked. The past will be all about him and clinging to his skin, treacly and pervasive as an oil-slick at sea.

'A student approaches you out of school hours in a provocative manner. She has clearly been . . .'

He falters. For a moment the words shimmer. He takes a breath and tries again.

She has clearly been drinking, and is quite demonstrative towards you.

Across the room there is a slight stir. A member of the art department puts up her hand at once and asks whether Lauren can explain why it needs to be stipulated that the teacher is male and the pupil female? Surely the general principles of how to deal with the scenario would be the same if the genders were reversed *or* – here she raises her voice triumphantly – if either the pupil or teacher were LGBT?

An elderly member of the geography department, not bothering to put up his hand, asks caustically what on earth she means, and the art teacher retorts that she means lesbian, gay, bisexual *or* transgender.

'For God's sake, Niamh,' snaps Rhidian. 'Can we just get on with this?'

Lauren interjects smoothly that it is a very valid point but actually, Niamh, the scenarios had all been drawn from experiences that members of the Senior Team have heard about personally; Niamh can rest assured that there is no *normative bias* in favour of heterosexual pairings.

It is then that her eyes wander around the room, and, to his horror, settle on Jackson.

'Dr Crecy,' she says, rather playfully, Jackson thinks afterwards. 'How would you handle a situation like this?'

But this time, when Jackson opens his mouth, he finds that no sound comes out at all.

XIII

After the phone call, Jackson had not heard from Tory again. Edie did not invite him to any more of her friends' dinner parties or *braais*, and Jackson didn't hear any more about Carly Nicholson.

A year passed.

Jackson turned forty.

Edie and her husband finally had a daughter, named Leonora.

'Your turn next,' said Edie's husband, Clem, in the hospital.

Jackson, holding the wrinkled little cocoon in the crook of his elbow, had shivered and not known why. The following week he had gone out to supper with the girl who Edie had always called what's-her-face. Sometimes, in the two years they'd been together, Jackson had toyed with the idea of an engagement ring. Walking home later, he thought ruefully that perhaps she'd hoped tonight would be the night.

It hadn't been.

'Oh God, why?' Edie asked the following day. 'She was a nice enough girl, wasn't she?' and Jackson hadn't really known the answer to that either, or else not enough of the answer to put it into words. He had looked at the baby's smallness, her tilted-up face, her fists soft as feline paws, and although it was not yet midday had gone to the kitchen to get himself a drink.

'Mid-life crisis,' he heard Edie mutter to Clem, and Clem had said Christ on a bike, shouldn't Jackson wait until he was fifty for that?

'You just need to grow up, Jackson,' Edie told him, when he came back from the kitchen with his drink. 'The girl of your dreams is only that, you know, a product of your imagination.' She'd been washing up and sterilising a breast pump at the sink – Leonora had had a condition called tongue-tie and often wouldn't feed – and her movements were terse and edgy. There was a slick of regurgitated milk on her dressing gown. She turned round to look at him, and he could see that her face was already a plane of exhausted hollows.

'Find a girl,' she said with a sigh, 'get married, and settle down. You'll be much happier.'

The sink had burped messily as she pulled out the plug.

A year later, Jackson had been sitting at his desk staring out of the window on to the immaculate lawns of the university laid out beneath him. An ordinary afternoon in autumn, sky neutral but a misty light from Table Mountain filtering through into the room, a light that Jackson always felt was flinted and mineral, bled from rock. On the back wall of his room, a Waterstone's poster with T.S. Eliot's face on it had reminded him that, on the whole, April wasn't much fun, and Jackson had been trying to take solace from the fact that, whatever other problems he had had, Old Tom had clearly never had any Problems Downstairs: that cold, square face with its metal-rimmed glasses and its large, flat ears, had by his own admission been *dependent upon female society*, even in his sixties. Maybe there was hope for Jackson after all.

Jackson, gazing at his poster, had been trying to remember if Eliot had had any children, when there was a knock on the door. It was clinic hours – students could come and complain that their latest assignment was too hard, claim an injury or bereavement and barter for extensions, or, as was becoming fashionable, hint darkly at their own mental health. It was only recently that Jackson had been told by his Head of Faculty that telling them all to brace up and bugger off was no longer considered to be best practice, pastorally speaking. There had to be some give and take; Jackson needed to be someone the students felt they could talk to openly.

'Come,' he had said crossly, and when the door remained closed, 'Come in, for God's sake!'

The door trembled, and then a round, pale face had peeped nervously around the edge.

'Tory,' Jackson said in surprise, and found himself getting to his feet.

He had taken her to the campus café, which after 5 p.m. was licensed. Tory said she'd just have a coffee, honestly, but when Jackson sighed, she'd sighed too and said, 'Oh, go on.

137

Twist my arm.' He ordered her a gin and tonic, and when their drinks arrived she'd raised her glass to him and said, with a nervous giggle, 'Well, chin chin, and all that.'

Jackson raised an eyebrow at that, and she'd blushed. 'I'm sorry – I've been in Europe for the last year.' Seeing his face, she explained, 'We – well, I, actually – found a decent school for Caroline, in London. Got her through her exams, and after that' – she shrugged – 'well, she wanted to travel. So she went off to Switzerland, and then Italy—'.

'The Grand Tour,' observed Jackson, taking a swallow of his own drink and spearing an olive. He wasn't going to think about Carly Nicholson gazing up at frescoes, transfixed by Michelangelo's *David*. And if she was as thick as she claimed to be, she wouldn't have managed to pick up the language, would she?

'Exactly. And I' – she gazed for a moment into her drink – 'well, I had some time to myself. Much needed, actually.'

'You look much better for it,' Jackson said, and found, to his surprise, that he meant it. When he'd last seen her, Tory had looked dreadful. Her skin had hung from her face and her arms as though it were melting and she'd had the stale and resentful air of a dog left tied up outside a supermarket; but now, some two years later, she had the landscaped look of the health club. And when she at last removed her hat he could see that her hair, which before had been lank and beginning to grey, now curled a soft reddish-brown, and her tight white trousers and short sleeves showed off the results of a relentless diet and exercise plan. He smiled at her, chinking her glass, and said, 'Welcome back.'

138

'I expect you're wondering what brings me to a university campus,' she said a while later, when they had ordered a bottle of wine, and when she had finally removed her wide-brimmed hat to reveal a pixie cut that she fussed with every few minutes. Jackson shrugged. He found he didn't want to bring Carly, inevitable as it was, into the conversation.

'It's all right, Jackson,' Tory said, looking at him over the rim of her wine glass. 'I'm not stalking you,' and when Jackson began to protest, she held up a hand. 'Carly's new boyfriend is a student. I dropped her off for the evening so she wouldn't have to drive.' She glanced, ruefully, at the glass sitting in front of her on the table. A pause. She fussed at the nape of her neck, and took a visible breath. 'I really came to say that I – well, I know how it looked that night, inviting you to supper just after Nicko had left. Honestly, I do. It was all about as subtle as a—'

'As a kick in the arse?' suggested Jackson helpfully, and Tory gave a little gasp. Then, to Jackson's surprise, she giggled.

'Yes,' she admitted. 'As a kick in the arse. I suppose it was. And I wouldn't like it to stop us being friends.'

Students were beginning to filter in. The sun was setting fast, and in the apricot light she looked, for a moment, very young, her hands still fluttering to smooth the strands of hair around her face that were no longer there. Jackson found himself looking at her mouth, which seemed fuller than he remembered, and which in that moment had gleamed with specks of oil from the olive bowl. Tory, realising she was being looked at, tilted her chin, and Jackson blinked.

Was it that? he wondered afterwards. Something as simple as a gleaming mouth, a suddenly tilted chin? Was he, after all, that *basic*?

'Come on,' he said, getting to his feet and holding out his hand. 'Let's go and find some supper.'

In the night, as he turned over in her vast white bed, he heard the back door bang, and voices in the kitchen.

'Just Caroline,' muttered Tory. Three-quarters asleep, she reached out and patted him. 'Don't worry.'

Some time later, he heard the footsteps coming up the stairs on to the floor below. When he heard the rumble of a male voice, laughing, Jackson had turned over and pulled the pillow tightly over his head. But he didn't sleep, and when he tiptoed out in the morning, closing the porch door softly behind him, he found himself glancing up for a moment at the first-floor windows.

And there she was, watching.

A figure silhouetted in one of the windows, a taller figure than Tory. Even at that distance, he recognised the round, cat's face.

He turned away before she could raise a hand in recognition.

Later that day, Jackson got back to his house to find an email from Tory. Last night had been so much fun, she wanted to say thank you to him for that, but also that there were really no expectations on her part. Really not at all. She had been sort of seeing someone in London and she

140

didn't know where that might or might not be going yet. So no pressure, Jackson. *Honestly.*

Jackson sighed.

'Why the *hell* did you do it?' Carly would want to know later, with a mixture of outrage and hilarity, and then Jackson would raise his hands, palms outwards to her in defeat. He didn't know, he said.

A lie, obviously.

Jackson had gone to bed with Tory Nicholson for the same reasons that hysterical students threw themselves down the stairs the night before an exam, or soldiers in the trenches had shot off their own feet. Because for that brief moment in the setting sun when her newly voluptuous mouth – 'Botox,' said Carly – had gleamed with oil from the olive bowl, Jackson had seen again, as if in the clatter of a camera shutter, the long shape of her daughter lying on the pastel sofa. He had seen the long line of her throat, her restless ankle with its silver bracelet. He had seen, above her and like a warning, the canvas of the Sharpeville massacre, with its spiked figures running from a broken sprawl of flesh. And he had known then, known he had to burn his bridges, jump into the frying pan in order to avoid the fire.

You fucking well stay away from us, Jackson, d'you hear? Nicko had said, when it was all ending. *Or I'll fucking well kill you myself.*

No, it wasn't Jackson's fault that his plan hadn't worked, was it?

XIV

Jackson is aware that someone is digging him in the ribs, and when he looks round, he can see Rhidian leaning forward in his chair and looking at him beadily.

'What?'

'We're meant,' says Rhidian gravely, 'to be discussing in our groups the best practice in fending off randy teenagers. Remember?'

He gestures to the young physics teacher, who has turned away from Jackson to talk to someone behind him.

'Christ,' says Jackson. 'Can't we just leave?'

'Well, *you* could. Given as how you're retiring – sorry, *getting out of teaching* – soon.' Rhidian leans towards him. 'Seriously, Jackson, what's the matter with you? You're behaving like a hysterical teenager yourself.' He puts his head on one side, like a bird. 'Or is it a menopausal house-wife? I can't quite decide.'

'Story of my life.'

'Yes, yes, bored already. What's actually the matter?' Rhidian narrows his eyes. 'I mean, I know we have our little jokes, but if you're trembling on the brink of a confession that you really are madly in love with Mercedes Solomon, may I remind you that I am your head of department and that—'

'That what?' says Jackson. 'You'll support me in any way that you can?'

'Christ, no. I was going to say that *as* your head of department I really couldn't give a shit.' Rhidian's mouth twitches. Then, seeing Jackson's face, he says, 'Oh God, Jackson, you're not—'

Jackson manages to smile weakly. 'No. I'm not.'

'Honestly?'

'Fuck's sake. Do I really look like Humbert Humbert to you?'

'Open brackets,' says Rhidian. '*Tactful silence*. Close brackets.'

XV

Carly said afterwards that she'd had absolutely no intention of running into Jackson that night ten days after he'd slept with her mother, and at first he had believed her.

Now, as the working party's chatter continues to eddy around him, and as he pretends not to be offended by Rhidian, Jackson finds himself thinking bitterly: *nine*.

Nine days it had taken her. Ten days since her mother had peeped around Jackson's office door, of course, but nine since he had crept out the following morning and, turning, seen Carly at the dusty landing window, watching him as he stood below on the drive.

Nine days. The length of one of the briefer English monarchies. And that evening, nine days later, had been a Wednesday, when all the current students knew that after consultation hours he often went to the campus bar, where after two drinks he was significantly more likely to be malleable to personal crises and fables about mental health. That night, Clem had been with him, had dropped in to have a quiet word about Edie's state of mind.

Nine days.

A student approaches you out of school hours in a provocative manner. She has clearly been drinking. How do you manage the situation?

He should have thrown a bucket of cold water over her, or perhaps himself, and run for the hills.

But he hadn't, had he? No.

Rhidian is nudging him in the ribs now, looking mildly penitent about his Humbert comment, but Jackson is looking away from him out of the window.

How had he managed the situation?

(I'll fucking well kill you myself.)

Not awfully well, as it turned out.

Clem had noticed her before Jackson had.

He came back from the bar the first time, to Jackson's dismay, with two foaming pints of lager – 'White wine's for poofs!' – and an expression on his face that reminded Jackson strikingly of Leonora when she was filling her nappy: a look that combined self-importance with a furtive sort of glee. When Jackson demanded what was the matter, Clem thumped the beers down and then tapped his nose with one finger. Jackson sighed. Clem was only five years older than him but in that moment looked more like someone's grandmother.

Eventually, after a slurp of his drink, Clem leaned forward. 'Chick at the bar's got the eye going.'

'On who?'

'On us, bro.' Clem jerked his head towards the bar, where

146

a girl in a white shirt and jeans was sitting with her back to them.

'She's not even facing us.'

Clem groaned. 'Christ, Jackson, for such a ladies' man you've got bloody poor skills.'

'I'm not a ladies' man,' said Jackson sulkily.

Tory had evidently told Edie about her night with Jackson, and Edie had told Clem, as well, it seemed, as anyone else who would stand still long enough to listen. It was because she was so pleased, she said, and had continued to hector him daily about when he was going to ask Tory out again. Clem thought it was hilarious: did Nicko know, he wondered, and if not could Clem tell him? It'd give the smug fuck one in the eye. Jackson had said Clem could not on any account tell Nicko and anyway, Nicko was somewhere in the Eastern Cape preparing to get married to his new girlfriend.

But Clem had nonetheless proceeded, admiringly, to call Jackson *racy Crecy* and *ladies' man* ever since. Jackson took a gloomy swallow of his lager. Clem was in the middle of explaining to him, with the conspiratorial animation of someone on his fourth drink, that the mirror on the back of the bar allowed punters to work the room even with their backs to it, and Jackson was trying to work out how to get the conversation back on to Edie without seeming unduly rude, when it happened.

A girl's voice at his shoulder had said, 'It's Dr Crecy, isn't it?' and, startled, Jackson had turned round, spilling most of his beer on to his trousers as he did so.

Later, she would say, laughing, *What, you mean you didn't see me coming?* And Jackson would wonder ruefully whether even if he had, it would have made the slightest bit of difference. Because Clem had been right after all, hadn't he? The chick at the bar with the eye going was Carly Nicholson, slender and smooth in jeans and a thin white shirt, and this time with a wine glass in her hand.

Clem had stood up when Jackson introduced her as Caroline, and had raised his eyebrows sky-high when Jackson added, 'Tory and Nicko's daughter.'

Carly said she hoped she wasn't butting in on anything, but she was waiting for her boyfriend, who was a bit late and—

'Of course!' Clem said expansively. 'Student bar's no place for a girl on her own. Can I get you another drink, Caroline?'

'It's Carly, actually.' She pushed back hair that was longer and lighter than Jackson remembered it, and smiled at Clem. 'Thanks. I'd love a glass of wine.'

White wine was for girls as well as poofs, apparently: Clem nearly fell over himself in his haste to get to the bar.

Jackson had taken a deep breath and said, 'So.'

She looked at him, expressionless, 'So.'

She was close enough that he could smell the shampoo on her still slightly damp hair, and he remembered then that the last words she had spoken to him – out loud, that is – were, 'I'm thick, you see,' before Jackson, stammering that he was sure she wasn't really, had been let off the hook by her mobile phone starting to ring in her pocket, and had

148

been able to escape to the kitchen. What should he say to her now? It was a toss-up, really, between *How was your holiday?* and *So yes, I did sleep with your mother*, and he'd been about to plump, cravenly, for the former, when Carly suddenly gave him a disarming smile and said, jerking her head towards Clem, 'Who the hell's he?'

'Him?' Jackson found that he sounded apologetic. 'Oh, him. He's just – he's my brother-in-law, Clem. He came by for a chat.'

We're not friends, or anything, he wanted to say, and realised then that he was no longer Dr Jackson Crecy, forty-one and a fully-fledged faculty professor. He wasn't racy Crecy, the divorcee's delight. No, he was once again just nerdy Jacksy-boy, the gangly boy with crooked teeth who'd been picked on so often at school that he'd developed a stammer and hadn't been able to address two words to a girl until he'd left for Cambridge, with a second-hand English accent and a scholarship and some painfully straightened teeth.

There was a pause, and then, in a rush, she put her hand on his on the table and said, 'Look, I just wanted to say that I'm glad you're looking out for Mum.'

He had looked at her in amazement. 'You are?'

She put her head on one side. 'Of course. Why wouldn't I be?' A pause, then she went on blithely, 'The divorce was shocking. Dad gave her a really rough time, you know.'

Jackson found he didn't know what to do with his head, so had another rapid swallow of his lager.

Carly said, 'It was my idea to go to Europe, but it was really for her. I thought she needed to get away for a while.'

Jackson blinked, and she withdrew her hand then, saying she really had to be going.

'You do?'

'I have to meet Sam,' she said. 'But I'll see you around?'

The slight tilt in her inflection then reminded him, again, of the way she had clutched the scatter cushion to her chest as she lay on her parents' sofa, her head turned away from the two photographs of her brothers on the mantelpiece. It was like a tiny loose thread hanging from a hem, a glimpse of something small which, with one unlucky catch, could unravel the whole. She was nearly nineteen, with a round cat's face. She was smooth and slender and beautiful and she was so close that Jackson could see the flushed gape of her sternum through her loosely buttoned shirt, could even see the tiny lace rosebud on the centrepiece of her bra. But it was that questioning in her voice that made something in him – in his heart, he would ask himself later, in his gut, in his groin? – flutter like a flag in a breeze.

And Jackson had found himself nodding again, speechless. *I'll see you around. Yes.*

When Clem got back to the table, Jackson, feigning insouciance, said, 'I'll have that,' taking the white wine from him.

'She gone, then?'

'Yes. Gone to meet her boyfriend.'

Clem had shaken his head. 'Lucky fella. Christ, if we were . . .'

Jackson said nothing. When he lifted the abandoned wine glass to his mouth, his hands were shaking. He downed it in one.

In time to come, Jackson would look back and find a way to blame everything that followed on that single glass of white wine, which Carly Nicholson had asked for and then left behind her, untouched.

XVI

The medical centre car park is full by the time Frances arrives, brimming with small accidents and emergencies, the ones not serious enough for the big A&E in town, but which nonetheless can't wait for a scheduled appointment.

Dog sits up when Frances at last gets back into her car, and looks at her, his head on one side. Together, they watch as an old woman is wheeled into the surgery by a carer, face pasty and vacant; together they observe, too, the young woman struggling to get a pram through the surgery door. Frances wishes she'd eaten some breakfast; she's feeling more sick than ever.

'Unfortunately,' the young woman GP told her, 'we can't take action on behalf of other people. Not until there's a proven risk to themselves or others.'

'Like what?' Frances asked. 'Like her crashing the car, or OD-ing on cat food?'

It sounded funny but it wasn't. Or was it that it didn't sound funny but actually it was, blackly, horribly funny? Frances wasn't sure any more what counted as funny, not funny ha-ha anyway. Things one might laugh at in a film or a book suddenly weren't so entertaining when they climbed off the page and happened to you.

The GP was sympathetic. It was always very hard on the family.

What family? wonders Frances bleakly. Her father was an only child, and Frances's only aunt lives in New Zealand, having long since ceased to speak to her sister and her niece. Family implies an immediate group, and this one's a group of two that's becoming more like one and a half. Her mother is disappearing like Alice, down a well to Wonderland, and Frances doesn't know how to follow her. The roads were disappearing. The map was never true. MAP, she thinks. Her father's initials.

She had taken an unsteady breath and said, 'She seems to have become confused about the circumstances of my father's death, you see.'

'Some people never get over a bereavement,' the GP said gently, and Frances had been opening her mouth to say that that's just the point, that her mother no longer seemed to believe that she *had* been bereaved, when she'd seen the GP discreetly looking at her watch. She had closed her mouth again, and got to her feet.

'Come back in tomorrow, try to bring her with you,' the GP had suggested, touching her forearm with her hand. Frances noticed the engagement ring, the wedding ring, others, perhaps, handed down from another generation. 'We can get an assessment done, maybe discuss some options for home care.'

154

And although Frances had made another appointment, she'd known she'd never get her mother to go, known all too well that her mother, lucid once more, would just tell her imperiously that she was being a drama queen, Far, quite honestly. Isn't she too old to go around turning every little thing into a three-act play?

Sitting in the car now, she rests her head on the steering wheel and bites down hard on her hand to hold back the tears that threaten, malevolently, behind her eyes, all the while feeling the warm, apologetic weight of Dog's muzzle resting gently on her shaking thighs. Opening her eyes to stare blankly at the car's dashboard, where the fuel gauge is almost at E for empty, Frances wonders whether she had wanted to tell the GP exactly what her mother seemed to believe about her father's death because she had hoped that, somehow, the GP would smile ruefully and say, 'Oh yes, that's quite characteristic of this disease.' Had hoped the GP might use words like *distortion*, *fantasy*, *confusion*. Might pat her on the arm and say that there was no need to worry, it was just one of those things that she would have to get used to as time went on.

But she had not told the GP, had she? At the last minute she had clammed up, gone quiet. Afterwards, when it is all over, Frances will ask herself whether, in her heart of hearts, she had already begun to wonder then. Had she and her mother been walking on opposite banks of the same slow stream for years now? She will wonder, later, whether she had begun to realise on some level that what has bound mother and daughter even more deeply than genetics is their unspoken sense that the bank beneath their feet is not solid ground but an overhang, hollow and tenuous, underneath which the river has gouged out troughs and hollows. As long as they tread quietly, they will be all right. But it will only take one missed step, one moment of inattention, and the bank beneath their feet will crumble and give way, casting them adrift into the currents below.

That afternoon, when her mother is safely engaged in listening to the afternoon play on Radio 4, Frances at last summons up the courage to slip out and see Jean. She has been delaying going round, making one excuse after another to avoid having to confront the awful truth that Jean will want to discuss, which is that her mother will soon need either home care or a nursing home. But the creeping feeling she'd had in the medical centre car park – that her mother's peculiar behaviour is perhaps more complicated than she could ever have imagined – will not go away when she goes back to London, will it? No, it will stalk her, run her to ground, until she ends up looping back in the end, like an exhausted hare, to talk to Jean anyway. Because Frances has a small, dark feeling that Jean is the only one of all their friends who has been around for long enough to have any idea of what is really going on here.

Jean has always lived only fifty yards further up the stony path towards the common, but when Frances opens Jean's front door, as usual she feels as though she is in a different world. The central heating is on, and the warm buttery smell of scones baking drifts out to meet her as she wipes her feet on the doormat. Because Jean does not have dogs any more, only cats, her house is carpeted, making Frances realise again, with a stab of guilt, how bleak her mother's old stone cottage really is.

Jean is delighted to see her – 'Sit down, love, near the radiator. It's nippy out!' – and bustles about putting cups and saucers on a laminated tea tray with a pattern of fluffy cats on it. Everything in the kitchen is cat-themed, just as it has always been, just as it was on the night the dog star went out. There is even a cat clock above the cooker, and Jean's own cats feature prominently in a collage of family photos that are framed and set under glass on the kitchen wall. There they all are, Jean and her late husband Brian, who had worked for the Water Board and whom Frances's mother is convinced died of hen-pecking; there are their two sons David and Robbie, and of course their grandchildren: 'You remember Mylene, she's four now and a proper little terror. And that's Andrew, still a darling.'

Looking at the grandchildren, Frances remembers now, with a pang, the birthday and Christmas cards, always with a far-too-generous banknote sellotaped to the inside. And then, when she'd got into Oxford, the way Jean had taken her on one side, said she knew money was a bit tight at home, and would Frances let Jean help out a little? No, Frances had said, laughing, not remotely, she couldn't take money from Jean! But Jean had shaken her head conspiratorially, because, truth be known, Frances, she'd come into a bit of money unexpectedly from her sister Margaret who'd died without any children, bless her, and now all

Jean's own children were grown and flown and making their own way, they didn't need help from their mum any more. Brian's life insurance had seen them all right, God rest his soul, and of course Jean had his pension which was very comfortable actually, thanks to the Water Board. No, Frances would be making Jean very happy if she'd accept a little something towards her university time. After all, what else would Jean do with it, give it to the Cats' Protection League?

The little somethings had totted up to about five thousand pounds by the time she graduated. 'Don't tell your mum,' said Jean, tapping her nose. 'Just tell her you took out a student loan.'

But in the end, when Frances did finally take out a student loan, with the express intention of paying Jean back, Jean had been adamant that she wouldn't accept it.

'I'd be offended, Frances, if you made me. It was a gift, and the Lord only knows things haven't been easy for you since your dad – well, you know.'

Now, as Jean puts the teapot down on the tea tray, Frances looks around the kitchen with genuine appreciation. You could laugh, she supposes, because the kitchen chair covers and the blinds are made from the same peach-coloured fabric. She can just imagine the sort of beady comment Rhidian would make – *guest-house chic, my God* – but nonetheless, Jean has always treated Frances as one of her own, has always made it clear that her carpeted and curtained home is Frances's home, should she ever need or want it.

And in London, of course, Frances's home is a studio flat in a communal building which is always untidy: there's almost always underwear and dirty wine glasses strewn everywhere and her bed's always full of dog hair. She's always put this down to being busy but it isn't that, is it? She can see now that when you have once had other people to look after, you might make more of an effort to make a home more welcoming. Frances's flat reflects a life that is largely made up of box-set nights in bed with Dog, or the flurry to get ready for a last-minute internet date. And in a similar way, her mother's house reflects not just her caustic disregard for housework, but something darker than that. As Frances accepts tea in a cat-themed cup and saucer from Jean, she wonders what it is. Grief? Is the house quite simply cold with sorrow, is it the absence of Frances's father that has over the years become a presence like some sort of chaotic and malevolent spirit?

She realises that Jean is offering her a digestive biscuit, and accepts one, mechanically.

'How is she?' enquires Jean carefully.

Frances dips the edge of her biscuit into her tea. 'I don't know. I think she took the dogs out early this morning, because they were covered in mud when I got up, but she's gone back to bed now, to listen to the radio.' When Jean raises her eyebrows, Frances adds, 'It's all right, she couldn't have used the car. It's at the garage for a service.'

'So how did she get to London, to see you?'

'In a taxi.'

Lord, says Jean, that must have cost a pretty penny, and Frances winces, thinking of the cash withdrawal she'd had to make on her credit card to pay for the return journey. Afterwards, she had wondered whether it might be possible to persuade Mr Singh of Singh's Cars in the village to please not take Mrs Pilgrim on any other long taxi journeys, but she supposes he is unlikely to concede to that, when a dotty old lady probably made him more in a day than he usually takes in several. But however brutal the thought of more taxi journeys is, it is nothing to the horror Frances feels when she contemplates her mother driving her own car, and she is opening her mouth to suggest to Jean that perhaps Jean might be able to take her mother to the shops in the future, when Jean puts down her teacup with the manner of someone who is about to broach a difficult subject, and says, 'Frances, dear. Has your mother mentioned your father to you at all since she, well . . .'

It is a difficult thing to pin down, isn't it? Since she what? Her mother has been going quietly peculiar for several years, seeing far fewer people, becoming more and more waspish and hostile to those she does see, taking less and less care of herself or the house. Then of course, more recently, there've been the mugs in the fridge and the flimsy grasp of names. There have been the endless, forgotten phone calls. But something more concrete and sinister than this gentle erosion of details has happened recently. She thinks again of her mother's slack jaw and outstretched, papery hands in the road last Friday, and then of the stringy hem of her bedtime leggings, peeking out from beneath her raincoat in the Green Café yesterday.

She looks across at Jean, and nods. 'She's been talking about him a lot. Only . . .'

Frances is still in the process of working out how to tell someone as sane and rational as Jean that one of the things that her mother's *something* seems to have wiped out is the very fact of her father's death, when Jean surprises her by saying, 'Has she spoken to you about what happened to Martin?'

It isn't the directness of the question that takes Frances aback so much as the fact that Jean has used her father's Christian name. There has been an almost thespian tradition in and around their home for years that her father is never mentioned by name, he's become almost the human equivalent of *Macbeth*. To other people he is the Absent Husband; the most intimate epithet he's ever received in Frances's hearing is a sniffy *your father*, emphasis firmly on the pronoun as if this quirk of chance and biology is somehow, nonetheless, Frances's fault. She is just opening her mouth to explain to Jean that the *something* that has happened to her mother recently is more like a circuit having fused, or a bulb exploded somewhere, taking out a great chunk of the past in a sizzle of sparks, when Jean says, 'I only ask, you see, because I think there comes a point in all families when enough is enough.'

She looks across the table at Frances then, and for a moment she is not a woman of eighty who smells quite distinctly of cats. She is a kind, plump woman of forty-six,

161

in a comfortable pink cardie, who is putting a blanket around five-year-old Frances's shoulders, and encouraging her long-suffering old Lab Mack to climb up on to the sofa so he can give a small girl, who is only now beginning to comprehend the extent of her loss, a cuddle.

Grown-up Frances has a sense then, like headlights approaching around a distant bend, that Jean is going to tell her something, and grown-up Frances also has a curdled and visceral sense that she does not want to hear it. She licks her lips and takes a breath to ask Jean if she could perhaps have some more tea, please, but nothing will come out.

Jean reaches out a hand to her then and says gently, 'What is it that you believe happened to your father, Frances?'

When she was fifteen, Frances had done a presentation to her GCSE English set on the disappearance of her father. She had been going through a particularly precocious phase at the time, and had privately entitled it 'The Pater Noster Project', mostly because Something-in-Latin seemed cleverer and more mysterious than something in plain English, but also because, on some level, she liked the idea that the name of the presentation was also the name of a prayer. Although well received by her peers, afterwards Frances's English teacher had summoned Frances's mother in for a 'little chat', and it was after that that Frances had noticed one or two of her teachers regarding her as one might a very small child venturing alone into the surf.

The problem, she supposed later, had been the lack of concrete and documented facts about her father's death which might have given her presentation a more respectable patina of authenticity and prevented any of her teachers from becoming so suspicious. Had she been able to access the internet, she might have been able to look for news reports, or naval archives. She might have been able to track down other officers who were on board HMS *Wanderer* at the same time as her father.

But it had been 1993. No one in Dryland had even heard of the internet. And because her father had been lost at sea there was not even a grave to visit, and as for Frances's mother – well. Her attitude to her husband's demise seemed to teenage Frances always to have been more tight-lipped than tragic.

Only once, when she was thirteen, had she attempted a proper conversation about her father's death. She had prepared herself for it as she would for an exam, practising her question as one might practise for dancing a pas de deux on a rough and muddy hillside. Given her mother's extreme reluctance ever to mention her father at all, she had sensed that the timing and inflection and carefulness of her question would be vital, as would be the circumstances in which she chose to ask it, so in the end had decided to surprise her mother at the sink after supper one evening when she was about to do the washing-up. At the time, Frances thought she'd been rather sly about this. The mountain of crockery, she knew, would exert a morose hold over her mother until the draining board was drearily cleared and the sink perfunctorily scrubbed, at which point her mother would retire to bed with the dogs and listen to a re-run of *Woman's Hour* with Jenni Murray.

So she had sat down at the kitchen table and pretended to do her history for a few minutes, and had then said, 'Mummy,' in a careful voice that must have instantly put her mother on the alert, because she had turned around, with narrowed eyes.

In the end, Frances had only got as far as, 'Do we know for sure that Daddy is—' before her mother had obviously seen her coming. Her father was *gone*, she said crossly, as if it were a tedious inconvenience like a power cut, and it was a terrible shame, of course, but 'God moves in mysterious ways.' She always used the words 'gone' or 'passed', as a polite euphemism, dead seeming, somehow, discourteously definite. Her tone had struck Frances even then as more sour than tragic, as if God's divine plans were far less to do with cosmic mystery than a really quite careless lack of regard for others. But when Frances asked her mother exactly how her father had come to die, her mother had tightened her lips and reached out to the windowsill for the Fairy Liquid. She didn't know the details, she said. There'd been a storm of sorts. Perhaps he had gone up on to the deck to sort something out. At any rate, he was gone, and his body had not been found, so perhaps Frances should finish her homework and make them both a nice cup of tea.

And Frances, who knew by then that a cup of tea was code for the end of a conversation, had been left to imagine a God with white pantomime wings who had evidently just sidled up to her father on the deck of HMS *Wanderer* and, grabbing him in His teeth like an eagle, had flapped cheerfully skywards before dropping him unceremoniously into the sea.

If she'd had relatives, she supposed she might have come closer to the truth of it all. But because there were no relatives left, the Extended Personal Contribution had become a useful outlet for all her unanswered questions: in possession of no facts at all, Frances had decided to simply buck up and use her initiative.

It was only years later, coming across her speech in a dog-eared coursework wallet at her mother's house, that she had supposed ruefully that the florid prose that she'd tried to pass off as an extract from a newspaper article about her father's disappearance had in fact been far closer to that of a Mills & Boon novel than a piece of journalism; and as for the heartfelt letter of commiseration from the captain of HMS *Wanderer* to her mother, outlining their attempts to locate and rescue her father at sea, well! *That* had owed far more to her obsession with *Mutiny on the Bounty* and *The Poseidon Adventure* than to any knowledge whatsoever of modern naval protocols.

Nonetheless, at the time, she had almost believed her own rhetoric, and so had most of her classmates. The boys in the set had been particularly fascinated by this story, and, while the young teacher sitting at the back and listening to Frances's lurid speech had looked more and more glum, they had asked a lot of questions. What did the navy believe had happened to Commander Pilgrim? How could

165

a naval officer simply disappear from a ship for hours without anyone noticing?

'Do you think he's dead?' one boy had asked her. 'I mean, if they never actually found a body?'

And the young teacher had raised her anxious face and said, 'I think maybe that's enough questions for now.'

But Frances had shaken her head. It was a good question, she said. Her mother at least had told her that *Wanderer* had been on a training mission before her father went missing, somewhere off the coast of Madagascar. Frances guessed that the waters were warm, that her father might have been able to survive for twenty-four hours. He had been a strong swimmer, although sharks were a distinct possibility.

'So, you think he's alive?' the boy had persisted.

And that was when she had run out of road, wasn't it? When she realised that, for all her fabrications about the ship's position, about radar and helicopters and rescue attempts, it all still came down to her father having fallen into the sea and drowned, his lungs filled with sea water and probably oil from HMS *Wanderer*'s massive engines, churning just beneath the surface. Frances had stood there with her mouth open, her eyes filling up with tears. On the wall opposite her was a poster advertising a recent production of *The Tempest*. On the stormy waters depicted, an elegant golden script informed her that, *full fathom five thy father lies . . . Those are pearls that were his eyes.*

Was it possible her father was alive? the boy had repeated, and she had opened her mouth and closed it again, like a goldfish.

Because the truth in her heart had suddenly seemed unsayable at the front of that tatty grey classroom, beneath posters showing the correct use of parentheses, or the definition of a subordinate clause. It seemed impossible, then, on the frayed green carpet beneath the peeling wall displays, to say that she believed that if her father were dead, she would somehow feel it, in her bones, like a cancer. That the black hole of his absence from the world itself would swallow her whole rather than simply nagging on the periphery like any piece of missing information in a sequence. That some part of her would simply have stopped by now, like a clock.

'And she's never talked about him since?' says Jean.

Frances shakes her head. Then, taking a deep breath she says, 'What did you mean before, Jean? When you said enough was enough?'

The cat clock's ticking seems to slow then, each individual tick punctuated by a roaring pause, as if the second hand itself is trying hard to hear what Jean will say.

And Jean has to look away for a moment before she starts to speak. Has to put down her own cup of tea before she can look back at Frances and draw a shaky breath. Has to squeeze her hand tightly as she tells her that her mother is evidently not very well. Clearly she needs to be assessed for vascular dementia, or Alzheimer's, and the sooner the better, for all their sakes. But what Jean believes that Frances should know – and Lord knows she's agonised about this over the years, Frances, she's prayed about it, she's asked the

Good Lord for forgiveness every single day – is that her mother has not forgotten that Frances's father is dead.

And she turns around then, half rising from her chair, to pull at a drawer just below the one where her cutlery lives. Frances watches her, wondering in a wild and hilarious moment whether Jean is about to roll open the drawer and produce her father, still in his naval uniform, coffined within.

But what Jean produces is a large and faded envelope. It's orange in colour, and looks as though it must have originated, once upon a time, from Brian's office at the Water Board. As Jean places it, carefully, on the laminated tablecloth, Frances can see that it is the sort of A4-sized envelope that is endlessly recycled in offices. There are rows of black lines on it, within which people's names have been written and then crossed out as the envelope is passed on to someone else. *Sue in HR. Finance Division. Mike in Billing.* Jean, however, has put a diagonal line in Biro through all these names and all that is written in the last, blank column is one word, small but clear.

Martin.

Frances looks at the envelope and then back at Jean.

Jean takes a breath, and then tells her, again, that Frances's mother has not forgotten that Martin is dead. What she seems to have forgotten is the more complicated fact that, thirty-four years ago, she had simply decided to let everyone believe that he was.

XVII

On Thursday afternoon, the office door is flung open as if someone has kicked it.

'Christ, Year 7,' says Rhidian, throwing his exercise books down on the table. 'You try and set them a prep, and they ask so many questions it's the end of the lesson before they've written it down. I'm moderately surprised they don't ask me to wipe their bums for them.' He cocks his head, lifting a limp hand to his cheek. '*Mr Sayer, can it be more than a side of our books? Can I write in Biro or does it have to be fountain pen? Can I word-process it and stick it in afterwards?*' He flings himself into his chair, spinning around so that he is facing Jackson's screen. 'I said you can write it on your *face*, Hatty Hengist-Jones, I don't give a toss.' He looks like he's about to say something else when the telephone rings. Snatching it up and saying, 'English,' he pulls a chair out from beneath the desk next to Jackson and starts putting his feet up on it.

Jackson looks at his watch and is supposing he ought to go and prepare something to teach Year 11, when Rhidian says, 'Oh, for God's sake,' and 'No, she bloody well hasn't,' and 'Did someone – oh, they did, good. Well, say thank you to him, and we'll owe him one for next time. Yes, yes. Good.' And then the sound of the phone being crashed back into the receiver.

Jackson turns round. 'Parent?'

'No, not a parent,' says Rhidian crossly. 'Pilgrim. She's not turned up to period five. Apparently Mercedes Solomon went and complained at the school office because this is the *second* time this has happened this term.'

Jackson raises an eyebrow. 'She isn't back? Hasn't she called in?' It makes him feel substantially better to realise that Frances is just as feckless and irresponsible as he's told her she is.

'No, Sherlock, she bloody hasn't, otherwise I'd have organised cover, wouldn't I? She promised she'd be back, and now I'll get an arsey message from Solomon *père*, saying this isn't what twenty grand a year is supposed to buy his little princess, and if he'd only sent her to Westminster she'd be applying for Oxbridge and blah, blah, buggery-*blah*—'

'D'you want me to call her?' Jackson asks. 'Ask her where she is?' That, after all, will break the silence in a benign enough way and will also give him the continued moral high ground.

'Yes, yes,' says Rhidian. '*Ask and thou shalt receive.* You can tell her she's got a right bollocking coming when she gets back, this happens far too bloody often.'

*

170

Frances's phone goes straight to voicemail, which irks him. At three o'clock, with twenty minutes before last lesson, Jen disappears to make booklets in the reprographics room, and on a strange impulse Jackson logs on to his computer and sets off through cyberspace, feeling like someone tipped out of a boat into a cold and unfamiliar sea.

He loathes social media. 'Face*fuck*,' he's always called it, tossing Katy's, later Frances's tablets and phones aside when he saw the familiar blue and white logo on their screens. But now here he is, logging on with all the trepidation of a man not knowing if he is about to tread on a landmine or dig for gold. They are all lurking down here, all his lost women, rising like pike through layers of memory.

Resisting the fleeting temptation to type in other names, Jackson simply types hers, and there she is, straight away, *Frances Pilgrim, University of Oxford, London.* He has dubbed himself Sigmund F, for a laugh, and posted a photo of Freud where his own was meant to go.

He clicks on her, and there she is, but because he's not her friend, she's just a ghostly outline to him, more absence than presence. Jackson can't help feeling disappointed, as if he's travelled miles to visit someone who turns out not to be at home. The page says she has 283 friends, but he can't see anything else about her.

If you know Frances, send her a message!

Who on earth has 283 friends, anyway? Jackson isn't sure his real friends would number the backwards shift of that decimal point. He peers at the screen, fumbling on his head for his glasses. Christ, what a gallery of shrunken heads! Many of her friends he only recognises through their names, their photos far too photoshopped to be real: other Hilltop teachers, carefully tanned and carefree, a distant relative or two, if the surnames are anything to go by. Then, others he doesn't know: ferret-faced girls on horses, an assortment of unknown men. He feels deflated. These are the people for whom she's turned him down, these morons with their identikit grins and sometimes-sinister chins? He pays special attention to the men, trying to remember individual names she'd mentioned. But Frances usually only referred to them with satirical avatars. *The Viking. The Banker. The Old Floppy Barrister.* More recently, of course, *The Love Rat.* Grouped together, they sounded like the names of public houses in the Square Mile, or the beginning of a school-yard tune, the sort little girls chanted as they clapped hands and skipped in formation.

The door bangs behind him and a shadow falls across his desk.

'My God, Jackson,' says Rhidian. 'Are you on Facebook?'

'No,' says Jackson, slamming his laptop lid down.

'Touchy,' says Rhidian. 'As long as it's, you know, legal.' It is an old joke, but Jackson suddenly finds it irritating.

'You shouldn't be so nosy,' he snaps.

'Oh, my dear,' Rhidian sighs, turning back to the chaos of his desk. 'You're mistaking me for an actress who *gives* a fuck.' A casual pause. 'Did you get hold of Pilgrim?'

Somewhere in the distance a bell starts to ring, like an emergency. *If you know Frances, send her a message!*

'No,' Jackson says, reaching for his Year 11 poetry anthology.

'Who's Dennis Scott?' demands Hector Duff, ten minutes later, peering at his anthology.

'Dennis. *Dennis . . .*'

They are, again, beside themselves. It never fails to amaze Jackson how easy it is to amuse his Year 11 set. The word *log* had held up progress for almost a week once; *wood* had been predictably worse, and the Ted Hughes poem 'Pike' had taken them almost six lessons because Danny McLellan kept falling off his chair as soon as they got to the bit about it being three inches long and perfect.

'We can't help it, sir,' Jack Blood tells him. 'We're tards.'

'Turds?' says Jackson, deliberately mishearing.

And Danny McLellan moans, 'Oh, sir, please, don't, I'll hurt myself.'

'Tards,' it turned out, was how the bottom sets tended to refer to themselves. It was understandable, Jackson supposed, in an academic school, to make the joke oneself before anyone else got round to it but, as he sometimes tells them when they are gloomy, bottom sets are usually much cleverer than they give themselves credit for.

'You know they call you C-Dog?' Frances said once.

'No, they don't.'

'Not to your face. But among themselves they do. *Who've you got? C-Dog. Oh, cool.*'

Jackson knew it was absurd to feel pleased, but couldn't help it. Now, as he writes the poem's title, 'Marrysong', on the whiteboard, he points at it and says, 'Significance?'

'Sir, what does that say?'

'Sir, your writing's awful!'

'Does that say *Barry*?'

'Oh God,' says Jackson. 'Can we just *try*?'

'But what does it actually say . . . ? Danny McLellan, short-sighted as well as dyspraxic, is squinting at the board from the back row.

'Why don't you move to the front so you can see, dickhead?' suggests Jack Blood, who is at least, Jackson notes, writing down the title with some purpose.

'Sir,' says Danny. 'He called me a dickhead.'

'Mmm,' says Jackson. 'Move to the front, Danny.'

'Sir, they *kick* me.'

'Who kicks you?'

'I do,' say Jack Blood and Hector Duff in unison.

'No one will hurt you,' says Jackson wearily. 'Until instructed, anyway. Come on, Danny. Move or copy from someone, it's already half past three.'

Danny peers around him, myopic as a mole until Jack Blood mutters, 'It's "*Marry*song". The title.'

'Oh, I thought it said "*Barry*song".'

In the row in front of him Hector Duff, groaning, bangs his head three times on the desk.

In the end, in order to give him something to do, Jackson makes Danny read the poem aloud. He makes it as far as the sixth line before letting out a snort of laughter.

'A new personal best,' murmurs Jack Blood.

'What's the problem, Danny?' Jackson, who has been tracing the poem with his pen as it's read, looks up. His nib touched the page, tracing an involuntary red line where they have stopped.

'He – he – he,' but Danny can't get the next word out, flattened beneath his own gale of mirth.

'*Charted*,' finishes Jack Blood for him. 'Oh that's it, sir. He wants to say *farted*.'

Danny howls.

'Can we hurt him now, sir?' asks Hector Duff.

Jackson puts his head in his hands. But at the end of the lesson, as he closes the anthology, his eyes are drawn back to the line on the page where Danny first stopped.

He charted. She made wilderness again.
Roads disappeared. The map was never true.

He snaps the book shut. Thank God, it's four o'clock. He's had enough of today, enough of Rhidian and Frances and Facebook and poetry. He wants to go home.

XVIII

XVIII

After she's said goodbye to her mother, telling her she has to go back to London to teach this afternoon but that she'll be back in the morning, Frances collects her overnight bag from her bedroom and Dog from the sitting room sofa, and makes her way out through the kitchen and towards the drive, where her car is parked.

As she unlocks the driver-side door, she has the strange tingling feeling of someone who has slept on a limb and can only dimly begin to feel the blood returning to it. As she had stumbled back down the stony path to her mother's house an hour earlier, she had found herself wondering if Jean was perhaps also bonkers – after all, she was even older than Frances's mother; is she losing her marbles too? Or is this extraordinary confession just part of some cosmic misunderstanding? Did Frances's mother once tell Jean that Frances's father was alive in some deluded moment of wish-fulfilment? Has Jean somehow faked the letters herself? Frances had even found herself chanting the possibility out loud to herself like a mantra, hearing her feet beating it out in a tantivy on the uneven surface, as though she's scanning a line of verse on the whiteboard at school. *They must both be ill.* (Look, iambus, anapaest!) *They're both confused.* (Two iambuses there, kids!)

But at the bottom of the path she had slipped and, turning her ankle, almost burst into tears. Because what she could not erase from her mind with any glib little rhythms was her mother's voice, high and wavering on the other end of the telephone. *He's gone. He's left me. Please, Far, bring him home, do.*

And, far worse, *Mum, do you know where my birth certificate has got to?*

Scarborough, I expect.

At home, just before she left, Frances had found her mother sitting up in bed, reading *Country Life* and looking quite composed. She had stood in the doorway for a moment, watching her before her mother noticed she was there.

They have never given each other an easy time, have they? As a child, Frances had simply been sad and confused, but as a teenager her confusion had hardened into rage against a woman who would permit nothing of a man who, after all, had still been Frances's bloody *father* to persist. In her darker moments, it had seemed to Frances that the heartless and beatific God with the white pantomime wings who had deprived her of her father in the first place had absolutely nothing on the woman who wouldn't even permit her daughter to talk about him, wouldn't even allow her a single sodding *photograph*! 'It was for your own good!' her mother had cried every time they argued. 'It wouldn't have

helped; you've got to move on! You can't be sentimental!'
No more tears, now. They won't bring him back!

No, it is only really as her mother has grown older, retired, retreated into her weather-beaten world of chickens and sheep and dogs that Frances has found herself feeling occasionally more tender towards her. It is only as, with each successive relationship failure of her own, she has begun to contemplate the spectre of her own lonely old age that she has remembered that look on her mother's face when she told Frances her father was gone: that almost preternatural strength and power. Her mother may be bloody-minded now, may be tough as old boots and difficult as hell, but what she has always had in spades is courage and resourcefulness. After her father's – well, whatever it was – her mother had gone to university in Canterbury, got herself a degree and then trained as a nurse, a job she'd done until she retired, bringing in about enough money to keep the house going, but not so much that Frances hadn't eventually succumbed to Jean's offer of financial help at university.

Now, as she watches her turning the pages of her magazine, her knees drawn up to her chest, one of the dogs stirring at her feet on the filthy duvet cover, Frances remembers the luminous young woman in the photograph album with her glossy hair, turning in the restaurant doorway to smile into the dazzling flash of the camera, her dark eyes and high heels, her long coltish legs and narrow shoulders beneath the shiny furs. Then she remembers the same woman, in a checked shirt and jeans, hair cut short and

179

severe, standing behind a beaming Frances on her tricycle and turning rigidly towards Frances's father. *Smile, Mary! That's it!* Her lips drawn back in what might just have been a smile but which looked to Frances much more like a snarl. *Dryland, October 1981.* The last photograph in the album, the rest of the pages bone-white, sterile, unused.

What had really happened between her mother and her father, Frances wondered, watching her mother turning the pages of her magazine, to transform that once sweet and expectant smile into the vixenish snarl of the photograph? And could whatever 'it' had been really have persuaded her mother to tell her daughter such a terrible, outrageous lie?

Once in the car, her first impulse is to do as she'd said she would and go straight back to London: not just to lessons but to noise and traffic, shops and people, to her untidy flat, to Silv and Jackson and Rhidian and Jen-Jen. To London, only fifty miles away, where after school she can walk on the Heath and phone Jackson and then lie in the bath and work out what the hell she is meant to do next. London, where there are people who are (mostly) in possession of their wits and who will be able to help her use the internet to disprove Jean's extraordinary thesis that her father is alive and well and living somewhere near Scarborough.

'London,' she says out loud to Dog, as she opens the passenger door of the car for him to jump in. But Dog is occupying himself in turning around several times on the seat, apparently to make sure it is as wet and muddy as possible before he collapses into dog-travel position for what, habit tells him, is probably the long journey home.

Frances is turning the key in the ignition when the orange fuel light flashes on the dashboard, and she realises she is out of fuel: *9 miles to empty*, announces the panel on the dashboard. *Metaphor alert*, says Jackson's voice drily, in her mind, and Frances grips the steering wheel until her knuckles go a drowned blue, like bone, and waits for the wave of nausea that assails her to pass. Saliva floods the inside of her jaw, and she swallows carefully, closing her eyes for a moment and breathing deeply. But the moment of stillness and quiet only allows the questions she'd asked Jean in the kitchen an hour or so before to ring out again, like church bells, in her head.

Because if her father had not, in fact, perished in the Pacific in 1981, if it were indeed her father who was the author of everything contained in the orange envelope and who had really sent her the money for university, then what on earth could have prompted her mother to have let Frances persist in such a grotesque enchantment? A story that she had seen disintegrate her five-year-old child into a sodden mess of phlegm and tears and bewilderment, a story in which they have all three of them, Frances and her mother and Jean, had to persist for thirty-four years?

Jean had looked at her for a long time before she answered that question. The cat clock had ticked loud in the kitchen then, slow, yes, but by then irrevocable.

'She was angry,' she said at last. 'He'd met someone else, you see. He couldn't call it off, he said. He had to go.'

Frances had blinked. That her father had had to go and be with someone who wasn't her mother she could have accepted: the photograph album had already begun to tell that story, after all. *Martin, can you just lean towards Mary a little more? Lovely!* But that her father, who had read her a bedtime story every night he was at home, who had tolerated her repeated demands for *Rapunzel, Rapunzel, please, Daddy!* and who shown her all the constellations in the sky, would have left *Frances*, Far, his very own Little, for someone who wasn't even his flesh and blood? No. It was inconceivable.

Frances was certain in her very bones, in that moment that this was wrong, certain in the same way that she had been on that frayed classroom carpet when the boys had asked her if she thought her father might, just might, be alive. She'd felt then that if he were really gone, she would feel it in her very bones like a cancer, and she felt the same way sitting at Jean's table that afternoon, listening to Jean tell her that her father had just left her behind like forgotten luggage at the airport.

See that, Little? The dog star isn't the brightest star in the sky, but it often seems so because it's the closest to the earth.

'No,' she said. 'He wouldn't have left us. I mean' – she looked down – 'he wouldn't have left me, Jean. I know he wouldn't.'

So when you look up at Sirius, sweetheart, you can think of me and be sure that wherever I am, when I look up at it, I'll be thinking of you, too.

Tears had threatened in her throat, as though she were about to be sick. She had swallowed desperately.

No more tears, now. They won't bring him back.

But when she looked across the table, Jean had been shaking her head sadly again. 'Your dad left you, love. I'm sorry, but there it is. Men are – well . . .' She folded her hands in her lap. 'I'm sure I don't need to tell you, you're a grown woman. They're different to us.'

Outside, it had started to rain, a light summery drizzle.

She reached out and squeezed Frances's hand again. 'You must try to forgive them, you know. Both of them. For your own sake.'

And when Frances had shaken her head furiously, Jean had gone on hurriedly, 'She always said she thought it would be easier for you in the long run, that at five you'd be young enough to put it behind you. He'd already been away so much of your life, you see . . .'

There was a pause, and then she said quietly, 'I always knew it was wrong, Frances. But once she'd told you, it wasn't my place to meddle. If I'd tried to interfere, she'd most likely have cut me off, too.'

Now, sitting in her car, Frances can feel her earlier tears subsiding and, in their place, a rage beginning to rise, sour as sick in her mouth. Is it the result of never having been allowed to cry, she wonders, this awful temper of hers? It's been the reason so many of her boyfriends have turned tail and fled, after all, isn't it? *I can't handle this, you know. You need to talk to someone!*

But could it be possible that her father was just another average and shabby love-rat, led blindly by the groin like Lucas and the countless other men she's known in her life?

And yet even Lucas went back to his wife when he was caught, Frances thinks dully. What is it about her that means she is always falling short; what makes her so completely, so uniquely leavable?

'It's not true,' says Frances out loud now, staring at the orange petrol light, at the panel that still says *9 miles to empty*. 'He would never have just left me.' But her voice sounds tinny and uncertain, as though broadcast through small and poor-quality speakers. Dog raises a weary head and gazes at her, and after a minute Frances shifts in her seat and with her right hand pulls out the sheet of yellow paper upon which Jean had scribbled down 'a few details, dear. Just in case you should, well . . .'

The sheet came from a neat pad on the table by Jean's telephone, and across the top of her father's address and telephone number, the word *Memorandum* is written in a swirly script, with a bunch of violets next to it.

Jean's writing is round and careful. Hairdresser's writing, Frances thinks cruelly. *Martin Pilgrim, 162 Brighouse Lane, Devil's Bay, N. Yorks.* Even a postcode and a telephone number.

Full fathom five thy father lies. Of his bones are coral made.

Looking at the address, she has that watery-mouthed feeling again, that sense that somewhere a long way down, something that ought to be solid is shifting. Her bones feel strangely hollow. *Those are pearls that were his eyes.*

Frances picks up her phone again, taps on Google, starts to type in the words Martin and Pilgrim and Scarborough. But her fingers feel, all of a sudden, like giant rubber sausages and in her shaky state she's pressing all the wrong letters so that what emerges on the keyboard is Maerty Pilhrim. A distant figure, mistily Welsh or perhaps Arabic and bearing no possible resemblance to the man who was once her father.

Frances looks at Jean's notepaper and then at her phone screen, at the Martin Pilgrim who lives and the Maerty Pilhrim who, if he exists at all, is unrecognisable, a stranger, neither kith nor kin. She looks, again, at the digital panel on her dashboard which, yes, still reads *9 miles to empty*. A wasp is buzzing at the corner of her windscreen, caught between the dashboard and the glass. She watches it try to rise into what it must think is the air, then bash, frustrated, into the glass.

Something, then, about the hot September air and that addled, frantic wasp, which cannot see its way out of its trap, stirs something. It is as if its thread-like legs are pulling on a memory, something to do with not being able to see – Frances closes her eyes and leans back against the headrest. Yes. There it is, emerging like a photograph from fluid.

It had been years ago. She was on a train, Clapham Junction to Waterloo, the packed carriage smelling of heat and salt and the insides of tins; spilled cider and beer drawing wasps through a high window; a child grizzling somewhere further down the carriage and a feral feel as the train swayed and slowed, pressing passengers against each other so that a low *whoooop* of anticipation rose among them, mostly Brentford fans heading for Griffin Park, and the opening match of the season.

Frances was jammed between two men. One was younger than her, head thrusting out in time to the beat from his head-phones. He was sweating profusely. As the train crested the corner into the station, she was thrown against him and he looked down at her, expressionless. She had looked around quickly for a bar or strap to hang on to.

It was then that she'd seen the man on her right, ramrod straight and very still against the wall of the carriage. Impossible to age, his white hair foiled against the brown crevasses of his face, and his milky eyes looking with dignity into nothingness. The motion of the train rocked her the other way as it came to a halt, and she realised she'd stepped on his foot.

'God, I'm so sorry.'

A cheer went up from the Brentford fans as the doors groaned open, and they began to flood on to the platform. The eyes continued to gaze over her shoulder, but a papery hand found her shoulder in the growing space around them.

'No problem, young lady.' A slow, measured inflection, scanned like verse; a voice like the small sneeze of a cat. She had given him her hand, and amid the fans still cours-ing from the carriage, they'd stepped down on to the

186

platform together. His right hand had crossed in front of his torso to take her left hand, his other hand resting on her right arm. They made their way slowly through the barriers then stood for a moment under the departures board, waiting for the jostling crowds behind them to move on. There was music coming from a lingerie boutique, there was spilled coffee and chewing gum on the floor but looking up, she'd seen the afternoon sun turning the skylight roof of the station a dusky gold, and had a mad vision suddenly, in the midst of that faux-marble floor, of the nave of a church, herself in white on a proudly proffered arm. She'd thought, defiantly, *Enough of this, Pilgrim*, and, *Not here, for God's sake*, but it was too late; in that moment the thought of her own father, now only a blurred gold-and-navy shape in her memory, had hit her like a murder blow. She'd taken a breath, been quite grateful the old man was blind. But she'd ended up walking him out of the station anyway, and all the way up the Cut, until he paused outside a blue door and said, loosening his arm gently from hers, 'Here we are now.'

'Really?'

He smiled, nodded. 'You've been most kind, most kind.'

Reluctantly, she'd let him go, empty hands falling to her sides. But as she turned to go, she looked back and said, 'How did you know that we'd got here?'

One corner of his mouth lifted, one eyebrow raised. He'd done this journey every day for forty years, he said, twenty of them with no sight. Knew the pavement like a schoolboy knew his . . . He chuckled, apologised, then tapped the side of his head with his hand. It was all in there, his map and compass, he said.

But how did he know? she persisted. Did he count the steps, so many this way then turn, so many that way then across?

His sightless eyes were laughing at her gently. Did she hear the trains, up there on the bridge? Could she smell the fish frying in that restaurant kitchen over there? Yes? And what about here, could she feel through her shoes the way the pavement shifted and sloped just here, then there?

'There are many ways to see,' he said, turning towards the blue door. Side-on his milky eye was just brow and lashes, his profile curved and proud like the prow of a ship. 'But sometimes you just have to feel your way.'

As he turned his key in the blue door she opened her mouth to say something else, but then he was through it, right hand raised in a brief farewell, and the door was coming towards her again and clicking shut before she could even ask him his name.

And it's in that moment that she can see that it's really quite simple. If she wants to know exactly why her father left her, and worse, why he never came back for her, she will simply have to go there and ask him. Will have to make him look her in the eye, will have to listen carefully not only to the words but to his tone of voice to know exactly who is right: the five-year-old Frances who sat with her father on the window seat looking out at the dog star, or the two women who had deemed her father so wicked as to be, by and large, better off dead. *Sometimes you just have to feel your way.*

So she taps on Google maps and enters the postcode. Then she props up her phone on the dashboard, between the fuel gauge and the speedometer, and watches as the route lights up between the simmering dot that is here, and the bright red pin that is Martin Pilgrim, at 162 Brighouse Lane, Devil's Bay. The fastest route is illuminated in dark blue, like a river seen from above, unravelling all the way to the sea.

XIX

On Thursday evening, Jackson is in the process of trying to work out how to get the three paper bags of food from Carlo's Deli down the road through his front gate without first putting them on the pavement, when Silv turns up.

The recent rainstorm has left the pavements slick and sticky, and he's convinced that if he puts the bags down they will disintegrate, and the one thing that's keeping him sane this afternoon is the thought of cooking and listening to Maria Callas. He's trying to balance one bag on his knee and keep one under each of his arms, while using his elbow to flick up the latch on the gate, when a pale hand pushes itself up from under his arm, like the lady in the lake, and he hears an ironic and lightly accented voice saying, 'Allow me, Dr Crecy.'

Craning round as much as he is able without dropping the bags, he can see the tops of some Doc Martens boots on the pavement, and, above, the slightly ragged hem of a long tweed coat. Between the boot and the hem is a short expanse of slim calf in fishnet tights, and he can smell perfume and wet hair and cigarette smoke. When the hand takes one of the paper bags off him, Jackson is able to straighten up and turn round properly.

'Silv,' he says in surprise. 'What are you doing here?'

Silv had been one of the first confessions Frances had ever made to Jackson when they became friends.

My lunatic friend, she had called her, and when Jackson had asked her good-loon or bad-loon Frances had smiled and said honestly? Sometimes she wasn't sure.

She'd known Silv at university, she said, she'd been at her college, busking through doing a degree in French and German which was a bit of a laugh, really, given Silv was half one and half the other. A half-caste, she'd always called herself, in every bloody sense! Bilingual, possibly bipolar, definitely bisexual. She'd come to the UK because she wanted to improve her English; she'd done a bit of modelling but was more interested in photography.

They'd met at a freshers' party held by the third years. Later, Silv said the Welcome Committee had bribed her with wine and grass so she'd let them use her rooms. 'I'm not into committees,' she'd told Frances from her window seat, where she had been reclining in ripped black tights and red velvet hot pants when Frances and some of the other first years arrived. 'But you're here now, so make yourself at home.'

For the whole evening, Frances had been aware of Silv's eyes following her, huge yellow eyes like lamps in fog, set off by her vivid and unbrushed red hair. Frances had been nineteen, straight out of Kent with no experience of anything. And there had been Silv, as glamorous and bedraggled as a supermodel left out in the rain. Yes, Silv, with her husky accented voice and her clove cigarettes, her white porcelain face and that beguiling smell, a twilight reek of earth and secrets. Frances had drunk so much red wine that night that her head had spun. And maybe at first because Silv's eyes were the colour of the city, an ancient yellowish-gold, or because of her husky accented voice, which promised not only London but somehow Berlin and Paris and Vienna too, Frances was caught, like a fish on a great gleaming hook. She'd been a virgin when the Welcome Committee flung open their doors to her that night, a tall and ungainly virgin with long unruly hair and make-up quite hurriedly applied.

But oh, how easily she had taken to sex that night, later, after the other freshers had gone, casting raised eyebrows over their shoulders as they sidled towards the door, bound for the college bar or for Fifth Avenue, the nightclub in town that everyone always referred to as Filth.

It was like discovering a language in which you were already quite fluent. And that night, in Silv's narrow bed, which reeked of cigarettes and scent and other people's bodies, Frances had found for the first time how easily she could make the white body writhe, the knees draw up as if for a birth, the neck fling up and back like a heron swallowing fish. It was as if she had always known how to navigate the contours of another body, knowing the puckered outcrops and hidden earths. She had known how to walk straight to the edge of the cliff, and with abandon step out, into the mist. Hearing Silv's breath quicken to a rasp and then a moan and then to nothing more than a series of deep animal grunts quite incongruous with her fragile frame had caused Frances, quite involuntarily, to grind herself against the other girl's knee, bucking and gasping until she could feel sweat seeping down between her buttocks and thighs.

At the time, the story had only heightened Jackson's excitable sense of Frances as being not only straight out of St Trinian's but *Trouble at Willow Gables*, too. Had they spanked each other with gilt-edged hairbrushes, he had enquired, and Frances had grinned, holding out her glass for more wine. They had not, she said, although she suspected Silv would have been quite up for that.

'So, what went wrong?' Jackson had wanted to know. Why had she not become a card-carrying friend of Dorothy, a woman who wore sensible shoes?

'Jesus,' Frances had said. 'You'd only need to meet Silv once to see she's not exactly the Birkenstock type.' She'd taken a swallow of wine, looked away for a moment and then looked him straight in the eye as she told him that, quite simply, she'd discovered boys. It had been a look at the time that had made Jackson want to lunge at her, jump her, rip off her clothes: a look at once comic and sly and secretive, a look that seemed to say, if only for a moment, *try me*.

'You discovered boys?' he said scornfully. 'What, scruffy, scrofulous, nineteen-year-old boys? And they were better than what you just described?'

194

Frances had shrugged. Silv had been a slut, she said, she slept with everyone, it was practically a rite of passage if you were a fresher with an even halfway open mind. With even a halfway open something, Jackson had muttered, and Frances had said cheerfully, well, yes, that too.

Silv had found her fifteen years later on Facebook, and when Frances moved to London they'd ended up sharing the damp, rambling building on Swain's Square, just the two of them in adjoining studios on the ground floor below Hilary, a clean-eating Canadian who kept cairn terriers.

'And,' Jackson had demanded, intrigued and also, to his slight shame, turned on. '*And?*'

Frances had yawned, lying back on his cushions. 'Once or twice,' she said. 'When drunk.'

'Really? She's okay with that?'

And this had been where Frances had frowned a little. She wasn't sure, she said, if she was honest. There'd been a small drama a year or so back when she'd discovered that Silv had hacked the code on her iPhone and had been reading her and Richard-the-TV-actor's texts. Silv had apologised in the end, said she was only looking out for Frances, wasn't she, because she had such utterly bumfuck taste in men. But ever since then, Frances had wondered. And to Jackson, as he got to know both women better, it seemed perfectly obvious. Because although Jackson suspected that, at forty, Silv had not so much aged as hardened, like enamel, there was a softness in the way she looked at Frances that Jackson recognised. It was the way he thought he probably looked at her himself, at any rate when she wasn't looking.

Now, inside, in his kitchen, as Silv lights a cigarette and accepts the glass of wine he offers her, Jackson says, 'Are you all right?'

Silv inhales and regards him steadily. Then, instead of answering, she says, 'Sorry for just, you know, turning up, but I didn't have your number.'

Jackson pours himself some wine. 'Apart from a desperate desire for my company, what brings you off the Hill?' It's a running joke between him and Frances. Why, she said, would anyone who lived on the very top of the capital ever want to come down? 'Sex,' he's always said, 'or booze, in your case,' and she would stick her tongue out at him and scowl.

Jackson watches Silv flick her ash into the coffee cup that's still sitting on the table from breakfast. 'It's Pilgrim,' she says at last. 'Think she's finally done her nut.'

And she proceeds to tell him about the call she's just had from Frances, who appears to be on her way to Yorkshire for a conversation with her very-long-dead father.

XX

Despite her earlier moments of clarity and resolution, for the first part of the journey north Frances is not entirely convinced that she will actually go as far as Devil's Bay. Even as she stands at the filling station on the edge of Dryland, she can feel the petrol pump shaking in her hands; she is conscious even then, as she often is in the heat of a moment, of the innate recklessness of the plan, of its many cracks and fissures. There are small but vital practical concerns: she will only get there at seven o'clock in the evening, according to Google Maps, which means that even if she turns straight round and comes back she won't be home until almost midnight. The return journey will be almost entirely conducted in darkness, if she doesn't drive off the road with exhaustion first. And then there are larger matters: if she does pluck up the courage to confront the Martin Pilgrim who lives at 162 Brighouse Lane, then what? Will they have a nice cup of tea and a digestive biscuit? Will he explain everything to her calmly, in the manner of an ex-naval officer, then politely offer his sofa, or a bed, perhaps, in the spare room? Will he see her off in the morning with a hearty cheerio, will he thank her for visiting, tell her to send his best to her mother? The whole thing is so absurd it is almost screamingly funny, she says to Dog, as she gets back into the car. Isn't it? Screamingly, killingly funny!

But Dog rams his nose into his tail, and screws his eyes shut.

And although as she gets going the act of driving itself is cathartic, although the whirr of the car engine and the mutter of the radio give her the synthetic sensation that she is, at least, on her way to *doing something*, by the time Frances reaches Cambridge the sky has clouded over and a torrential downpour has set in. The tarmac in front of her, hot from the sultry weather, steams, and each arrow of water ahead of her hits the road so hard that a sizzle of steamy splashback seems to jump off the surface from every single drop that falls. By Nottingham, the drive, which she had anticipated being one long, fast, mostly motorway slog, has already taken two hours and suddenly seems a completely absurd undertaking. As the sky darkens and flickers through the frantic back-and-forth of her windscreen wipers, she sees an exit looming, and with relief hits the indicator. She can get a coffee here, then turn around and go home.

Because what on earth is the point of this, anyway? Frances realises as she gets out of the car, promising Dog a treat, that although she may be currently consumed with a shivery, pins-and-needly rage towards her father, it is undercut by something colder and murkier like oil in a freezing sea.

Her father cannot have loved her all that much, can he? Frances has an absurd vision of her father trading her in like a Cabbage Patch Kid card, for an image of another young woman, lissom and graceful as her mother had once been, in her fur-coat-wearing youth.

Because inside the gaudy orange envelope, that faded commercial palimpsest that Frances already hates with an intensity quite out of proportion to the item's size and shape, had been a packet of letters, insulting in its slimness. Inside were mostly cards, sent to arrive on her birthday or at Christmas. The cards were clumsily chosen, kittens or puppies or flowers, mostly, but the writing was the same black, spiky hand that had labelled the hidden photograph album.

Dear Frances, the cards always began. Breezy but formal, almost as if he were persuading himself that the distances of space and, later, time were quite ordinary. As if he were simply away at sea, as if the circumstances were, by and large, quite propitious. *I'm sending this to you on this special day because—*

One letter, which she had not been able to finish, had begun in this vein but then become oddly, opaquely halting, as if in an attempt to speak honestly and translate the circumstances into something a five-year-old would understand, and had lost its rhythm completely. *I've had to go away. I expect that's very hard to understand, and I'm afraid it is likely to be for a long time, but I hope not for ever. If you ever need me, Jean will know where I am.*

It had struck her, bleakly, as she put the letter to one side and reached for her empty teacup, that he had not tried very hard, nor for very long, but when she said so, Jean had shaken her head. It was he who had sent the money for university, she said. After thirteen years of silence he'd given up on the letters, resorted to something practical instead. Jean had pretended it was her all along, but honestly? She shrugged, gave a faint smile. She'd always been an only child, she said. Margaret had been the name of a teacher she'd once liked at her school.

He'd been banished, Jean said, shaking her head, exiled from the family because he'd met someone else. It wasn't right, was it? But as she locks the car, Frances finds that she can very easily see how her mother might have gone mad with jealousy and rage when her father told her he loved someone else. As she crosses the tarmac of the car park, she finds that she knows, in her own small way, what it's like to be humiliated, to be left. (*Elsie, love! Get your dad, will you?*) It's easy enough when you're in a fury to lose the plot, to rant, to swear, to break things. She thinks of the shattered phone screen and the compound nouns of her own recent rages against Lucas. Only a phone screen can be repaired in the way that a little girl's understanding cannot. Once her mother had let that narrative take hold, had watched her daughter crumple and grieve but then (*no more tears!*) lift her wobbly chin and continue, had it perhaps seemed untenable to take that story from her small hands and present her with another, perhaps even harder and more painful to comprehend? *He's alive, but he doesn't love us as much any more. He's got another family now.*

As the electric doors of the service station slide open to let her in, Frances can see herself reflected more clearly for a moment: bedraggled and dripping from the violent rain, pale-faced, with a set jaw, a cross between a mutinous teenager and an exhausted middle-aged woman. Is this the vision that her mother has tried to save her from, with her niggles about weight and highlights, and her endless paranoia about Frances's love life? Had her mother looked at her only child and seen providentially, in her sweet curiosity and her impetuous, reckless heart, the inevitability of her course? Has she always known that Frances, like her, is destined to be betrayed? *I have done nothing but in care of thee, Of thee, my dear one, thee, my daughter!*

And as she walks into the cool interior of the service station, it strikes her afresh that there is nothing to be achieved here, nothing to be done, that this is a typically stupid and quixotic quest, as risky and impetuous as one of her internet dates. If she feels like it, tomorrow, she can go online and have a proper look for the Martin Pilgrim who lives in Devil's Bay. If it is him, perhaps she can write him a really savage letter, and tell him she doesn't want anything from him except for him to stay away, stay gone, stay fucking *dead*. The word itself makes tears well up in her eyes as she turns blindly into Starbucks.

Standing in the queue, she takes a deep breath and squares her shoulders. The events of the day are surreal and awful and now that the latest cycle of rage has burned itself out she feels limp and shivery, close once more to tears. She realises in that moment, with the familiar smell of coffee and panini in her nose suddenly making her feel both hungry and queasy at the same time, that the only person she wants to see is Jackson, that the hurt and humiliation they've caused each other is, at least, forgivable and mendable. She wants, suddenly and more than anything, for Jackson to put his arms around her in the warmth of his flat, to tell her that she's daft as a bloody brush, Pilgrim, come on, isn't she? Even Dog thinks so, don't you, Dog? (Dog, ever-treacherous, will probably wag his tail, and agree.)

But just as she is opening her mouth to ask the barista if she can have a skinny cappuccino, please, *grande* to go, there's a commotion behind her.

Someone has dropped a tray, sending mugs crashing to the floor, and making a woman sitting nearby snatch up a toddler and shout that people should be more bloody careful, for God's sake, there are *children* in here.

As if in a dream, Frances stands watching as baristas leap out from behind the counter and run to the aid of the woman who has dropped the tray. She is in her seventies or eighties, nicely dressed but standing frozen to the spot, looking terrified. One barista sets about re-seating and pacifying the mother and toddler, while the other takes the older woman by the arm. She does not move. Frances watches as her hands come up to her face. Then the barista is turning, in relief, as a grey-haired man in a Barbour jacket strides from the door marked Toilets and takes his wife's arm. 'It's all right, Sian,' Frances can hear him saying gently, 'it's all right. We'll just get more coffee. I'm sorry,' he says to the barista, 'I'll help you clean up.' His shoes click on the laminate floor as he leads the woman to a table, his arm protectively round her shoulders. The woman is shaking her head, and Frances hears her saying, 'It's worse today, Jack, my hands just don't work the way they should . . .' Her voice breaks.

What is it, Parkinson's? Multiple sclerosis? Click, click, go the grey-haired man's shoes. One-two, one-two. She doesn't want to be caught staring, so she looks away, towards the counter. But even then, she finds she can see them, smudged and distorted in the gleaming frontage of the coffee machines. The husband is ex-forces, Frances finds herself thinking: the neat short hair, the straight back, but most of all the sound of the shoes. He walks like a man who knows the voice of the drill-sergeant, left, right, left, right. It reminds her of a poem she had taught to her Year 10 about the Roman legion marching along Hadrian's Wall. *Sinister, dexter, sinister, dexter.* Slipping into the picture now is someone else, a woman of about her own age. As Frances stares at the reflected family, the younger woman leans down and gives the older one a hug. The grey-haired man puts his finger, just for a brief second, on his wife's nose. Her reflection looks up, and smiles.

When she goes to collect her cappuccino from the end of the counter, Frances's hand is trembling so much that she squeezes the lid off the cup inadvertently, and spills most of the coffee down her front.

Back in the car, she realises she is shaking violently, and for the first time in a long while she finds herself thinking, with a surge of sudden and unexpected love, of her mother, the once sweet, pert young woman with the luminous skin and the big dark eyes, who only through and because of marriage to Frances's father has become the abrupt, weather-beaten figure in her seconds leggings and her slipping headscarf, affectionate only to dogs and chickens, bearing her guilt and her humiliation and her sadness in silence all these years. Only letting anything slip at all now that her mind has started to disintegrate and betray her, like a small and leaking boat that is beginning to sink. She should have someone by her side, Frances thinks, now that her carapace is crumbling. Like poor Sian in Starbucks, she needs, no, she *deserves* to have someone standing by her. She should, all along, have had not only a daughter to give her a hug, but a husband who would stretch out his hand to her when she faltered. Who would put his finger, gently, on her nose, so that she could look up, and smile. That man should have been Martin Pilgrim, and suddenly Frances is consumed with an even redder and more violent rage than before. Martin-bloody-Pilgrim, who just upped and left with his fancy woman, who traded them in like second-hand cars and is now, no doubt, living the life of Riley up north with not a care in the bloody world, while Frances's mother is wandering the lanes in her nightie and turning up in London in her pyjamas. *He's gone. He's left me!*

Damn him. How can Frances deal with her mother's mind, with its blown-out fuses and its showers of sparks, unless she understands for herself why he left?

Please, Far. Find him. Bring him home, do.

Frances turns the key in the ignition and reverses out of the parking space, watching as her headlights sizzle the tarmac ahead of her.

It is five o'clock when she reaches Doncaster, where her phone tells her she will need to turn right and start moving towards the coast road. The M1 becomes the M18 and then the M62, and for a moment the rain gentles and the clouds roll back, allowing her to see that she is approaching higher ground. As she passes a sign saying *Driffield*, Frances realises that what she can see to her left are the moors, rocky and rusted with bracken, while to her right the horizon is flattening out into the blue distance of the sea. There are hills in the distance on her left, *sinister, dexter*, although between Frances and the coast all there seems to be is a darkening expanse of sky and telephone wire. She shivers. If she had turned back at the services, she would have been almost at Jackson's by now. But then she sees again the grey-haired man stretching out his hand and touching his wife's nose. *It's all right, Sian.* There must be a missing piece, she thinks. Something more than A.N. Other woman, something more than the flush of romance, the pull of sex. Had her mother simply kicked him out on learning of an infidelity, perhaps, told him never to return? Is it possible that it was all, quite simply, some terrible misunderstanding that has unravelled over the years quite out of control?

She sees the sign just then – *Robinsbridge and Devil's Bay* – and takes the exit in a hurried swerve. Beside her, Dog sits up, swaying groggily on the seat, and looks out of the window in amazement.

'I know,' Frances tells him. 'But we must.'

Dog's ears droop, and a moment later he lies down again with a sigh.

Brighouse Lane is three streets down from the cattle grid you have to cross to arrive in Devil's Bay (population 11,000), and Frances slows down instinctively as she sees parked cars and pavements ahead of her. On her right is a low wall that boundaries a stream, running alongside the edge of what looks like a small park, and to her left a row of terraced cottages that seem to be made out of the same sort of sandstone. Everything here is so small, and so quiet, compared with London! Even Dryland seems more lively. But nonetheless, as she pulls over to let a bus get by her, Frances can feel her heart starting to thrum in a thready rhythm, as if she's about to sit an exam. On the seat beside her, Dog is curled up sulkily, and she realises then, with a pang, that she had not honoured her promise of getting him a treat at the services. Although she's made better time than expected, Dog has still been in the car for most of the day, and now she's missed his tea. *Crack-whore mother*, mutters Rhidian, in her mind. But all of a sudden, on her right, is Brighouse Lane, its sign a little mossy, but clear enough. They have arrived.

'How is *going* there going to prove anything?' Silv had demanded, when Frances rang her from the service station. She had been, in typical Silv-fashion, fairly unbothered by

206

the minutiae of what Frances is doing – trekking off to see if a long-dead parent is actually still alive and thriving – and it occurs suddenly to her that this may be more to do with Silv having long ago decided that Frances is engagingly crackers, than because her story holds any objective water. No, it is the *point* of the venture that concerns Silv. Will Frances even recognise her father, thirty-four years on? And if he had buggered off and left her mother in 1981, who's to say that he's going to admit that to some random woman who turns up on his doorstep? Frances would do much better to do some actual homework before fucking off up the motorway in the middle of the week; after all there are websites, Silv pointed out, where you can look up marriages, births, deaths for free. Wouldn't it be better to have some proof other than some nebulous names on Google and Facebook?

Frances knows she's right. But something like a tide within her is pulling her so strongly that she can't resist it, and in the back of her mind she can hear again the blind man saying, 'Sometimes you just have to feel your way.' And more than that, she can see poor, bewildered Sian in the motorway service station, with her husband on one side and her daughter on the other, and she can't explain to Silv, or to anyone, that what consumes her more than anything else is the raging unfairness of it all. Her mother is old, she is ill and frightened, and how can Frances ever begin to know how to deal with her, how to offer her any consolation at all until she knows the truth about their past?

She pulls the car over into a gateway, just opposite the turning into Brighouse Lane. Although of course there is no way in the world that anyone is going to recognise her, Frances feels better knowing she can get away promptly if she needs to. Opening the passenger-side door with trembling hands, she slips on Dog's lead, and together they cross the road, into Brighouse Lane.

As they make their way along the pavement, Frances can see curtains being drawn in a house across the street. Somewhere further down, an indoor light is switched on. How much time does she have? It strikes her that she doesn't know what she's here for: just to get a look at the man who is meant to be her father; to talk to him in a low voice and then leave; to shout, cry, rail? She finds herself thinking, irrelevantly, of Ariel in *The Tempest*, coming to fly, to swim, to dive into the fire, to ride on the curled clouds. Overhead, gathering clouds are creating a premature darkness, and just for a moment she hesitates, pausing with her weight on one foot. For an instant she feels thirteen again, marking the shooter on a netball court, trying anything she can to stop the ball sailing over her head and slipping, swishily, through the net. She looks down at Dog, who pricks his ears and looks back at her, eyes shining in the fading light. Dog thinks they are going for a walk, and for a moment it occurs to her that maybe that would be the better course, to veer off the pavement right here, down one of these ginnels between the houses and climb up on to the moors. But they are right outside the gate of 162 Brighouse Lane, now, and far off there's the faint groan of thunder. *For still 'tis beating in my mind, your reason For raising this sea-storm?* She finds herself looking up, perhaps because of the thunder, she isn't sure. But the sky's dark with clouds, so she drops her eyes and focuses instead on her father's house.

Unlike some of the other houses on Brighouse Lane, number 162 is in darkness, and Frances's first thought is the inevitable irony that she will have chosen to come on a day when there is no one at home. Its frontage, which had presumably once been white, has faded now to grey, and even in the gathering darkness she can see that the garden is unkempt: to the left of the garden path, cow parsley grows tall along the fence that divides the garden from the neighbouring one. To the right of the front gate, two bins, one green and one brown, stand neatly, and, it seems to Frances, quite deliberately, although when she looks up and down the road she can't see that any others have been put out. September is still holiday season, isn't it? *I fucking told you*, says Silv, in her mind. They've gone away, her father and his fancy woman, maybe – her stomach wobbles – their children, too. Where to? Walking in the Lake District, a villa in Tuscany? Or is her stepmother more of a beach holiday sort, does she lounge on a recliner with a copy of a celebrity magazine while Frances's father looks out to sea?

She has realised there are tears in her eyes even before she looks down and sees, first, that there is moss growing on the top of one of the bins, that scummy water has gathered in its plastic pivots. But it is only when Dog pulls forward to lift his leg, delicately, on a wooden post stuck into the soil beside the gate that Frances looks up and sees the sign at the bottom of her father's path.

For Sale.

She looks again at the moss-covered bin, and for a moment sees the sodium light of the street lamps on Brighouse Lane gleaming on its green surface. *Oh, Pilgrim*, sighs Silv, further off now. *What did you expect?*

Her father is not on holiday.

Her father, once more, has gone.

XXI

At six o'clock that evening, Jackson's phone beeps plaintively, and he snatches it up immediately. But it is only a message from Silv. *Any luck?* And he has to text her back, saying that Frances would not pick up her phone when he rang, and last time he'd tried, about an hour ago, it had gone straight to voicemail.

Stupid cow won't have charged it, comes Silv's reply, and Jackson's heart sinks because he knows just how likely that is. In fact, whenever Frances came over to his, she would ask him if she could borrow his charger. When he asked her why she never got organised to charge her phone, she'd look shame-faced. It was because she was on it all the time, she said, she drained the battery and he knew what iPhones were like, crap battery life at the best of times. Button junkie, Jackson had called her. It had only dawned on him later that she probably used her phone for her internet dating sites, for hooking up with those useless men who made her so miserable. All those men, none of whom understood what made her so delightful or what made her tick. All those men, none of whom were Jackson.

And now his phone is ringing, its face lighting up, and his heart is plunging with disappointment again when he sees that it is only Silv, of course it is, they've only just been texting a moment ago.

'I'm going to wait till the morning,' says Silv straight away when he picks up, 'and then if she isn't back, I'm going after her.'

When Jackson points out that Silv doesn't even know where she's gone, Silv says grimly, 'Oh yes, I bloody do.'

And she tells him that she has managed to locate the only Martin Pilgrim anywhere near Scarborough. He's on the electoral roll as living at 162 Brighouse Lane, Devil's Bay, ten miles from Scarborough.

'And you think that might actually be him?' says Jackson incredulously. 'The dead father? Risen like Lazarus from the grave?' He finds it hard to believe that hard-nosed Silv is even countenancing this. It's perfectly clear to Jackson that Frances has, as usual, gone off madcap and wrong-headed at something. It's like her fevered pursuit of other men she finds online, he thinks angrily. She so much wants to believe that they're something they're not that she gives them their own fucking mythology, like an evangelist or a hippy. When will she ever learn to just look around her and see that what she needs is right there, under her nose?

On the other end of the phone Silv is admitting that it does sound like bullshit. Then there's a pause, and she says, 'But it's going to be awful for her. Whether it's him or not.'

'How do you mean?'

Silv sighs gustily down the phone. 'Because either it isn't him, and she'll have to face up to the fact that he's dead all over again, or else . . .'

Here she pauses, and in his mind's eye Jackson finds that he can see, again, a girl's face turned away from him towards a window, can see the sinews beneath the skin of her throat tightening as she swallows, the cushion clutched close to her chest.

At the other end of the phone, Silv is saying, '. . . or else she has to face up to the fact that he never wanted her, anyway.' There's a pause. 'Do you see what I mean, Jackson?'

Jackson says that he does see. He manages to get off the phone before he says anything else, so it is only to Callaghan, landing on the windowsill a moment later, that Jackson confesses that he really doesn't give a fuck about girls with father complexes.

Callaghan blinks his yellow eyes at him, and yawns.

Later, after he has fed Callaghan, Jackson wanders about the flat in his bare feet.

Pausing at the open window through which the cat had arrived half an hour previously, below him on the pavement he can see a young man in a navy blue shirt and jeans hoisting a little girl in a red dress up on to his shoulders, the child screaming with glee. Even as he closes the window, Jackson can hear her laughing and laughing, calling, 'Daddy! Daddy! Daddy!'

Beyond the glass, the cheek of Primrose Hill continues to swell gently through the evening, the curve of the land dark

213

and sharp against the white cheek of the sky, as if the land has drunk up the last light of day and holds it for a moment, throbbing bright like blood in its silhouette. Jackson finds himself shaking his head, although against what he isn't quite sure, and decides to go and talk to Callaghan.

But when he goes through to the kitchen, where only minutes previously the cat had been crouching over a chipped china bowl of leftovers, he finds the bowl licked clean. Callaghan has gone.

XXII

It takes Frances only a matter of minutes to decide what she needs to do.

Standing beside the moss-covered bin, even on the lightest part of the street, she feels exhausted in the way that she sometimes does at the end of a long teaching day that has culminated with her lowest ability Year 7. Her thoughts themselves have been shimmying and fidgeting for so long that she finds she no longer has the energy required to bribe or subdue them with logic, to shock them with a sudden roar of outrage. So she lets them go, and for a moment they explode in malevolent glee, and the cooling adrenalin that had pooled in her gut now makes her feel nauseous. Frances puts her hand out and holds on to the wooden stake of the *For Sale* sign which, a minute earlier, Dog had cheerfully pissed on. What should she do?

There is no answer at 162 Brighouse Lane. The Pilgrims whom Jean claimed lived here have gone, upsticksed, put out their campfires and moved on. The truth has drifted on, still somewhere ahead of her and confounding her rebel courage; her mother's spell, although beginning to dissolve, still holds, for now.

She knows she should go home. It is still relatively early, she could be home by midnight, even if she stops on the way. In the morning, she'll knock on Silv's door as she goes down the hall and Silv will groan and tell her fuck off, Pilgrim, too early; she'll go into school as usual, and teach her lessons; maybe she'll talk to Jackson if he's still in the mood. She'll phone Jean and get her to check on her mother and at the weekend she'll go home and start looking into options for care that don't straight away involve the government seizing her mother's home and depositing her in a care home. That, after all, is her future, isn't it – her job, her friends. Her mother.

Frances has had these fleeting instincts a lot, recently: these self-preserving ones, her adult self perched like a grey parrot on one shoulder. She's had them at the door of a taxi at the end of an iffy internet date; she's had them at the mouth of that disused tunnel underneath Alexandra Park when contemplating a shortcut home from a walk with Dog, the one that stinks of fag ends and piss and dead leaves but which will save her half an hour. *Go home, Pilgrim. Be sensible, there's a good girl.* She'd even had one the night she jumped on Jackson. But something has happened to her in the last year, hasn't it, something she's been putting down to her desperate and possibly pre-menopausal hormones. The old grey parrot's voice has faded to a scratchy squawk, it's increasingly been shouted down by a different voice, furious and shrill, a child's voice. As she

216

clings on to the wooden stake of the *For Sale* sign at the bottom of her father's garden, Frances has a sudden vision again of Jean's peach-coloured, camellia-scented bosom, the one she'd been sick on that night when the dog star went out. Only this time she isn't crying or being sick, she isn't snivelling and quiescent, this time she's thumping her fists against the comfortable bosom. She's shouting, *No! I shan't, I shan't, I*—

At her feet, Dog lets out a gusty sigh.

'You're right,' she tells him. 'We need a drink.'

There are several pubs in Devil's Bridge, although none of them conform entirely to Frances's flat-cap-and-ferret expectations of a small Yorkshire town. The first one, just past the Co-op, is more of a wine bar. Frances and Dog stand outside it, and quite apart from the sheer unlikeliness of such a Farrow & Ball establishment admitting a dog, she knows it isn't where she wants to be. Two women sit at a window table with a bottle of Pinot Grigio in a translucent cooler between them. The stripped-back floorboards present too open a space, somehow. The bar shines. No one in this establishment makes impulsive decisions, no, not even after two bottles of after-work Pinot. This is a place where people contemplate adultery, a risky bet, a minor office rebellion, this is where they rehearse how they'll, like, just tell her to fuck off, you know, then sigh and go home afterwards, wobbling a little in stylish-but-affordable heels from Zara or Mango. If she goes in here, even supposing they let her in, she'll end up being engaged in a discussion with the over-manicured girl at the bar about the virtues of threading versus waxing, or who they think might win *Strictly* this year. After an hour in here, Frances will end up being pointed in the direction of a beige B&B down the road. That or she'll commit suicide, who knows?

The next pub is too full of men in suits jostling for pints at the bar. Sky is broadcasting football.

Finally, at the end of the street, just as she's beginning to think that she might as well make do with a pint of Starbucks and a packet of crisps on her way home, she finds it. The last pub in Devil's Bay.

The Star and Garter.

Afterwards, Frances will argue to herself that her decision to go into that particular pub was not in any way fortuitous. After all, the outcome would have been the same in the end, wouldn't it? She'd have found out one way or another. Maybe the girl with the falsies and the orange tan who'd been serving in the first place would have been able to give her the same answers. You never could tell.

But whether the rest of it would have panned out as it did, Frances will never, really, know. All she will remember when she looks back afterwards is the intense and dizzying relief she had felt as she tugged on Dog's lead and pushed against the pub's heavy front door, the thought that her first glass of Merlot was now only a matter of seconds away.

XXIII

The phone wakes him abruptly in the night. Jackson comes to from a shadowy dream which slithers away, leaving only a trace imprint of what he suspects, uncomfortably, is Mercedes Solomon, in gold body-paint. She seems to be singing one of Ariel's songs from *The Tempest*, something about lurking where the bee sucks, and Jackson has a strong feeling that in the dream he isn't wearing any trousers.

'Christ,' says Silv, 'you took ages. I thought you must be dead, or shagging someone.'

Jackson refrains from saying that the two probably aren't exactly mutually exclusive these days, and says instead, 'What time is it?'

'Just after midnight. I tried you three times,' she adds accusingly.

As he gropes for the bedside light, Jackson finds himself wanting to describe his dream to her – well, to anyone, really, Callaghan would do if he were there – in an attempt to divest it of its varied frissons, but before he can say anything at all, Silv says, 'It's Pilgrim.'

Of course it is, Jackson thinks. He finally locates the switch on the bedside lamp and winces as light floods his pillow.

'She's in a mess,' Silv informs him.

'She *is* a mess,' says Jackson, and blinks to dispel the lingering image of Mercedes Solomon coming crab-wise at him across his bedroom carpet, her belly-button sticking out at him like a nut. *Where the bee sucks, there lurk I—*

But there is a stony silence at the end of the phone and Jackson realises that Silv isn't interested in hearing about his dream. He sighs.

'Go on,' he says.

'She rang me at closing time, dead drunk,' Silv says matter of factly. 'And crying.'

'In *Yorkshire*?' demands Jackson, to whom this is the only part of the information that seems unfeasible.

'She said so.'

'And this was all because Daddy didn't want to welcome her with open arms?' Shit, he hadn't meant to sound so savage.

'No,' Silv says. 'Daddy wasn't there. Apparently the house had a *For Sale* sign out front. But she said she got talking to the barman in the pub she was in . . .' Silv tails off for a moment. Jackson can almost visualise her shaking her head in bewilderment, reaching out for her tobacco and papers. Eventually, she says, 'I couldn't really make much sense of what she said. The signal was really shit and she was walking, and, you know, a bit *gulpy*, and then the fucking line went dead. I tried to ring her back but it went straight to voicemail. I left a message telling her to get in her car and lock it and sleep it off, but . . .' There is another pause, and this time, when she speaks again Jackson can hear the first note of a very un-Silv-like anxiety in her voice. 'But you know what she's like.'

Jackson sits up. 'You don't think she'll try and drive?'

Silv sighs. 'I have absolutely no idea. But I can't just sit around waiting for her to get into trouble.' There's a silence then. Jackson can hear people stumbling out of the pub down the road from his flat. They are laughing. A girl is calling to some others, something about *going back to Hatty's, guys!*

'So?' he says.

'So we have to go there.'

Hadn't that been the Specsavers logo? Jackson wonders. He has a dim memory of a TV advertisement involving two sloths in a tree. In that moment he feels some sympathy for the one he remembers being elderly and, presumably, short-sighted. *Oh, poor fellow!*

'I am not driving to Yorkshire in the middle of the night,' he says flatly.

'But she'll—'

'Probably sleep in her car,' says Jackson firmly. 'And if she does intend on doing something as bloody stupid as driving her car when blind drunk then we won't get there in time to stop her anyway.'

He has a discomfiting vision of blue lights across a central reservation, of ambulances, emergency cordons, a stretcher.

'It's four hours to Yorkshire,' he points out, when Silv doesn't say anything.

'You've got a Jag,' Silv says bleakly, and puts the phone down.

Jackson punches his pillow several times in his attempt to get comfortable, and tries to distract himself by hoping that his dream doesn't descend upon him afresh. The last thing he needs at this moment is Rhidian in lilac tights and Mercedes Solomon coming towards him dressed as a large golden crab.

XXIV

Afterwards, drunk on the hillside, she can't quite remember how she got talking to the barman in such an intimate way, but let's face it, in recent times she's slept with strangers on fewer hours' acquaintance. At least she didn't do that. (Did she? No, she bloody didn't.)

In the moment, though, it seemed quite natural. As she ordered her second glass of wine in the dim interior of the pub – no Sky Sports, but old notes in different currencies taped up above the bar along with an extensive collection of beer mats; a 1920s cigarette advertisement propped up beneath a line of dusty liquor bottles hanging upside down, like bats awaiting nightfall – the barman, who later turns out to be called Tim, and who's had to come out of the army recently, said, 'Bad day, is it?' and Frances had been about to say, old-grey-parrot-fashion, that oh no, she was fine, thanks, just a long drive.

But then something happened, the pummelling child within her must have reached out and pulled the old grey parrot's tail, making it squawk and fly away, because that's when Frances heard herself say yes, bloody bad day, actually, and that was when Tim had smiled at her, reached over the bar and topped up her glass way past the rim that said, rather smugly she thought at the time, *175ml*.

'Go on. Boss or boyfriend?' he said.

'I'm sorry?'

And Tim had said well, let's face it, it was usually one or the other, wasn't it? She must have looked indignant, because he added hurriedly, 'Oh, don't get me wrong, it's the same for blokes. Boss or girlfriend.' He winked. 'Or Mum.'

Frances looked down at her glass. The Merlot was a startling red. The label on the bottle said it had *a fresh nose of plum and blackberry, with striking notes of oak and smoke*, but in her glass right then it looked bright and dangerous. If she picked it up, she knew she would probably spill it, but she wasn't drunk enough then to just lean down and slurp off the excess, either, like you sometimes saw people do with the top of a pint.

'Actually, you were closer on your last guess,' she said, and Tim raised his eyebrows.

'Row with Mum?'

'Not exactly,' said Frances, and although at that point Tim-the-barman had not yet told her about Helmand in 2011, although it would be another bottle before his clumsy attempts to sympathise with her would include the smoke and the light and then the fucking *crying* – Jesus, you never heard anything like it, like an animal it was – she thought in that moment that she saw something in his face: something prescient, as if he had already known that she was about to tell him her own tale of scorched and glistening flesh, about the pink shock of a stump. About the search for the pieces.

And she had only been a few minutes into her explanation that she was here to try and track down a long-lost friend.

'Oh yeah,' said Tim, winking. 'Like that, is it?'

'No,' said Frances, annoyed, 'it isn't.' She cast about wildly for a moment and then said, 'He's a friend of my dad's.'

Tim raised his eyebrows. He clearly still thought this was bollocks, that this long-lost friend stuff was cover for a boss-or-boyfriend tragedy that Frances was too proud to share. But he was willing to humour her.

'What did he do, then, this friend of your dad?' His eyes crinkled, as if he were encouraging a child in a fairy story, and Frances said in a rush that he had been in the navy although that had been years ago, he'd be long retired now.

Which is when she had seen the tiny furrow on Tim-the-barman's forehead.

'What was your friend's name, if you don't mind my asking?'

'Martin,' said Frances absently, thinking how polite he was, pretending to be interested. She took a chance on the over-filled glass and drained half of her Ribena-like wine in one contemplative swallow. 'Martin Pilgrim.'

'Shit,' said Tim-the-barman, and Frances looked up.

Because as tired and miserable and drunk as she was on her way to being, something in her knew, right then. Just as her developed mind was throwing the pieces up into the air and watching them spin – *small town, ex-forces, military always know each other, don't they?* – some deeper animal instinct, the sort that stood apart from death and disease and injury in others and which took itself off into the woods to die in private when the time came, knew the note in his voice.

Not merely mournful, not just polite.

It wasn't the soothing expletive of simple sympathy, a *shit* uttered on the down-beat, the outbreath. No. Tim-the-barman's *shit* was flat and angry and resentful.

It took him a moment to look at her, but when he did, she could see the helplessness in his tanned boy's face. How old was he? she found herself thinking in a rush, as if hectic speculation could somehow block off whatever it was that he was about to say. How old was this scrubbed young man with his clean fingernails and his not-quite-shaved hair – twenty-six? She might have taught him, eight years ago. If he'd done A-level English, that is. But thinking of A-level English made her think suddenly and unaccountably then of her classroom back at school in Dryland, of the frayed green carpet and the curling *Tempest* poster on the wall. *Full fathom five thy father lies*, sings Ariel to Ferdinand.

Frances looks again at Tim-the-barman's face. His lashes are short and sandy, his eyes a clear, light blue, the colour of shallow water, a dawn sky.

But in the play the death of the king was only a charm cast by Prospero for his daughter Miranda's good, wasn't it? Because everything he had done – or she, in some recent productions – he had done *in care of thee, Of thee, my dear*

226

one, thee, my daughter. In the play, it was only Prospero who had called forth the mutinous winds and between the green sea and azured vault set roaring war. It was only his power.

Or hers.

In the play, Ferdinand's father lived.

But Frances could see in Tim-the-barman's face, in his quieter, muttered '*Shit*,' and in the way his clean square hands, with their neatly buffed nails, clenched for a moment on the surface of the bar, that this was not the case. When he looked up at her, he could see that she knew.

He took a breath. 'I'm sorry,' he began.

Frances shook her head, and pushed the glass across the bar towards him. When he turned round to get another bottle she could see the defeated stoop in his shoulders.

At closing time, she'd thanked him, and he'd asked her if she had somewhere to stay. There was a room over the pub, he said, staff used it sometimes after a lock-in. But Frances shook her head. She was fine, she said, she was going to stay with a friend.

'Don't get in your car,' he said, and she managed to refrain from laughing. She knew then, feeling his hand on her shoulder, that she had to get away from Tim-the-barman, not just because he was tainted with the sickly pall of the messenger, but because over the past few hours a nauseating intimacy had opened up between them, a force-field that had emerged not simply from their drinking but from the way in which, in his attempts to provide her with companionship in her grief, he had flung wide the gates of his own private troubles. As she stumbled from the pub with Dog loafing at her heels, she thought that she would rather sleep in a ditch with Dog than fall into the swampy territory of sex with someone who was still daily enduring the horror of having to put bits of their friend in a body bag. Frances hiccupped. And anyway, she thought defiantly, Dog would never forgive her. Half a plate of chips and the greasy bap of a pub burger had left him salivating mutinously, and fidgeting because he badly needed a wee.

Outside, it was surprisingly cold. A few doors down, some mid-week drinkers emerging from the Sky Sports pub were turning up their collars and talking about kebabs and taxis. From further down the hill she could hear the thrum and swish of the main road, see car lights like falling stars across the cattle grid beside which, she knew, was the sign that said *Devil's Bridge*, twinned with – oh, who cared. Places.

Dog raised himself on to his haunches and clawed at her elbow. The gesture made her teary again.

'Sorry,' she said to him, 'sorry, Dog. I'm sorry.'

Her vision was blurry with wine and with pointlessly threatening tears, but she could see that there was no convenient patch of green on this road that might soothe Dog into relieving himself – even the terraced houses had no front gardens into which he might, perhaps, slip if she looked the other way. Unlike the houses on Brighouse Lane with their neat rectangles, their deceitfully straight paths that led so neatly to their front doors. But then Brighouse

Lane, she thought, is a cul-de-sac. Or was it a crescent or a close? It certainly wasn't a lane, in the conventional sense of the world. It didn't lead anywhere.

He'd lived there all my life. Partner was Indian, he said. They had a little boy but he wasn't right, Down's, I think it was. They found out before he was born, kept him anyway. But it was never easy between them and Sanjeet went back to her family in the end. Took the little boy with her. He said he had a daughter from his first marriage but she wouldn't see him. I think that's why he did the cadets, he missed his kids. He was a good teacher. Fair, you know?

And a little later, *We asked him, at the end, if there was anyone we could get to come. He said there wasn't. What about your daughter? I said.*

And that was when Frances had given a little cry, her hand going up to her mouth as if she were going to be sick. Tim looked at her, startled. There was a pause.

'Oh, *no*,' he said.

She had balled her hands into fists and shoved them against her eyes.

'You're Frances,' Tim stated, and Frances had moved one hand down to her mouth and bitten it, to stop herself from crying.

And now she found herself on a strange pavement, alone and still in the process of getting drunker, the second half-bottle gaining on her steadily like a wiry cyclist on a fatal hill, and the tears wouldn't go away no matter how much she blinked. She was lost here. She'd no idea where there might be a turning or a footpath or a stile, and so all she could do was swing around and retrace her steps. Back towards Brighouse Lane, and her car.

She needed to talk to someone but couldn't stomach the idea of Jean. And much as she wanted to call Jackson, the connection between them was too brittle, somehow, too much like a fuse whose plastic covering had melted and which might belt and throb into life in her hands, throwing her even further off-balance.

So she had dialled Silv's number for the second time that day, and only then set off down the road, unshed tears fat and lumpy at the back of her throat.

XXV

In the end, of course, Jackson does not sleep.

There are grey phases to his restlessness, moments when the floor of his consciousness begins to become less solid and the edges of his awareness warm and blur. But just when Jackson feels himself slipping, as if over the lip of a vast enamel bath, into unconsciousness, yet another image washes up on the surface of his mind, and bobs there, dried and faded and defunct like a missive from a long-sunk vessel. But these moments are not whimsical or surreal, like those in the dream from which Silv had woken him. These ones seem grainy and factual as memory, as photographs from a crime scene.

Frances, drunk-struggling to get her car key into the lock.

Frances, balancing on one leg in the office and laughing at something he'd said.

Frances crying in the dark on an unknown street.

Jackson himself, rolling off her that night, breathing heavily.

(You *were embarrassed? Christ!*)

The tail-lights of her car, disappearing down an unknown road.

In the end, he gives in and gets up. In the kitchen, the kettle seems to take an age to wheeze into life, and so Jackson finds himself pacing the sitting room in his bare feet, past and future flapping around him like a torn sail. He pauses at the window, resting his palms flat against the glass. What had he said to Silv? *If she does intend on driving, we'll be four hours too late to stop her.*

True, of course, logical and rational, but, well . . .

Beneath him, the pavement is stained orange by street lamps.

Good-looking, of course, his Great-Aunt Vi observes from the fireplace behind him. *But quite useless, of course.*

Jackson feels something cold seep through his chest cavity, and as it does, he sees in his mind's eye not Frances, now, but a speeding sequence of other images, real ones, like a fast-forward of the seasons in a nature documentary. The trailer to his own life, in box-office technicolour.

There's Carly, lying beneath him.

There's the ghostly ululation of that fish eagle from the harbour, trembling between terror and ecstasy.

There's the Kurt Cobain poster on her wall, and the gasp of the door opening and, oh *fuck*, there's Tory again, her hand still frozen in the act of pushing her sunglasses up on to her head, looking across at what she had probably thought would be her daughter, lying on her bed reading a magazine. Jackson had thought afterwards that she had looked, in that moment before she saw them, strangely boyish, like a sea captain competently scanning the horizon for rocks, pirates. The end of the rainbow.

You fucking well stay away from us, Jackson. You hear me? Or I'll fucking well kill you myself.

And Carly, days later, shaking her head sorrowfully as she told him she simply couldn't carry on distressing her father like this. He'd been in such a *state* when her mother told him, Jacksy, honestly! Her inflection tilting as it tended to on some words, but not tilting up this time, not asking for an answer only he could give (*I'll see you around?*). No, when Carly Nicholson told him about the terrible state her father had been in about her and Jackson, her voice had actually pitched down an octave. She had sounded conspiratorial and womanly, then, consumed with triumph. He'd known then it was over. Of course it was. *Oh, poor fellow!*

As she reached across the café table to pat his hand that day, Jackson had seen again the mantelpiece in the Nicholson sitting room: the photographs of her brothers, one in a cap and gown and one scoring a try. He'd had a mad vision, then, of a new photograph appearing between them, a centrepiece in which Carly, naked, straddled a dazed-looking Jackson with one hand curled, cowboy-style, above her head. *Look at me, Daddy! LOOK AT ME!*

She started it, he thinks desperately, she knew what she was doing.

But somewhere in the darkness outside his window Edie is turning away from him, with Leonora propped on her shoulder. *Eighteen years old, Jackson, eighteen. What the hell is wrong with you?*

The shriek of the kettle from the kitchen makes him jump. Jackson blinks, then turns away from the window.

XXVI

Frances has been walking for about ten minutes when Dog goes on strike.

She had stumbled down the road away from the Star and Garter, checking over her shoulder from time to time just in case Tim-the-barman, consumed with that primal intensity occasioned by female sadness, had been following her to insist again that she use the bed above the bar.

He wasn't.

She had just rounded the corner from the High Street on to the peripheral road that wound back towards the cattle grid and then the slip road, and with relief seen her car still parked where she had left it. The moon gleamed for a moment on the old grey sign that read Brighouse Lane, and it was at that moment that Frances had stopped in her tracks, pulling Dog to a reluctant halt too. He looked up at her, eyes gleaming resentfully: surely not another detour? But Frances found she did not want to go back to the house, with its moss-covered bins and overgrown garden, or indeed anywhere near it. Even though she was still a hundred yards away up the road, she could feel the house sitting there like a darkening tooth. Even at that distance, its emptiness rolled at her like a wave, the peak rising and curling towards her while the base moved away towards an unreachable horizon.

He'd stayed at home for as long as he was able, Tim-the-barman had said. He'd been lucky: the local health authority had been piloting a mobile chemo unit, so after the initial diagnosis he hadn't had to travel, and afterwards someone always volunteered to stay with him, monitoring the sickness, keeping him hydrated. Watching for signs of the infection that could set in at any time. He'd been much loved in the local community, Martin: the sea cadets, the church, the neighbours. Sanjeet hadn't come back, though, had she? Took his alimony payments, fucked off back to Delhi and stayed away, didn't she? Even when he was bloody dying.

On the second bottle, Tim had reached across the bar and touched her hand.

'I asked him if he wanted me to try and find you,' he said. 'But he said it wouldn't be fair. Does that make any sense?'

Frances had stared at his hand, resting on top of hers. It was an intimacy that she assumed was meant to be compassionate, but it occurred to her then that she hadn't been touched by a man since Jackson, and so she waited a moment, then withdrew her hand.

Tim had still been watching her, waiting for an answer. She picked up her glass. 'Yes,' she said. 'And no.'

After all, what was sense any more? Her father had left them for Sanjeet, and the child they had even then known was

– how had Tim put it? – *not right*. That was the missing piece she'd come for, wasn't it, the reason, the mitigating circumstance. And it fitted what she had always believed about her father, the man Tim described as having *loved kids*, the man he had admiringly called *fair*. But whether or not it made *sense*, Frances wasn't sure. She had finished the glass.

Along the road, on the pavement just before her car, Dog comes to a stop and sits down. She tugs at him impatiently, but he tugs back. She can hear the scrape of his claws on the pavement, feel the collar beginning to slip forward over his ears. He's had enough. He's telling her it's a walk or nothing, enough of all this farting about in cars and pubs. Frances can see a gap in the shadow cast by the hedge: a gateway, she supposes, or a stile, up on to the fells. She looks down at Dog, slumped mulishly on the pavement, and sighs. A walk might do her good. After that she supposes she and Dog could roll themselves up in the back of the car and wait for daybreak. Six hours would be enough to clear her to drive, surely? She clicks her tongue at Dog, who gets up, ears twitching instantly, and as soon as they are within sight of the gap in the hedge, she bends down and slips off his lead.

The green sign beside the stile shows a white stick figure, bent forward against a gradient, and in neat white lettering announces *Devil's Bay, ¾ mile*. Dog wriggles through the gap beside the stile and pauses for a moment, muzzle lifted and both ears cocked, as if he has picked up the voice of a long-lost friend on the breeze. Frances, watching him, hears it too, and reaches out towards his collar.

'Careful, Dog.'

But Dog, banged up for hours in the car and then pub, is already bounding away up the hillside, stopping only to relieve himself on a rock. Frances knows that truculent tempo, the way he puts his nose down and lopes like a hare. He has no intention of coming back straight away, and, sighing, she sets off after him, stumbling a little on the uneven ground. But even over her quickening breath she can hear it, closing on them all the time.

The melancholy, long, withdrawing roar of the sea.

XXVII

Jackson is in the middle of wondering whether it is, technically speaking, either too late or too early for a drink, when he comes across the earring.

Tea, as usual, hasn't helped. It's a disgusting drink, he thinks, as uniquely British as Spotted Dick or sprouts. At school and then at Cambridge, Jackson had regarded the benignly offered cuppa with alarm, but over the course of his marriage to Katy he'd become quiescent to its consoling rituals: the filling of the kettle, warming of the pot, even, he observed once to Rhidian, the demure sound of the pouring spout. That Christmas Rhidian, who professed to loathe all forms of so-called *warm beverages*, had given Jackson a tea cosy, 'In honour of your new enthusiasm.' Of course, it had taken Jackson some time to realise that the tea cosy wasn't just round and pink, it was actually designed in the likeness of a bottom and was therefore, as Rhidian cheerfully pointed out, guaranteed to make sure Jackson never looked at his *spout* in quite the same way again. Rhidian and Frances had laughed uproariously about the bum-cosy for months, carolling *Cup of tea, vicar?* and clutching themselves in fits of glee every time the drink was mentioned, and Jackson had largely stopped drinking tea after that. Nonetheless insomnia, if only by dint of its tedium, called for a crisis response.

He has just taken a tepid mouthful and put the mug back down on his bedside table, when he hears a faint, tinny scrape and feels the mug rock, minutely, between his fingers, as if he has set it down on a drawing pin, or a nail. But when he moves it, the lifted base of the mug of cooling tea reveals – of bloody course – the same tear-drop earring that two days previously had caught Katy's eye when she walked into his bedroom unannounced. Now, he picks it up and holds it up, for a moment, against the light from his bedside lamp.

He knows little about geology. As a boy he had eschewed most boyish pursuits, in fact it had been Edie who'd been the fossil-hunter, digging with a special knife into rocks found on holiday beaches or mountain tracks. Edie, he thinks with a pang, would have known what sort of stone this was. It is milky pale in colour, but surprisingly dense between his finger and thumb. What is it, an opal, a moon-stone? No, he muses, feeling the granular surface beneath the surface polish. Quartz, perhaps, some mineral exca-vated from igneous rock, compressed for millennia beneath infinite strata of sandstone or shale. Edie's husband Clem had been a mineral prospector in South Africa and Jackson can almost hear his voice as he examines the stone. *Milky quartz, bro. Quite pretty to look at, but common as muck, no real value.* Still, it was an unusually demure and elegant piece of jewellery for a fly-by-night like Frances, who most of the time seems to regard brushing her teeth and her hair as the limits of day-to-day grooming. Who had given her the earrings? Jackson wonders bleakly. A previous boyfriend, on an anniversary? A grateful pupil, a relative?

It is then, as he holds the discarded stone up to the light, that the truth strikes Jackson quite plangently. Frances has no relatives. Well, she has her mother, of course, but it seems to Jackson that Frances's mother is to family as an avalanche is to a Himalayan walking holiday, an inevitable risk factor rather than a design feature. And as for her father . . . Jackson puts the earring down and, unthinkingly, picks up his mug of tea again. He finds he feels baleful about Frances's father, *the drowned Phoenician sailor* as Rhidian always privately refers to him. Dead or alive, he has become more of a presence for Frances in his absence than any gently ageing parent could have been. Jackson sighs, and resolves to put the earring, along with its partner, in an envelope and return them to her when he sees her. *When*, not if, because Frances will be fine, of course. She'll come into work, probably not tomorrow but on Monday and Rhidian won't be able to bollock her because Jackson will, after all, tell him what's going on.

And yet again, as he takes another mournful swallow of tea, Jackson finds himself brooding restlessly on the last time he spoke to Frances. She had been sitting against the edge of her chaotic desk in the office, hands clenching the work surface on which her computer sat. She had been white and glassy-eyed, silenced for once by the precision of his stored-up vitriol. She asked for it, he tells himself fiercely. She started it, she's behaved like a complete bitch since the summer. Jackson has a self-pitying vision of himself, then, sitting at his sister's bedside over the summer, checking his phone repeatedly for any reply from Frances. Nothing.

But somewhere at the back of his mind he can hear Silv's voice, unusually tense. *You know what she's like.* And of course Jackson does know: reckless, impulsive, often hilariously wrong-headed. But in that moment, prompted perhaps by the earring at which Katy had looked askance when she visited, he has another, quite different recollection of her. He pauses, letting it unspool in his mind, his hand still reaching out for his rapidly cooling mug of tea.

It was the morning after Katy and he had decided to separate.

He'd been unable to sleep that night, either; had lain on his back staring at the ceiling until he'd got up and come in to work at seven, just to get out of the house.

The school had been stirring quietly as he walked in through Hilltop House: cleaners in maroon overalls mopping the stairs, maintenance men unlocking classroom doors and turning on computer monitors. The air smelled of disinfectant, and he couldn't stop thinking about Katy, or the coldness, that morning, of the sheets on the spare room bed.

He'd opened the office door expecting to find the place in darkness, or, perhaps, to find just Jen McGarrick, photocopying briskly in the quarter-light with her iPhone earplugs still in.

What he hadn't expected was for the lights to be on, or for there to be pop music playing. He hadn't expected a lone figure, dancing, in the small space between the desks. When he came in, the figure's back was to him; she'd kicked off her shoes, and her arms were raised above her head as her long body undulated with the unmoored urgency of a sheet hung out in a high wind. Afterwards, he'd reflected that it wasn't a graceful display; it hadn't at that moment made his breath catch in lust. But as the music reached its chorusing crescendo, and as she spun round, hands still above her head, Jackson realised.

It was Frances Pilgrim who was dancing in the office like an ungainly schoolgirl at seven in the morning. And as she saw him standing watching, her hands had flown to her mouth in embarrassment, but her face had been bright with joy. Later, she told him that she'd been out all night on what she grinningly called *an iffy internet date*, hadn't even gone home to change. And in that moment, emerging sleepless from a sterile spare room and stunned with failure, all Jackson could see was her energy, her abandon. Her very great capacity for happiness.

She'd come to a halt, and grabbing the computer mouse on her desk to turn down Madonna's 'Papa Don't Preach' had said breathlessly, 'Sorry, Jackson – didn't expect anyone to be in . . .'

It was only when she glanced up at him a second later that her smile had vanished. 'What's happened?'

243

He had shaken his head, not trusting himself in that moment to speak, and she had stretched out her hand and touched his arm. It was an unthinking gesture, he thought afterwards, a reflex. She had seen someone in pain, and her first thought was to comfort. Never mind the fact that she didn't know him that well, nor was she entirely sure whether she liked him. Her hand said, *You are sad. Let me help.* And so he did; he let Frances take him out for coffee in a place he hadn't known then on the High Street, called the Green Café; he let her ask him questions which he answered with an honesty born out of the weariness of never having told anyone else the story of him and Katy and his Little Chaps. It should have been too humiliating, but Frances had listened, and nodded, and even made the occasional wry joke, until he realised, at one stage, that he was actually almost laughing.

And although it was only coffee that day, although then she was just a colleague being kind to someone in a crisis, he remembered as they emerged from the café at half past eight that the air already seemed warmer. He had noticed snowdrops on the triangle of grass on the traffic crossing, had felt her hand brush his arm on the kerb as though he were a feckless child who might, in his current condition, walk out in front of a car. He remembered that as they reached the other side of the road, he could see that the sun was coming out.

Now, Jackson leans back against his headboard and closes his eyes, remembering again the shape of her sitting on the edge of the bed in the summer, her misery broadcast a thousand times the size of itself by the midsummer dawn seeping in through the cracks in the curtains. She'd had a lousy time, she must have done, to have withdrawn from him so completely. Did he apologise to her at the time, jokily suggest they try again when they were less drunk? He can't remember. Can't remember much about any of it after the kitchen is the problem, they really must have had a ridiculous amount of wine. Is it possible he just hammered away at her and passed out? And if so, shouldn't it really have been him who made some overture to her afterwards? I couldn't, he thinks self-pityingly. There was Edie. I had to go, there were suitcases and taxis and the airport with a hangover, and then when I got to South Africa my phone didn't work . . .

But in his heart of hearts he knows that really, he was just ashamed of himself, ashamed that he'd been a brute, ashamed that he'd disappointed or even offended her in the course of what had perhaps only been to her a generously offered portion of pity sex, anyway. He'd been too embarrassed that night to say: look, I know that was crap. Can we try again, some time? And then she'd been gone and the first she heard from him was a self-pitying text several weeks later. No, it is as plain as the nose on his face that he's fucked up, but there isn't a lot he can do about it now, is there? Frances is probably asleep in the back of her car by the side of a road somewhere. Jackson's stomach turns over. Does she have a blanket, a coat? You could bet your bottom dollar she wouldn't have a bottle of water in the car either, to quench what is likely to be a belter of a hangover when the sun comes up. Jackson gazes at the earring, and finds, suddenly, that he is shivering.

She started it.

But in the distance, again, Edie, with the baby in her arms. *What the hell is wrong with you?*

Jackson gets up and starts to look around for his trousers.

XXVIII

At first, Frances thinks Dog is just playing a game.

He has done this before, she thinks vaguely as she climbs higher, away from the road; it is a type of payback when he is feeling ignored. He just buggers off on his own, causing her to shriek herself panicky and hoarse, at which point he usually materialises from somewhere behind her, head low and ears drooping, an expression on his face that seems to say sulkily, *I was only having a walk!*

And so, to begin with, she does not panic. The air is crisp and fresh, cooling as she moves higher, towards what she assumes is the bay, and although she's still drunk, she can feel the threatening tears receding enough for her to see more clearly. In front of her the land rears straight up in a sheep-nibbled gradient towards a ridge, the other side of which, she assumes, must be a sloping path down towards the beach. The sign back on the road had said the bay was only three-quarters of a mile away, but Frances thinks the distances must be way off, because although the sea sounds a little closer than it had on the road, it doesn't yet sound anything like a matter of yards away. Anyway,

247

she tells herself, Dog's not that much of a swimmer, he tends to stay in the shallows even of ponds and rivers these days. There is no way he will plunge off into the sea for a swim, however close it turns out to be. So Frances takes a shaky breath and keeps putting one foot in front of the other, one eye on the skyline so she can see Dog when he finally emerges from the trees. Walking uphill after Dog is, she reflects, perhaps as good a way as any to deal with everything she has learned.

My father is dead. She tries out the words in her head like a child with a new language. The phrase comes easily enough; but after all, it isn't new, is it – she's been repeating it to friends and lovers for decades now, she's hardly experiencing the shock of the death for the first time, is she? No, Frances has already taken that bullet, and more importantly, she has grown up around it. It's priced into everything she does, a knowledge by now more like an instinct, primed through a hundred thousand repetitions. She has learned to move up and down through the gears of her established loss quite competently, all things considered. Nevertheless, as she pauses to catch her breath, she finds herself wondering whether the factual chaos of the day has, somehow, left her dislocated, unaligned from herself. Her emotions have whip-cracked from incredulous hope to anger and then to a smarting numbness with such speed that she wonders if her true feelings are actually up in the air, hovering somewhere above her, like the far-off falling debris of an air disaster. *Shock*, Silv had said on the phone, although the line had been really awful. Perhaps she had actually been trying to say, *Pilgrim, you pillock?*

Nothing has changed, she tells herself. You are still Frances Pilgrim, an almost thirty-nine-year-old teacher, whose father has been gone since she was little. Last week an old man you never really knew died in a town you'd never visited. *Nothing has changed.* She stumbles forward quicker, as if to outrun herself, but the land has suddenly grown less tussocky and more rocky underfoot. She staggers a little, her arms going out in front of her to re-balance herself, then pauses for a moment, looking automatically back down the sheep track she's climbed up for any sight of bloody Dog.

It's then that she realises that, while blindly following the sheep track uphill, she has drifted quite a considerable way to her right: even from this height, she can no longer see the dark outline of her car, nor the flashing lights of the night traffic on the slip road. She is only a matter of yards from the bay, which must be somewhere the other side of the rocky ridge in front of her, but which way then is left or right, north or south? The hillside has turned crafty in the darkness, it has deceived her. She reaches for her phone, but Google Maps had already devoured most of its battery even before she rang Silv earlier, and now the screen only responds with a red-and-white lightning-flash symbol, exhorting her to plug it in. *Shit.* The darkness is thicker here, with the rocky incline rearing up in front of her like a tumbled-down wall, and no street lights or lingeringly lit windows to cast a comforting glow from below. She shivers, and starts to move back across the hill, going diagonally left now, like a crab to correct her error, and then stops short, listening.

Funny.

Somewhere across the uncertain distance of her mind, she can hear Cal Smith's husky voice again, just as she had before she fainted yesterday afternoon. *Come to the window, sweet is the night air.* Frances is wondering quite absurdly whether she is developing some sort of highly inappropriate crush on Cal Smith as she cocks her head. What is it? She realises again as she stands there, her thoughts panting to catch up on themselves, that it isn't the sound itself that surprises her. She recognises it, of course she does, as any tiny island-dweller would, that tremulous cadence slow, which begins and ceases and then again begins. But it's something about the direction of the sound that jars, which sits wrongly, somehow, with her assumptions about where she is and where she's going.

And although she doesn't know why, something in Frances's stomach flickers and starts, like a lizard shooting suddenly across a rock. In two or three ungainly strides she is up on to the rocky outcrop and looking straight out, as if over the wing of a plane, into a swooping gape of sky.

Her heart staggers in her ribcage.

Then she looks down, and sees it. *The folds of a bright girdle furled*, crashing against the livid striations of what Frances only now understands is a vertiginous cliff. The sea.

Immediately, she swings back again to the hillside below her, scanning and scanning for a loping dark shape.

But there is nothing.

Dog is gone.

XIX

XXIX

Under ordinary circumstances, Jackson would rather not have taken Silv with him to find Frances. Under ordinary circumstances, in fact, he can't think of many things he'd rather less have done. Gnawed off his own arm, perhaps, put his tits through a mangle, slammed his genitals in a drawer. But when he gets Silv on the phone some time after 2 a.m. and asks her, in the manner of an apprehended thief showing his palms to an arresting officer, to confirm the name of the village Frances has gone to, Silv says simply, 'Take me with you.'

'Oh, look,' says Jackson, 'perhaps it would be better if—'

'If what?' demands Silv.

Jackson pauses. He can't after all claim that Frances would prefer to see him to Silv at the moment; after all, Frances didn't ring him in her drunken state, did she? Nor does he feel any particular compulsion to explain to Silv that somehow, this is *his* errand, his sole act of repentance, although for what he's not yet quite sure. For behaving like an opportunistic old man in a mac, perhaps? For mocking

Frances's mother's illness? For claiming world rights to outrage in the cock-up that their friendship had become? Or is this tokenistic gesture of apology perhaps on an entirely more cosmic scale: to Tory and Nicko; to Katy and the child he'd been unable to give her; to Edie, who had been days beyond being able to recognise him, let alone acknowledge his apologies by the time he arrived in South Africa in July; sod it, perhaps to all the places and people he has left behind in his life because of his varied and monumental incompetences?

So Jackson sighs gustily, and says he'll be there in twenty minutes.

'I need coffee,' Silv says, when she gets into his car, 'and cigarettes. There's a petrol station that'll be open just beyond the North Circular.'

So much for *Thanks, Jackson, you're a brick*, thinks Jackson, as he turns the ignition again and switches on his headlights. Other than that, they don't speak much for the first few miles of the journey, past Hilltop and, opposite it, the Rat and Gate, windows heavy-lidded with blinds down and curtains drawn. The pavements are quiet and smooth with only the occasional skirl of maple leaves drifting down as they pass, and as Jackson increases his speed down the steep hill towards the ring road, the streets seem more like a deserted discotheque than a sleepy city suburb. Perhaps this is always how London seems in the dead of night, a still-lit stage on which the curtain has quite incidentally fallen for a swift scene change. He glances sidelong at Silv, about to share this insight with her, but Silv is hunched down in the passenger seat, chewing a nail. Before he can speak, she says suddenly, 'Why didn't you want to go and get her?'

Jackson is taken aback. He restrains himself from making the sort of elaborate gesture towards his steering wheel that would inevitably result in the car swerving into the kerb, and says instead, 'What do you mean?'

Silv looks across at him, eyes only slits in her white face. 'I thought you'd be dying for a chance to play the white knight.'

Jackson blinks. 'You did?'

'Course.' Silv lies back on the headrest and closes her eyes. 'You've been after her for ages, we all know that.'

Who is we? wonders Jackson, trying not be rattled by her truculence. Of course, Jen and Rhidian and probably others at work have guessed intermittently at his interest in Pilgrim, had initially inflicted Friday night banter on him when she'd been at the bar, a habit that had quietened down to meaningfully raised eyebrows when Frances complained as she did frequently about the state of her love life. But Silv is not close to them, is unlikely to have discussed it on her occasional appearance in the Gut on a Friday. If she'd simply meant that she as well as Jackson knew about his feelings for Frances, she'd have said *both*, wouldn't she? But she'd said *all*. Jackson squirms a little in the driver's seat. Does this mean that Frances has known all along about how he feels, that she has – Christ – discussed it with Silv? Jackson steals a glance at Silv, notices the mocking smile playing on her large mouth. Have they *laughed* about him? He is fleetingly tempted to pull a U-turn and drive her straight back to Swain's Square, but instead he finds himself shrugging and hunching a little over the wheel, paying exaggerated attention to the road.

'It's okay, Jackson,' says Silv, grinning wolfishly. 'I'm pretty sympathetic, you know.'

Jackson glances across at her. The brighter lights on the dual carriageway light up her profile for a startling second at a time, making her white face seem even more deadpan and sinister than usual, like a flick book revealing, at speed, the same image on every page. She looks about as sympathetic as a snake hunting a rabbit, and the fact that she is lolling, lazily, against his car's padded headrest as she launches her attack pisses him off almost more than the things she's coming out with. He grits his teeth, and says, 'Is this the petrol station you meant?'

'Yes.'

Jackson pulls in. As she gets out, Silv says, 'Do you want anything?'

'Apart from you not to be here?' says Jackson, before he can stop himself. 'No.'

Silv raises her eyebrows, and as she walks away from him across the forecourt, past the empty newspaper racks and the bunches of yesterday's flowers wrapped in cellophane, Jackson curses himself. Now he's augmented rather than dissipated exactly the atmosphere that Silv has been trying to create. Rhidian is right, he thinks crossly. She is a bit like Mrs Thatcher. Perhaps in a moment Silv will throw him out of his own car and tell him that *it may be the cock that crows, but it's the hen that lays the egg*, while she waltzes off to find Frances on her own. It crosses his mind that when she comes out of the petrol station he could just chuck his keys in her face and tell her to fuck off and find Pilgrim herself, good fucking luck to her. But it strikes him simultaneously that quite apart from everything else, Jackson would probably never see the car again, so he stays where he is, hunched broodily over the steering wheel, until the passenger door opens and Silv slithers back in.

'Here,' she says, handing him an unfeasibly large coffee.

Jackson takes the coffee grudgingly.

'What are you waiting for?' she asks a moment later.

'For you to put your seat belt on.'

Silv, who is in the act of lighting a cigarette, raises an eyebrow. 'I didn't think you were exactly concerned for my safety.'

Jackson says glumly that he doesn't give a toss about her safety. 'But if you go through the windscreen you'll make a mess of the paintwork.'

There's a pause, then Silv grins. 'Okay.'

They are on the M1 before she says, in a more conciliatory tone, 'I didn't mean to wind you up, before.'

'Yes, you did.'

'Okay, maybe I did a bit. But I didn't think you'd be quite so touchy about it.' She's looking ahead of her now, not sizing him up any more, so he is taken by surprise when she says, 'You love her, don't you?'

257

Jackson's hands tighten on the steering wheel, and the Jag swerves a little.

'Do I?' he says, affecting a nonchalance he doesn't feel. 'Why do you think that?'

'Easy.' She glances across at him, not mocking now. 'You wouldn't be so angry with her, otherwise.'

'Wouldn't I?'

'No. In fact' – Silv roots around for another cigarette – 'if you'd only shagged her and left her, you'd have been much more prepared to get out of bed and go and get her.'

'I would?'

'Yes,' says Silv simply. 'You're her friend, after all. If you'd just stuck one on her because you were pissed and miserable, you'd be feeling guilty. You'd have been feeling responsible when I rang you, not resentful.'

Jackson can feel hysterical laughter flowering up through his chest. He has a sudden and absurd urge to tell Silv that he was once top of his year at Cambridge, the darling of the English Faculty, that there had been a time – several decades ago, granted – when girls had not always made a fool of him. But here he is, nonetheless, not that far from sixty and being lectured about his own feelings, in his own car, by the lesbian love child of Greta Garbo and Mrs Thatcher. *Be cheerful, sir. Our revels now are ended!*

Silv, however, seems to read his mind. Exhaling, she says, 'Why didn't you just tell her how you felt at the time?'

Jackson sighs. Outside, a large blue motorway sign approaching on the left-hand verge of the road: *Cambridge, 37 miles*. All roads tonight lead to the past, it seems.

258

'It's not that interesting,' he says.

Silv glances at the satnav. 'Well, we've got another three hours and forty-seven minutes,' she says drily. 'I can always stop you when it gets boring.'

And so Jackson, to his surprise, does tell her, about his disastrous past. Not about Katy, but about Tory Nicholson, and Carly. About knowing for months, years even, that he was going to fuck things up, and trying quite hard to do all he could not to. About the blank paralysis that had seized him when his niece was born, as if he had suddenly seen his own youth inevitably unravelling into mid-life . . .

'Oh,' says Silv with interest. 'Now I see.'

Jackson glances across at her. 'You do?'

'Of course.' Silv lets down the window to tap her ash out into the darkness. 'Mid-life crisis. There you were, not wanting to settle down, but hitting forty nonetheless, and everyone around you, you know, *spawning*—'

'You speak with some authority.'

'I do,' agrees Silv. 'Anyway, along comes baby Chloe—'

'Carly.'

Silv waves her cigarette dismissively. 'Whatever. Anyway, so suddenly she isn't just this little minx who's flatteringly got the hots for you, she's also your opportunity to, like, become a father.'

Even trapped behind a steering wheel, Jackson recoils. 'That's grotesque.'

'No, it isn't. There you were, hanging about your own life like a spare prick at a wedding, and suddenly here's your chance to be a big hero.' Silv gives him a ghost of her earlier, truculent smile. 'Real white knight.'

Jackson wants to tell Silv that she's talking complete and utter crap, but can't help remembering Carly standing beside his table in the student bar. *I have to meet Sam. But I'll see you around?* The way something in his heart had started to unfurl, then, like a flag, just as it had when she'd turned her head away from him in her parents' sitting room to look at the mantelpiece upon which she did not feature. The way she'd been sprawled there like lost luggage underneath that vast and gaudy canvas of the Sharpeville massacre. *I'm thick, you see.*

'So,' Silv is saying, with interest, 'what happened then? After you saw her in the student bar?'

Clem had already gone home to Edie and the baby, and Jackson was halfway back to his car and wondering how the actual fuck he was going to get home when Carly stepped out on to the concrete path across the green ahead of him.

It was the part of the campus that everyone referred to as the Palms, because of a large bronze of two outstretched hands that had been commissioned by the new chancellor several years before. The hands were crudely sculpted, each about ten feet across and cast in what Jackson guessed was probably clay, but one painted black and the other white. The plinth on which they stood lifted them to an overall height of about eleven feet, and Jackson had always found them sinister. They might be meant to herald the new dawn of the rainbow nation, but to Jackson they'd always loomed, fingers splayed out like so many swords of Damocles waiting to fall.

The plinth had been installed on the grass next to the point where the path that ran from the first-year residences to the dining hall and the bar crossed with the path leading from the English Faculty towards the car park. Jackson had been weighing up the merits of sleeping in the cramped back of his vehicle, and driving home swiftly in the morning for a shower and change, with the possibility of attempting to drive, very slowly, home after four hours of solid boozing. He was so drunk, however, that he only seemed to get halfway through the merits of sleeping in the car before he started to think with a blind longing of his bed.

It was then that Carly stepped out from behind the Palms, a moment that later he argued to himself to have been so fortuitous as to have been almost magical, really.

She was in profile to him as she stepped out, for all the world as if she were simply crossing from the residences where, no doubt, the moronic Sam lived, to the bar area to get herself a Coke or some cigarettes. Jackson, head down in debate with himself, only saw the lower half of a pair of denim legs at first. The legs seemed a bit blurry to begin with, but they seemed to have stopped moving, and as he drew closer he saw that the ankles that protruded from the neatly tailored ends were slim and brown. One of them had something tattooed on it, and for a moment Jackson found himself focusing on the tattoo, trying to work out what it was. A seahorse? A phoenix? A tremulous falling star?

261

'Hi, Jackson,' said a calm voice then, and when Jackson looked up he saw for the second time that night the tawny hair and see-through white shirt of Carly Nicholson.

(She told him later that he'd been unable to speak at first. I was drunk, he protested, but she just smiled.)

After a moment, he said, 'Where are you going?'

'Home,' she said. 'I'm about to call Mum.'

'I'll drive you,' Jackson said stupidly, and Carly had raised one eyebrow, just as she had that first evening as she lay on the sofa.

'Is that a good idea?'

Jackson admitted that it probably wasn't, and then Carly said, quite casually, that maybe it would solve both their problems if she were to drive Jackson's car. Jackson must have looked confused, because Carly added, 'You can crash at ours.' There was a pause and then she said, 'Like before.'

Oh, said Jackson, that was very kind, but he'd probably have sobered up in an hour or so.

Carly shrugged. 'Whatever,' she said, and held out her hand. Jackson stared at the hand for a moment, and was about to reach out and take it, when he realised. She was waiting for his car keys.

'Little minx,' says Silv admiringly. 'She had it all planned.'

Jackson shrugs. The ungallant thought has long ago crossed his own mind, of course, but so has the simultaneous thought that it is quite a convenient thought for him to have, exonerating him as it does from at least part of the responsibility for what happened next. He glances across at Silv.

'Aren't you bored yet?'

'Not likely,' says Silv, leaning back in her seat and putting her feet up on the dashboard. 'This is even better than *Bake Off*.'

The most salient thing Jackson remembered about entering the Nicholson house that night was the entirely easy way in which Carly told him it would be better if he slept in her room because the alarms had all been set in the sitting room, and turning off the beams was too complicated for her, she always got them mixed up and ended up hitting the button that called out the security firm by accident. Jackson had found the idea of two burly Afrikaners with red faces bursting in on them with guns drawn actually quite funny, but he had said okay.

'Isn't there a spare room?'

Carly shrugged. 'Yes. Right next door to Mummy's room.'

Jackson had paused sharply at the idea of Tory hearing the landing creaking and emerging in her nightie, perhaps. Carly watched him coolly.

'Okay,' whispered Jackson, tripping over a shoe rack beside the back door. 'Perhaps your room is better.'

Had he really assumed, then, that *she* would be going to sleep in the spare room, next door to her mother? Afterwards, he was never sure. There was something so innately and almost unbearably transgressive, to his mind, about going into Carly's room at all that Jackson could never adequately decide afterwards on the precise grid

263

reference of the thrill that overcame him as he stepped over the threshold, breathing in the smell of deodorant and perfume, wet towels and shampoo. There were discarded magazines on the floor near the door, and he always remembered afterwards that he slithered a little on the slippery pages, as if he had stepped on a banana skin. The red light of a CD player winked at him from across the room, and in the moonlight coming through the window just then, he saw a vast black-and-white poster of what he thought at first was a woman, with wild blonde hair and large, diamond-shaped eyes. Then he saw that the lettering underneath spelled out *Kurt Cobain, 1967–94.*

'How old were you in 1994?'

Carly had turned around, then, removing her shirt in such a fluid movement that Jackson almost didn't notice her doing it. Her manner was so brisk and unselfconscious, so like someone stripping off in a changing room that for a moment he had thought, with simultaneous relief and disappointment: of course, she's going to throw me a blanket and let me sleep on the floor.

But then she was standing right in front of him in her jeans and the bra which earlier he had been able to see through the white shirt, and smiling.

'I was thirteen,' she said.

She's going to turn away, Jackson had thought then. I'm drunk, this is all a misunderstanding.

And in a way, he had remained convinced that she was teasing, even as he kissed her and pushed his hands through the wings of tawny hair behind her ears and felt the goose pimples pucker the downy flesh on her upper arms. Even in bed, when she reached down and touched him, and laughed until he put a hand over her mouth, whispering, 'Your mother,' and even as she said, 'Oh, fuck my mother,' and they both dissolved into fits of silent, hysterical laughter, a laughter that if anything only cemented a sense of their being equals, conspirators in a transgression that she initiated but in which Jackson without hesitation participated, deeply and swiftly and . . .

Yes, even inside her, Jackson had not really believed she meant it. It was only at about 4 a.m., when he woke to the first misty light of a new morning and heard the trembling scream of a fish eagle from somewhere below them, in the bay perhaps, that he recalled with disbelief and amazement and fear her closed eyes and tilted-up face. Her legs scissored up around his shoulder blades and the hungry rock of her hips.

Eighteen years old, Edie would say later. *That's practically child abuse, Jackson.*

And Jackson would hear his own voice, shrill and self-righteous. *Nineteen. She's nineteen, Edie.*

'So it was good, then?' Silv says, and Jackson looks at her in disbelief.

'Well,' says Silv, feeling around for her cigarettes. 'In my experience, which shall we say is quite considerable, nineteen-year-old girls are often quite shit in bed.'

'Are they?'

'Mmm.' Silv, unable to find her lighter, presses in the cigarette lighter just below the car radio instead. 'They're usually either clueless about what they want, or too shy to ask for it. So they end up faking it to please you, and you know they are but you can't ask them if they're faking it because that makes you sound either rude or, like, massively insecure.' She pulls out the lighter and applies it to the end of her cigarette. Jackson keeps his eyes on the road but out of the corner of his eye is aware of the red glow, and then the warm smell as the tobacco heats up and takes.

'Carly didn't fake,' he says.

'How d'you know?'

Even now it seems like a betrayal to tell Silv exactly how he knows. Because of the way, afterwards, she had carried on, moving with delicacy and precision against what was left of him until he heard her cry out, a trembling and urgent sound, and was too late and too amazed to press his hand to her mouth. Because of the sudden slackness of her mouth, the way she held herself over him on arms which, at the very end, suddenly shuddered.

Silv gives him her wolfish grin.

'You lucky boy,' she says. Then, 'So, what happened?'

'What do you mean?'

'I mean how did it end, of course.'

Something in her voice, then, as if it isn't just that logically Silv knows it must have ended, otherwise why would Jackson be here. As if, to Silv, like Jackson himself, people and endings are really one and the same thing.

He had half expected, if there was any such thing as cosmic justice, to turn as he left the house that morning, and see Tory standing on the landing, looking out. But the windows

266

remained dark. Carly had stood on tiptoe to kiss him in the kitchen.

'Thanks for the lift,' she said, grinning, and Jackson had just stared at her, wanting to demand when he could see her, wanting to apologise, wanting to tell her it was all impossible. She'd opened the fridge, then, taken out a carton of milk and drunk a mouthful. It left a faint white moustache on her upper lip, and he'd wanted to reach out his hand and wipe it with his thumb.

There was a pause with a tug in it like a tide, and then she'd said, as if remembering, 'Oh! Your keys,' and left the room. He'd heard her bare feet cantering up the stairs, and across what he now of course knew were the floorboards of her bedroom just above the kitchen. Then she was back. Breathless, the keys in her hand.

'The car's just beyond the gate,' she said. 'Remember?'

She appeared in his office later that day, as he was grading papers with his fourth coffee cooling on his desk. He'd got up, automatically, as she came through the door, aware he was grinning like an idiot. 'Hey!'

'Hey.' She remained by the door looking much younger suddenly, and uncertain, all conspiracy evaporated.

Jackson remained standing, becoming aware that his smile was fixed in place like a brace. Outside, there was the whoop of a rounders game on the grass beyond the Palms; a radio was playing in the seminar room on the floor above them. Carly fidgeted for a moment. She was wearing a red dress and white sandals and suddenly Jackson remembered. Sam. His smile faded.

'Are you all right?' he said, and she shrugged.

'You left this,' she said, and pulled his watch out of her pocket.

'Oh.' He didn't know what to say. 'Thanks.'

She fiddled with the strap of her dress and then said, in a rush, 'It's Sam's birthday.'

'Oh,' said Jackson. 'Well, happy birthday, Sam.'

'It's difficult,' she said, 'he's—'

'I am not,' said Jackson, 'all that interested in Sam.'

But Carly had hung her head then, and Jackson had thought of a yellow crocus on a broken stem. His voice softening, he said, 'Look, last night was – well.'

'It was amazing,' she said in a small voice. 'It's just . . .'

'You're with Sam.'

She had said then that it wasn't just Sam, not that he wasn't nice and all, it was more that, well, they needed to maintain the appearance of things, didn't they, if they weren't to attract attention. The strap which she was turning over and over moved further and further across her collar-bone, and he remembered the way it had felt under his tongue, and shivered. She was offering him a half-share, and much as he wanted to turn away, to have dignity, to pat her on the shoulder and tell her to have fun, go and be young, *live*, he couldn't. Two years ago she had looked up at him from her parents' sofa and without speaking something in her had said, *Hi, Jackson*, and something in him had responded. And now they were having that conversation, damn it, the conversation was in full spate, and Jackson knew that if she had to break it off to take another call that he would hate it, would fidget and agitate and fret. But he would wait.

'Do you sleep with him?' he said, as she was turning to go, and she looked back and shrugged.

'He's not very good at it,' she said, and then she was gone.

The rules emerged between them over the coming days and weeks. She never came to his office when she was on campus, and he never rang her cell or even texted it. Sam was jealous, she said, and her mum was fucking nosy. Instead, she emailed him and texted him. Messages. Photos. Sometimes videos. He was furtive and horrified and delighted, would put the blinds down in his office to look. Lock the door.

How many times did they actually meet? Five, six? Always at his house.

Almost.

'Almost?' says Silv. 'You mean, apart from the time when—'

Jackson sighs. 'Is it that obvious?'

'Jackson, you're a twat, you know that?' She's laughing at him now, feet still on the dashboard, head flung back like a heron, swallowing smoke. 'You're a complete fucking *twat*.'

The last time, he tells her, was the week before Nicko's wedding. Carly was going to be away in Plettenberg Bay for a week, she wanted to see him before she went.

269

'Come over, it'll be fine,' she texted him. 'Mum's gone for the day. Mani-pedi, hair, the lot. She'll be hours.'

And so, like a fool, he had gone.

Afterwards, it wasn't the sex that he remembered – did all sex with one partner after a while achieve the same remembered gloss, he wonders, the same motifs and key signatures, even when the notes were different? No, it was the pattern of light through leaves playing on the ceiling as they lay on the floor under the window. The pale, tormented face of Kurt Cobain on the wall, which Jackson had seen again as he turned his head, suddenly, towards the unexpected sounds below. The bang of the door. The cantering feet on the stairs. ('Shit,' whispered Carly.) Tory's voice calling imperiously (*Caroline!*) and the dim squeak of the rubber finish on the bottom of the door as it began to be pushed back against the varnished floorboards.

Jackson's eyes had flashed desperately to Carly in that moment, expecting her to shout out *Mum*, or *No*, or *I'm getting changed*, perhaps to pull the duvet down off the bed and over him. Something, anything, to save him from what was coming.

But Carly had lain beside him, pliant and still. Her eyes on the moving door. Waiting.

'Boom,' says Silv softly.

'Boom,' agrees Jackson, eyes on the road.

'And what happened then?'

'What happened then,' says Jackson, 'is that I left. I went to live in Italy. And even my sister never spoke to me again.'

270

Eighteen years old, Jackson. And Tory's bloody child, what the hell is wrong with you? Christ, I can't even look at you. Just go, will you? Just get out, go. Go.

Even Silv takes a while to digest this information, and when Jackson looks across at her, she is chewing her lip contemplatively.

But up ahead of them on the road, a blue sign flashing by announces Doncaster and the North, and despite everything, Jackson can see that at last, the sky is beginning to lighten into dawn.

XXX

Frances knows, in her heart of hearts, that there is no real point in searching the cliff path for Dog, knows that were he up here he would have come back by now, but in the end she does it anyway, because doing something keeps her rising panic at bay.

A long time afterwards, when she looks back, she will wonder what she had really thought in those moments about what had happened to Dog. Had her gut instinct even then been that he'd gone over, nosing curiously over the outcrop near the cliff edge, seduced by the oil and salt smell of the sea below? Had she already been aware in her bones of how it would have happened? So easy in the dark; his old eyes not what they were, night vision, as the vets had warned her, always the first to go. Had she envisaged the way in which one greying forepaw, claws splayed and brittle, might have skittered over an out-jutting stone, a little slippery perhaps with the light mist rising from the water below? How his whole body would then have gone, heavily, taken by the gape of gravity below before he could even yelp with surprise?

The path does not wind too close to the edge, and at intervals she passes red signs that issue tepid warnings. *Danger, unfenced path. Venture on to rocks at own risk.* Once or twice, although it makes her feel sick, she drops to her knees and crawls across the outcrop to look down over the drop. Even as she does so, she wonders what the point is. If Dog's gone over, she won't be able to see him. His body – she blinks, seeing it in the air, limbs strewing and flailing like string, blind eyes staring – will have hit the rocks below and been washed away by the tide. Even if it is still bobbing in the surf, it is too dark and she is too far up to really see. But oddly, once she's down on all fours, she finds she can't stop looking down, can't take her eyes away from the giddy dark swell as it heaves and turns on the rocks. There must be many more rocks concealed under the surface, she thinks, because the waves do not seem to roll over, to crest and break, in a rhythm. Instead the water seems to roil and heave, back and forth and side to side, like a line of horses waiting to start a race, manes and tails twitching. Further out, the water is dark and calm, seeming almost to pull backwards, away from the blank sneer of the cliff face. As she watches, Frances has the distinct sensation of specks of light surfacing, further out, as if some prehistoric creature is awakening from slumber. She looks up, again, into the night sky. But clouds have rolled over the moon, and the stars are surely too dim tonight to be casting their light on to the water's surface? She rocks back on her heels, balancing herself on the granular surface of the outcrop.

274

Once, at school, in a geography lesson, she'd read about how some sorts of marine life – sharks, wasn't it? – and some plankton exuded a particular sort of chemical when they died, which became something called *bioluminescence*. It lit up the surface of the water in whirls of blue, or green, like a firework. For a long time, she had consoled herself with the idea of her father, transformed into phosphorescence, a scrawl of green light on the parchment of the water. Of course some time later, a new girl in her class who knew nothing about Frances's hang-ups about the sea had pointed out that humans don't contain the same chemical at all, that a human body in water would probably just bloat, then break down and sink, in the end. Nonetheless, the image had remained, green light glimmering in the sea like code or a message, perhaps, to those left behind. *The sea, the snot-green, scrotum-tightening sea!* Before he knew the whole story about Frances's father – story, she thinks now, being the operative word – Jackson had never let up in his attempts to make light of her anxiety about the sea. And Rhidian, glancing anxiously at Frances, would then kick Jackson on the ankle and change the subject, saying crossly that all his allusions were so fucking *miserable*.

'Not all,' Jackson had said cheerfully, promptly launching into more Eliot, as he was prone to doing when feeling whimsical.

Frances closes her eyes for a moment, swaying a little in her squatting position, feeling the damp rock between her fingers.

What seas what shores what grey rocks and what
  islands
What water lapping the bow
And scent of pine and the woodthrush singing through
  the fog
What images return
O my daughter.

Her eyes burn.

Jackson, she thinks, but it's another voice that comes to her then, which seems to flower up from the cliff like samphire.

O my daughter.

But of course when she opens her eyes all there is in front of her is the shifting sea, behind her an empty hillside. *He lived with it for years. Lots of men do, these days. But it got into his spine in the end.* Frances balls one of her hands into a fist then and stuffs it into one of her eyes. She won't, she bloody won't, because nothing has materially changed after all and she's just a fucking idiot, she needs to grow up, she's got to get up and on and find Dog and then, somehow, she's got to make her way home.

She shakes her head, and stands up, swaying a little. She's still a bit drunk, that's for sure, but a headache is threatening in the base of her skull which will drive the fog away before long.

'Dog,' she calls again into the descending darkness of the hill. And then, desperately, 'What d'you say, Dog? What do dogs say?' An old trick for a biscuit, back from when he was

276

a puppy: she can see him now, younger and sleeker, sitting and lifting a paw before throwing his head back and barking. Ever since, even the word *say* has evinced, at worst, a hopeful grunt. She tries again. 'Say, Dog, say!'

Nothing.

She tries everything she can think of, then. Old commands from puppy class. 'Here, Dog, close, close! Come up, come up, *hi-lost!*'

The sea wind takes the words from her mouth, and gives her nothing in return, and she stands there, helpless. Her mother and Matthew Arnold, she finds herself thinking. What a pair. But they were both right, weren't they? The world had really neither joy, nor love, nor light and now she's lost, somewhere above the naked shingles of the world.

XXXI

The rain sets in at Howden, just as they are turning off the motorway towards Scarborough. In the distance it is getting light gradually, the dawn seeming to rise from the far-off blue horizon which must, Jackson assumes, be the sea. Nonetheless, above them and inland, clouds are lowering so gloomily that Jackson has to keep his headlights on, and it is another half an hour before the satnav instructs him, peevishly, to *turn left*. Silv stretches, like a cat, and yawns elaborately.

'Are we here?'

The car rattles over a cattle grid and then a bridge.

'We're here,' says Jackson as they pass a sign announcing Devil's Bay.

Silv is saying thank fuck for that because she really needs a wee when the Jag's headlights illuminate something standing in the middle of the road, fifty yards ahead.

'What's that?'

'I don't know. Sheep, wolf,' says Silv, shrugging. 'Large rat?'

Jackson slows the car. Ahead of them, the hunched shape stands still, standing with head slightly lowered but facing them straight on. As the car comes closer, the headlights pick out two green points of light that seem, eerily, to be looking right at him. Silv leans forward against her seat belt.

'Shit,' she says, and turns to Jackson. 'It's Dog.'

At first, as he gets out of the car, what Jackson feels is relief. She's still here! She must be close by, dog lead swinging in her hand, taking Dog for a leg-stretch before heading for home. He starts to feel loose-jointed and light-headed with adrenalin, has to resist the temptation to laugh as he walks towards Dog, who for some reason does not come towards him but remains in the road, watching him carefully.

'Dog,' he says gently, 'come on, Dog-oh. Where is she, then? Where's your mother?'

Which is when he realises that something is not quite right with Dog.

Jackson stops, and, squatting down, examines him carefully. He is soaking wet, for one thing, as if he's been caught in a storm. But it's the look in his eyes that pulls Jackson up short. It's a look of exhaustion and defeat, the look a much loved animal might have if . . .

Behind him, the passenger door slams, and Silv appears beside him. Dog looks up at her pathetically, ears flat to his head, abandoned, and she squats down to him, cradling his wet head against her coat. When she looks up at Jackson, he can see the tension in her face.

'He's been out here all night,' she says tightly. 'He's lost.'

'He can't be,' says Jackson, pointing a hundred yards further down the road, where they can both see the car parked in the gateway. A navy VW Golf. But when they reach the car, they see that the driver-side window is down, and, when he looks inside, he notices that rain has collected in the leather pouch around the gearstick. Worse than this, Frances's bag is sitting, in plain view of the road, on the dashboard.

The car has been here overnight, that much is obvious. But much, much worse is the glaringly obvious fact that when she left it, she hadn't meant to leave it for long. Frances might be scatty, but she's lived in London for long enough to be jumpy about break-ins and car-jacks. How often at his has she jumped up from the sofa and said, 'Just need to check the car's locked,' or, 'Oh, God, where's my wallet?'

Jackson looks across the bonnet at Silv, but Silv is looking down at her phone. When she looks back at him, she shrugs and says, 'This is it.'

'Don't be defeatist,' snaps Jackson. 'She'll be here somewhere, she's just—'

'I mean it's the address.' Silv slips the phone back into her pocket, and then, unravelling her scarf from round her neck, bends down and slips it through Dog's collar. 'This is where Martin Pilgrim lives.'

And she jerks her head across the road, at the partially moss-covered sign they can see at the bottom of the lane, which reads Brighouse Lane.

XXXII

Towards dawn, and almost by accident, she finds the cliff path, and makes her stumbling way down and down on to the beach. She is cold, and damp, from the sea air, she assumes, as well as the wet grass she has periodically been sitting on. A brisk wind cuts across the face of the cliff and she plunges her hands into her pockets, her chin into the front of her jumper.

Down below, the tide is out, the breakers a hundred yards away from the base of the cliff, and in front of her the sand levels out, pale and smooth, marked only here and there by rocks, seaweed, driftwood. Flotsam, she thinks, dully, is that what you call it?

She isn't even sure why she's come down here. If Dog has fallen, it will have been at high tide; there's no certainty at all that his body will be here, it could have been taken far out to sea by now; it could already be being nibbled by basking sharks. It could just be floating.

But Dog has not fallen, she tells herself, and to prove it, she opens her mouth to call for him again.

'Dog,' she tries to call, but all that comes out this time, on the empty beach, is a bending caw, like a baby's first attempt at a new syllable. *Dah! Da!* And that's when everything that has henceforth been theoretical becomes real, somehow, the word made cold and breakable flesh. She has a sudden and absurd vision of being Tim-the-barman watching his school friend get blown sky-high by a landmine, has a scattered moment of lightness and hilarity at the grotesque cartoonery of it all, the leering pinkness, the foamy flight, the ridiculous swiftness of the change from being to matter.

Frances stands on the beach, feeling her face frozen in the first spasm of grief. *Dog*, she hears herself whisper inside her skull, although something clinical on the edges of her knows that the word itself is only a panic signature, the catalyst for a reaction that between them she and her mother have held at bay for over thirty years.

Because as she draws the desperate breath in that she knows will only fuel what's coming, she can see it all, as clearly as the silhouettes of rocks and the dark shapes of seaweed: her father, gone, dying at home with no family near him, the curtain now having definitively fallen on a past she might have known. And in that moment as she stands there, just another piece of flotsam or detritus herself, it strikes Frances that the loneliness she feels in this moment is no passing spasm, no ghost going over her grave, that this is just the *beginning*. Her mother is becoming more absence than presence, an accelerating process that she's powerless to halt, and other than that she has no one, no one who is bound to her, no one from whom she might not conceivably find herself cut adrift. She is a spinster schoolteacher with one dwindling parent, no partner, nothing. Jackson was right: she should have grown up sooner, she's too late now for everything. Too late for her own children, probably. Too late even to help her mother. *Please, Far, find him. Bring him home, do.*

And before she can do anything about it she can feel the sob working up through her chest like a weed, flowering tightly in her throat. She retches, takes a deep breath, but it's no good, the muscles around her cheeks and jaw are working and the sob blooms like bile in her mouth. Frances crouches down on the sand. Then, wrapping her arms around her knees, she buries her head in her folded arms and weeps. The tears rock her from side to side and make her choke and retch and, some time later, when she is done, all she can hear is the ring of wind against rock and, from further off now like a sigh, the retreating sea.

At dawn, as the tide is turning, she climbs back up the cliff path.

Crying seems to have emptied her of most sensation. Her eyes feel bee-stung and swollen, for sure, and now and then in order to breathe she has to blow her nose, messily, into her hands and then bend down to wipe her hands on the wet grass. But apart from this, as she walks away from the cliffs and the sea she feels nothing, no sense of catharsis. Her fear and dread about Dog have been strangely absorbed by a mute, cotton-wool feeling, a bitter understanding that her mother has been right all along. Life would come for her in the end, and it has, hasn't it? She feels desiccated, sterile, finished. Below her, in the valley, lights are beginning to flicker on in the houses either side of 162 Brighouse Lane. Inside those houses, she thinks, alarms are going off, families are getting up. They're bickering about the bathroom, about the bins, being late for work. Radios and TVs are going on in the kitchen while mothers chivvy older children to the bus and fuss with toddlers' bibs. Washing machines are setting off on early morning cycles in time to catch the mid-morning heat, socks and pants and skirts and trousers tumbling together in a tangled wheel. Shopping lists are being made, evening meals planned, in these lit windows couples are negotiating about who will take Peter to football practice and collect Jane from orchestra, and can you remember to pick up the car from its MOT, love? Ordinary families who probably don't even think about the small comforts of their daily rituals, the consolations of proximity and routine.

In between them, the windows of her father's house remain dark.

The ground is at last becoming flatter, and ahead of her she can see the low hedge that surrounds her father's back garden. She can cut across here to her car, and then use the car to continue looking for Dog. Dear God, but she's tired, though. Frances drags her hand across her face, realising too late that it is smeared with grass and dirt. Once over the hedge, she walks through the wilderness of garden – did the estate agents not think it was worth their 15 per cent to cut the fucking grass? – noticing the ragwort and yellowing cow parsley that spring almost waist high from the cracks in the patio. The patio door is cheap, she notices, just glass in a white plastic frame, and within it she can see herself, a smudged and ghostly silhouette in the watery light of the morning. From a distance her face looks old and gaunt, but as she comes closer she can see that the new hollows are really only grass stains and tears. The carpets within the house are dark green and remind her, for a moment, of the surface of the water she'd seen from the ridgeway. She stops in front of the patio door and leans forward, until her forehead rests on the glass. Her tired eyes burn and blur, and for a moment the carpet roils and heaves. What was it she'd learned about waves in those geography lessons at school, before swotty Alice had told her the facts about bioluminescence, and the terrible-seeming significance of the subject had evaporated? She frowns. Something about a wave moving in two directions at once, that was it: that as the crest peaked and rolled forward, the base of the wave was actually moving backward.

Frances closes her eyes, feeling the chilly relief of the glass pressing on her face. She wants to pull herself upright, to keep walking away, forward and towards her car, but her grief is all around her now, lapping her, treacly and pervasive as an oil slick at sea. She's so tired of crying; the rims of her eyes are stinging and she hasn't got the energy either to do it properly or to hold it back, so she simply sags against the door, letting the tears roll down her face, holding on to her father's plastic door handle to keep herself upright and squeezing her eyes shut so she doesn't have to look at the emptiness inside, the pale squares on the walls where pictures had presumably once hung, the gaping holes where once a refrigerator, once a washing machine had sat.

A little later still, she's aware of the footsteps on the patio: a man's tread, and the lighter click of heels. Neighbours, of course. They probably think she's a burglar, or perhaps – she's almost moved to laugh – a homeless person, stumbled in off the hill after a night on the grog. The footsteps have come to a stop somewhere nearby but still outside her blurry field of vision and she is drawing in her breath, wondering whether she can face telling them the truth about who she is. Wouldn't it be easier to take the rebuke and obey the probable advice that she should piss off out of it, this is private property you know? But before she can lift her head or drag her hand again across her eyes and turn to face them, Frances blinks.

Because reflected in the dark panes of the patio door there are shapes, emerging as if from water, one on either side of her. Two tall bright shapes, in glowing shades of purple and green and red, which enfold and surround her snotted and grass-stained silhouette, lighting it up like a scene painted on stained glass. They are a distance behind her, this jewelled family, still swimming through the darkness towards her, with something smaller standing at their feet like a calf or a baby deer.

Frances watches them, drawing her forehead back off the grass to see them more clearly. It takes her a while to be able to see what they are. That the red is a mane of hair and the green is a man's trousers. That the purple is a scarf, which one of the figures has looped through the collar of what is neither a calf, nor a deer, but a dog.

She can hear a man's voice talking, a husky girl's voice breaking in over it. But she can't hear what they are saying because her head's full of foam, of the sound of seagulls wheeling and crying somewhere overhead. Her eyes are burning as she turns around, away from the reflection, to face them, and it's a moment before Jackson reaches her, putting his arms under hers and catching her as she staggers a little. She wants to tell his scratchy shoulder that it's over, she understands it all now, the charm's dissolved apace – but she can't get any words out because, of course, she's bloody crying again.

Even later, when Silv has gently peeled off her wet jumper and coat and replaced them with her own, and when Jackson is coming back from somewhere with plastic cups of coffee and chocolate, Frances sits quite still, listening to the far-off sounds of the bay. Weeks, or will it perhaps be months or years later, when she tells him about it, Jackson will tell her gently that of course she had been distraught that day, she had been traumatised. That all she had really heard was the sound of seagulls in the distance.

But in the present, as she clutches Dog to her like a stuffed toy, she is convinced that she can hear Ariel again, speaking in a voice which is strangely familiar and rather like a child's, patchy and far off, as if it were being borne away on the relentlessly tugging breeze.

Was it well done?

289

And then what seems to her to be not an aged magician's voice but a young woman's, coming from far beyond the cliffs and far out at sea. For a moment, Frances has a vision of her, turning with her narrow shoulders in her dark furs, her face pert and luminous and sweet.

Bravely, my diligence. Thou shalt be free.

Acknowledgements

Very many thanks to my agent Sue Armstrong, and to Emma Finn and the rest of the team at C+W Agency, as well as to Mark Richards, Becky Walsh, Rosie Gailer, Jess Kim and Morag Lyall at John Murray.

This is a book in part about teachers and teaching. Over the years I have been fortunate to have worked with, and learned from, too many wonderful teachers to list in full here, but special thanks must go to Sos Eltis at Brasenose College, Oxford; to Clare Morgan and Sam Thompson amongst so many other tutors on the Oxford MSt in Creative Writing; to the inimitable Gordon Catherwood in London; and also to the memory of John Ferris at Hereford Cathedral School, who told me one dusty afternoon in 1992 that, one day, I would be an author.

I am very lucky to have grown up in a house full of books, and to have parents who always encouraged me to read and be read to. Thank you, both, for those endlessly-demanded readings of *Rapunzel* and *I Had Two Ponies*, and later for Tolkien, T.S. Eliot, and all manner of books featuring stoical or heroic animals. More than that, thank you for continuing to support and encourage me in my writing.

Many other people were kind enough to offer advice and encouragement on very early drafts of this book, including Maggie Traugott, Philip Hensher, Jo Hogan, Cordelia Feldman and James Ellis. My last and most heartfelt thank-you, however, must go to my husband John, without whom this book would have been neither started nor finished. Thank you for your wise words, your insightful reading and, most of all, your belief that yes, this could be done, and that *no*, giving up was not an option. Quite simply, this book would not exist without you.

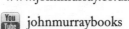

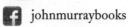